Speculations

Also edited by
Isaac Asimov and Alice Laurance

WHO DONE IT?
An anthology of mystery stories
with authors' names concealed

SPECULATIONS

◇ ◇ ◇ ◇ ◇ ◇ ◇ ◇ ◇

EDITED BY

Isaac Asimov & Alice Laurance

Houghton Mifflin Company Boston

1982

Library of Congress Cataloging in Publication Data

Main entry under title:
Speculations.
1. Science fiction, American.
I. Asimov, Isaac.
II. Laurance, Alice.
PS648.S3S6   813'.0876'08   81–13369
ISBN 0–395–32065–8   AACR2

Printed in the United States of America

S 10 9 8 7 6 5 4 3 2 1

For
Old Dull and Prosaic

Contents

Authors
(in alphabetical order)

Isaac Asimov
Scott Baker
Alan Dean Foster
Phyllis Gotlieb
Zenna Henderson
Joe L. Hensley
R. A. Lafferty
Alice Laurance and William K. Carlson
Jacqueline Lichtenberg
Roger Robert Lovin
Rachel Cosgrove Payes
Bill Pronzini and Barry Malzberg
Mack Reynolds
Joanna Russ
Robert Silverberg
Jack Williamson
Gene Wolfe

Story introductions by Isaac Asimov

The Scope of Science Fiction

by Isaac Asimov

When I was young, I thought of science fiction in terms of the classification of pulp magazines that filled the newsstands. There were detective stories, western stories, air stories, sports stories, jungle stories, love stories, horror stories, and so on.

Right down there along with all the others were science fiction stories. That was one of the categories and, as a matter of fact, the least of them, with the fewest magazines, the fewest readers, the fewest monetary rewards, and the lowest esteem.

I didn't really care that science fiction was at the bottom of the pack, because I loved it and wanted to read it and to write it and nothing else mattered to me.

But I came to wonder, as time went on, at the amazing stamina of this ugly duckling of literature. All the other categories withered; all the pulp magazines vanished — all except science fiction.

Fiction in general dwindled — but not science fiction.

Walk into any paperback store today, and you'll find

shelves of science fiction novels. Each day brings new arrivals to crowd those shelves. Many are old standards that have been selling steadily for up to thirty years. Science fiction has overtaken mysteries and far outstripped every other "genre."

Why?

Perhaps because the easy classification of literature into genres was wrong. The genres are a vertical classification. What if we try a horizontal classification?

Suppose, for instance, we deal with the here and now — ordinary fiction. You can concentrate such fiction on the relationship of the sexes and produce a love story. You can concentrate on crime and produce a detective story. You can concentrate on human beings facing a hostile environment and have an adventure story. You can concentrate on various elements of suspense and produce a tale of international intrigue or of mystery or of terrorism. You can deal with the human condition generally and have a "mainstream" story.

But not all stories are here and now. Suppose you consider the three categories of time: past, present, and future. Then add a fourth category that lies outside of time altogether.

Present-fiction is the "ordinary stories" of the here and now. Past-fiction is the "historical stories"; future-fiction is "science fiction"; and nontime-fiction is "fantasy."

Each of these horizontal divisions can be divided into the usual genres. You can have a love story set in the court of Louis XIV, or a tale of international intrigue, or of crime, or of suspense, or of the human condition. And the same is true for science fiction and for fantasy.

From this standpoint, science fiction is not just a variety of genre fiction, but a much broader class of fiction embracing many genres.

Nor are the four horizontal divisions entirely equal. Science fiction is not condemned to imprisonment in the future. A tale set in the present can have its science fiction elements, and since we live in a world of rapid scientific advance, this is becoming more and more common.

There can be science fiction elements in tales of the past. What of the talking head Roger Bacon was supposed to have invented in the thirteenth century? Tales of prehistoric man create one of the lesser staples of science fiction; time travel into the past one of the greater staples; and tales set in the youth of the universe can be nothing but science fiction. Finally, there are few possible fantasy plots that, with a little ingenious tinkering, can't be made into science fiction.

One might suppose that this just means that there are hybrid forms of fiction, which is not surprising. What is surprising, if you think of it, is that any hybrid that includes science fiction as part, even a minor part, *becomes* science fiction. Write a straight love story, but give the heroine a robot servant and have it add a kink or two to the plot — and you have science fiction. Set up a tale of fast-paced spy adventure and add a cold-blooded villain with a weapon that will blow up the world — and you have science fiction.

There is something broader and sturdier about science fiction than is true for any other category.

Another point. Historical fiction is rather moribund these days. It is used mostly as a device for frothy romance verging on soft-core porn. Ordinary fiction is dwindling, too. It is widely recognized that we live in a changing time and that today is obsolete even before the Sun has quite set. Fantasy is utter escape, and people are troubled by a sense of guilt when they read it.

Science fiction, on the other hand, is of its own essence when it deals with change. It accepts the necessity of change, the inevitability of change as the prime characteristic of its being science fiction — and this in a world in which change is indeed necessary and inevitable. It considers the consequence of change — in a world in which the consequences can be enormously exciting or devastatingly catastrophic. It is, in short, the one form of literature that is peculiarly adapted to the problems, fears, and hopes of today — the one truly topical literature — and is slowly being recognized as such. Why else has it flourished when all other categories have remained stationary or are dwindling?

In this anthology we have a collection of science fiction stories written expressly for us by a number of established writers. We did not direct them in any way, or suggest themes. We took potluck in that respect, feeling secure about the quality of the writing and willing to have the content wander freely through any part of science fiction's ample domain.

The result?

We have an intense love story, "Nor Iron Bars a Cage" — a love story that could not possibly exist in the here and now but that illuminates the human condition all the more brightly for looking at it from a new angle.

We have a crime story in "The Hand of the Bard"; a historical romance — of sorts — in "The Man Who Floated in Time"; a tale of international intrigue — of sorts — in "A Touch of Truth"; a horror story — of sorts — in "The Winds of Change"; even a completely unclassifiable story in "Tom Fool."

Read the seventeen stories of the anthology, and judge for yourself how you might divide them into genres, or fail to do so, within the illimitable spaces of the field.

And if that sort of scope is not enough, we have supplied you with an additional dimension. Science fiction, unlike any other variety of popular fiction, challenges the writer to present outlandish settings and outrageous assumptions and to force the reader to accept them not merely as entertaining (as in fantasy) but as *plausible*. This is by no means an easy thing to do, but, if it is successfully accomplished, it is a *tour de force* for the writer and a source of intellectual zest to the reader.

Each writer, moreover, has his own way of bringing it about, his own way of wriggling his settings and assumptions into the mind of the reader with minimum friction and discomfort. And perhaps no two writers do it in precisely the same fashion.

The experienced science fiction reader may learn to recognize the style of particular authors even if he or she hasn't looked at the name under the title. Just to test your ability in this respect, and as an added feature for your amusement, we haven't put the name of the author on the title page.

The names are given in a code that you may crack to see whether your judgment was correct. Failing that, you may read the instructions for working the code in the back of the book. You will, in either case, enjoy the stories.

So read on!

Speculations

Nor Iron Bars
a Cage

by 0040333413232421230443212441 1323

We tend to pity ourselves a great deal for the harm we do ourselves. "Man's inhumanity to man / Makes countless thousands mourn!" said Robert Burns, sorrowing. And yet we are cold, most of us, to what man does to other species — to the soulless, impersonal way in which we enslave them, bend them to our purposes, kill them for our hunger, or amusement.

But at least the nonhuman species of the world are less than we in intelligence and (we can hope) neither anticipate nor apprehend as we do, so that they are free from the kind of subtle suffering that intelligence makes possible.

But what of the future, when across the vast gulfs of space different intelligent species meet? What will they do to each other? How will they react?

It was an encounter typical of those early collisions between the Human Empire, expanding inward down the spiral, and the races of the Bright, the star-dense galactic center. There were four Empiremen, light, fast corsairs, wolves of space. They came by chance upon a lone but massively armed *Korunnar* Flowmotor lumbering like an atomic bear through the diamond night. It was the first contact either race had had with the other, and neither knew how much alike they were in their xenophobia, their pugnacity, their territoriality. Within a heartbeat of sighting, both opened fire.

For a hundred and nine seconds, the space around them became an actinic hell of coruscating energies, of fear and hatred made manifest. Then there was only silence and darkness, and ever more tenuous clouds of expanding vapors filled with charred flesh, fused metal, burnt lives pinwheeling away in the emptiness.

Among the flotsam was a suit of battle armor, scorched and dented, one foot partially melted. It tumbled end for end, stiff as a robot. Blistered red paint on the helmet identified the suit as belonging to *Friddle, James T., S/Sgt.* But Staff Sergeant Friddle wasn't inside. He was an erupted mass of blood and gristle somewhere far behind.

The man in the suit was a radar technician named Jake Miller. He had been marginally nearer the suit when the alarms had gone off, so he had lived and Friddle had died. His last conscious image had been of the sergeant clawing desperately at the suit's seals. Then a flash of impossibly bright light had seared his eyes, and a giant's fist had sledge-hammered him into unconsciousness.

The suit had done its job with the relentless efficiency common to Terran technology. It had cushioned Jake Miller's body against the explosion well enough to keep most of his bones inside his flesh. It had diagnosed his injuries and treated them within the limits of its ability, plunging home the needles and tubes and catheters, feeding in the nutrients and medicines and stabilizers. Then it had activated its locator beacon and prepared to sustain life until rescue arrived.

But in that time, in that place, nothing remained to hear the beacon's faint signal; nothing lived to come in aid. So the suit, with Jake Miller inside, not quite dead, not quite alive, fell away into the aching infinity between the stars.

Far, far ahead were the Q'Linn.

The Q'Linn . . .

They were an ancient race, sure in their wisdom. In their youth they had been conquerors, explorers. They had quested to the far edges of things in their saucer-shaped vessels, proclaiming themselves and growing mighty in their knowledge. They had perfected science, tamed emotion, defined their paradise. And in their young maturity, their pride and strength, they had created that paradise and made it real.

First they had built themselves a sun, a blue-white giant. Then they gathered in all the matter in near space, all the worlds and worldlets, the moons and seas and motes of dust, and hung them in a great globe around their sun, a globe made of a million million worlds, a sphere half a billion kilometers across, its skin-of-worlds a quarter-million kilometers thick. Then they set the million million worlds, the moons and asteroids and rocks, into motion, in infinitely complex interweaving orbits round about each other and the blue-white sun. And they wrapped the whole in a single, shared atmosphere, through which they flew on their graceful, gray-feathered wings. For it was the Q'Linn belief that all things worth knowing could be known within that enormous sphere. No longer interested in the universe outside, searching less for answers than worthy questions, they shut themselves away, taking notice of the universe only to the extent that it impinged upon them by chance, only when whim brought some piece of flotsam, some galactic curio to them.

But they were a prudent people, and patient. They set machines of ceaseless attention to watch the emptiness outside their sphere of worlds. And when Jake Miller was still a tenth of a light year distant, the machines noted his presence and cried alarm in electric voices. The Q'Linn noted the alarm and dispatched a vessel to examine the oncoming object.

It had been long in the void. Its surface was pitted, scoured, its faceplate yellowed by age, spiderwebbed with cracks. The desiccated face inside was covered with frost.

But life is persistent, and a spark yet existed in Jake Miller. So the vessel gathered him and his suit and bore them into the sphere, to a place of science and study. Such of the Q'Linn as were interested or qualified or curious came to see this thing from Outside, came winging from near places and riding swift devices from far ones. They gathered about the blackened suit, chirping in their high voices as they probed it with skill and radiation and sophisticated technology. And when they understood the suit, they caused it to open and they extracted Jake Miller. They touched him with their taloned hands, pumped their serums and gases through him, put thin wires in his brain, connecting him to a strange colloidal computer. They waited while the computer asked its questions, gathered its data, drew its conclusions. And when that was finished, the Q'Linn knew everything Jake Miller had known, and much more besides. They knew his name and race and tongue, his fears and dreams and taboos, his social organization and politics. Their historians knew whence he came, their predictors whence he was bound. They knew his place among living things. From this and other knowledge, the wise among the Q'Linn knew the state of the universe Outside, and that was sufficient. They gathered their instruments, their devices and tools, and departed. Jake Miller and the suit, being of no further use, were discarded.

They were taken to a place of storage and put upon slabs in a dark room. An attendant catalogued them, filed them away, and forgot them. From time to time, Q'Linn who were

4

interested or qualified or curious came to the place of storage to see some discarded thing. Occasionally, the object would be Jake Miller or his suit of battle armor. A student of measurements came to measure both the suit and the body. A warrior-general in pursuit of some question about weapon grips came to take a hand and a set of tendons. Revelers took the head for a centerpiece at a festival roosting. A geneticist rummaged through the remains and took the reproductive organs. A poetess came to sing a song over the battle armor. In time, that which had been Jake Miller was reduced to little more than mummified meat, without recognizable form.

The geneticist's name was Bwee K'Torr. He had taken the reproductive organs for no particular reason save that he was a geneticist. He took them to his roost-world and forgot them.

Later, while casting out clutter in his place of work and study, he came upon the organs again, and an elegant amusement occurred to him. He placed the organs in complex machines and caused them to function, to spasm and produce sperm. Then he gathered ova from ego-indentured females of his species, for it was his whim to construct a new creature, an avian/mammalian crossbreed capable, at least in theory, of reproduction with either Q'Linn or Human.

It was not a particularly difficult undertaking. He had at his disposal all of Q'Linn science, infinite patience, and the focused zeal of the trained dilettante. From these resources he built monsters live and stillborn, failures grand and ignoble, and three creatures which had both wings and navels, and lived. Two were male, one female. He separated them on nearby worldlets and set machines to tend and study them, then turned his mind to other amusements.

The worlds and moons and floating seas of the Q'Linn sphere danced their endless permutations of place and gravity, of weather and season, and in due course Bwee K'Torr's creatures matured into puberty. The tending machines reported this occurrence, and the geneticist returned to his experiment. He gathered in his creations and mated first the female, then one male with ego-indentured Q'Linn. The Q'Linn female did not conceive. K'Torr dismantled her and the male of his creation to find out why. His female creation died in agony at term, delivering her burden, a tiny, stillborn thing with a bloodless umbilical cord and a crumpled, flaccid shell.

But it did not matter. K'Torr had found the problem in the male creature. With an air of tidying up, he disposed of all his failures, made the necessary organic and genetic changes in his remaining male, and admired his work. He returned the male to its worldlet and went about his business. It had been an elegant amusement, elegantly carried out.

The male grew, isolated by K'Torr's design, tended by the machines. Chance sometimes brought a flight of Q'Linn to his worldlet, and from these he learned such things as it was their amusement to teach him. He had no wants and few desires. He came into young maturity, all in all, healthy and happy.

◊　◊　◊

Zylla K'Cee almost died in her fifth season. She had taken a traveler-disk from the crèche and flown it through the thickness of the globe of worlds, all the way to the cold outer airs where the sky was black and filled with faraway stars. She had ridden the disk as high as it would go, and when her urging would coax it no higher, had beat upward on her little wings, fighting, until exhaustion and anoxia felled her, sent her falling back, inward, where she was found floating comatose in a gravity sink between two moons. When asked why she had gone to that cold outer darkness and flung herself

6

against the stars, she could not say. Her child's mind did not yet hold the concepts to define her yearnings.

But her guardian, the warden and protector of the K'Cee crèches, understood the aberrant nature of her actions. And as was both necessary and proper, he caused her to be brought before him. He regarded her sternly from atop a perch of authority. "Zylla K'Cee," he said, "do you understand that you are a Q'Linn?"

On her own small perch, she made a gesture signifying "of course," a slight lifting of one wing.

"Do you know what it means to be Q'Linn?"

"It means you get spanked if you're a *little* Q'Linn."

A brief smile, no more than a quick opening of the beak, crossed the crèche warden's features, then was gone. "We are a free people, Zylla, the freest in the universe."

"What's the universe?"

"The Outside." He ruffled his feathers at her, a shushing gesture as if to command her attention. "We are free of want, Zylla, free of fear, free of labor. We live out our lives in unending beauty, in the joy of contemplation. Do you know that this is so?"

"Yes," she replied, annoyed as children are always annoyed at the stupid questions of adults.

"And how do you *know* we are free?"

Zylla blinked her lilac eyes, taken off balance. "I don't understand."

"How do you know that the Q'Linn are the freest people in the universe?"

This was just like school. "Because you tell us it is so?" Her small voice was tentative.

"Ahh, that is close, Zylla. But not yet the true reason." He shifted his grip on the perch. "The real reason, little eggling, is because you *believe* me when I tell you it is so, as I believe the councilors of the Wise who tell *me* it is so,

7

and as they believe the wise who came before them."

Zylla watched the crèche warden earnestly, not understanding any of it.

"And we believe, all of us, because those wise ones who came before us *knew*. They went everywhere, Zylla, and learned everything. They built our sphere of worlds and made the Q'Linn immortal." He gazed at some far place past the confines of the room. "They learned that races, like worlds, burn their youth away in quest of useless knowledge, vain emotion; grow old and feeble and die. So they made us a home where the race need never change, never age, never waste itself in pursuit of false questions, needless disturbance." He seemed lost in reverie for a time, and Zylla made impatient motions. He drew himself back with an effort. "Yes," he said briskly, then fixed a hard gaze on her. "There are worlds enough within the sphere, Zylla K'Cee, questions enough for a hundred lifetimes. You must forget the Outside."

"Why?" she demanded, half petulant.

"Because it is unhealthy, and unQ'Linn, and because if you persist in aberrant behavior I will have the crèche mistress spank you."

"Oh."

Zylla K'Cee grew, beautiful of her kind, quick and intelligent. She took her place among the egglings of her cycle and attained stature with them. She showed skill at the use of words and concepts, and was adept at games and puzzles. She proved graceful even in a species of exceptional grace, and became expert at the aerial poetry of gravity ballet, the most difficult and respected of Q'Linn arts. She was liked and admired by her peers. But to her elders, those whose amusement it was to watch over and teach and discipline the young, she was a matter of quiet concern, for there was an aloofness to her, a distance she kept about herself. She spent a great deal of time alone. And when, in her fifteenth season, she was found before a knowledge-accesser, attempt-

8

ing to order it to produce information about Outside, it was decided to bring her existence to the attention of the Wise.

A council was summoned, far on a golden world. Six of the Wise sat on high perches in a golden hall while an advocate and an antagonist argued.

"She is an aberrant," the antagonist said, "a danger to herself and the harmony of the race."

"She is exceptionally intelligent," the advocate replied, "of the ancient and stable eggs of the Line K'Cee."

"Aberration is infectious."

"Redirection is simple."

At stake was Zylla K'Cee's life, though she did not know it. Nor did she know of the debate itself, for she was yet on the K'Cee roost world, moving with her hatch-group through the rituals and studies of youth, guided by the crèche warden who had called her existence to the attention of the Wise, and who, should the Wise so decree, would be charged with destroying her.

The advocate and the antagonist argued long. The Wise retired to take counsel among themselves. Three of the Wise voted for Zylla K'Cee's death, two for her life — for the reason that the pride of Line K'Cee should be maintained untainted. All then looked to the Eldest, who spoke last, as was his right and duty. "She will live," he declared. "Not for the pride of Line K'Cee, but for use to Q'Linn wisdom."

The Wise gave him their full attention.

"For a thousand generations, we have believed the laws of our ancestors, accepted their choices. We have believed because the proof was with us; a hundred thousand years of unchanging life, of growing knowledge and wisdom."

There were gestures of acknowledgment, murmurs of agreement.

"And yet, what proof have we that we are still fit to judge our own proofs?"

The murmurs of agreement became a chorus of shock, for the thought was blasphemous.

The Eldest spread his hoary wings for silence. "How if we allow this child her aberration? How if we permit her her unhealthy interest in things Outside?"

The Youngest But One spoke, deferentially. "To what purpose?"

The Eldest spoke slowly, making certain they followed. "To learn, ultimately, if the dream of our ancestors still holds. To learn if, at root, the genes are still true." He looked to each of them in turn. "We who are without blemish, chosen for our wisdom, we who are the best of our race . . . we do not doubt the dream because we cannot. It is bred into us to believe. But this child, this flawed eggling, what of her? She seeks a freedom which our ancestors knew to be unhealthy, destructive."

"Then she should be destroyed!"

"No. She must be given her freedom! She must be allowed the choice between what she thinks she desires and what we hope she is, for we must know the choice she makes. If she, an aberrant, finds in the end that she is Q'Linn, that the way our ancestors chose is, despite all, her way, then we shall know that the dream still holds."

There was a moment of stillness as they absorbed the implications of the thought. Then the Eldest But Two spoke. "A testing, then."

"Yes. Of her and ourselves."

"And how shall we accomplish this testing?"

"Elegantly," the Eldest of the Wise replied.

◊   ◊   ◊

In her eighteenth season, as was the custom for unmated Q'Linn, Zylla K'Cee left the roost-world on her Great Flight, her journey to explore herself and the sphere of worlds. She followed many amusements. For a time she sang, and for another time studied the crystallography of the floating icebergs of the outer airs. For yet another time she studied the propulsion systems of the ancient saucer-shaped vessels in which her ancestors had traveled the galaxy. And seemingly by chance, she was offered the pastime of reorganizing certain records, among which she found — again, apparently by chance — a small memory-egg containing a list of everything from Outside which had come to the Q'Linn sphere of worlds in the previous thousand seasons. To Zylla K'Cee, it was the key to a door long denied her.

She found record of a piece of a broken planet which had come drifting in six hundred seasons past, a piece of a planet with the ruins of a civilization still clinging to it. She found echoes of an incorporeal terror which had come like static two hundred seasons ago, fleeing a greater, incorporeal terror. She found a cloud of dreaming seeds which had, disturbingly, proven incomprehensible to the Wise of the Q'Linn and had sailed on past the sphere without taking notice of it.

And inevitably she found Jake Miller, come tumbling comatose and nearly frozen, less than thirty seasons before, almost in her own lifetime.

As with her previous discoveries, Zylla probed the machines for access and information, though cautiously, for she was yet under supervision and not permitted freedom of choice, and all knowledge of Outside was reserved to adults. But she managed to discover another memory-egg dealing with Jake Miller and the research that had been done using him. Thus she found out about the geneticist Bwee K'Torr and his creations.

It was a season and a half before the Great Flight period ended, and Zylla performed the rites of passage that made her an adult and freed her of supervision. She spent that time absorbing surreptitious knowledge, probing the depths and breadths of the records and researches having to do with Jake Miller and his history, with the strange race of bipedal adventurers whence he came, who called themselves *Huumnns*. By the time of her adulthood rituals, Zylla K'Cee knew everything about Jake Miller's race that the Q'Linn knew. She was, though she did not suspect it, the authority on humanity among her people.

Within three *skree* of achieving adulthood — and freedom — Zylla took a traveler-disk around the inner curve of the globe of worlds, skirting the fringes of the blue-white sun in her haste, and came to the roost-world of Bwee K'Torr. After some thought, the geneticist remembered his experiments and directed her to the worldlet where the surviving male lived. K'Torr was a scientist, and very nearly a Wise One. He noted the light in Zylla K'Cee's lilac eyes, the intensity of her voice. He cautioned her. "Study the creature if you wish, Youngling, but do not give it imaginary qualities lest you be disappointed. It is an experiment, nothing more."

She made a gesture of understanding and acquiescence, but her lowered eyes were unrepentant. Her plans had been formed much earlier.

She took herself to the worldlet, a blue-green jewel with a necklace of moonlets and floating seas strung around it, and rode a gravity-spiral down, her heart unexpectedly tight, her beak dry.

He was beside a lake when she found him, squatting on his haunches, eating a fish with his fingers. K'Torr had not bothered to make visual records of his experiments, and Zylla K'Cee was unprepared for the physical reality before her. He was grotesque. He had no beak, only the pulpy slash of a human mouth; no earholes, just the gnarly knobs of human ears. Patches of naked skin showed, for his body was feathered only at chest and groin, on skull and wing and stubby tail. Worst were his hands and feet, which were properly taloned, the skin properly scaly, but which were too broad, too fleshy. Such hands would never easily manipulate the precise and delicate tools of Q'Linn technology, such feet never authoritatively grasp limb or crevice.

In two aspects only was he undeniably avian: in his beautiful wings and his round, purple-irised eyes. And even here his human blood had betrayed him, for his eyes were set forward in his head after the manner of ground-hunting predators, denying him the encyclopedic vision of the Q'Linn. And despite the ten-meter spread of his wings, despite his hollow bones and huge pectoral muscles, his mammalian heritage had bequeathed him a body nearly twice as heavy as it should have been. His flight would be forever clumsy, forever awkward. The Q'Linn had no word for the image he created in Zylla K'Cee's mind, but Terrans did, and it rose unbidden as she looked at him. *Gargoyle.*

But Zylla did not find him repulsive. Ugly, yes, in an inoffensive way. Alien and perhaps a little frightening. But she could see a vein pulsing beneath the skin of his featherless neck, and in that vein, she knew, flowed blood from Outside. Outside! And that was all that mattered. She made the feather-display of Q'Linn greeting and introduced herself. "Zylla K'Cee."

"Awk," he replied.

While Zylla sat nearby, disconcerted, he performed for her as he had been taught by earlier visitors. He waddled along limbs and ledges for her amusement. He performed parodies of aerial dance, somersaulting clumsily through the currents. He mimicked the lovely songs in his slurred, growling voice. He juggled bright stones for her. And came at last to stand before her with his hands out expectantly, awaiting the customary reward.

K'Torr had been right. She was not prepared for this. But she was determined, her dream long considered. This was perhaps a stroke of fortune, for she had before her a slate unwritten upon, hers to inscribe as best suited her purpose.

She removed a bauble from among her decorations and held it out. But when he reached for it she withdrew it behind her.

"Awk?" His eyes were confused.

"Zylla," she said. "Zy—lla."

Comprehension came. This was a game he understood, had played before. "Zyrra! Zyrra!"

"Good," she crooned, giving him the bauble, "very good."

She applied for a roost-world and was given a small planet which served as satellite to six larger ones, moving around them in turn in slow figure eights. She took him there and began to teach him, causing machines of learning to be brought, and chemicals to assist and speed his comprehension. His speech smoothed, and if it was not the lilting chirp of the Q'Linn, it had a certain rolling beauty to it. If, when he cruised above the waters of the globular seas, his glide was flatter than that of the Q'Linn, his dive for the silver fish more angular, there was power in the strike, authority in the capture. If his misshapen hands held tools with no grace, they used them with considerable skill. And early in the training, she named him: T'Miller, after the fashion of his father's people, Honn, after her hopes — He Who Completes the Dream.

In time, he came to her with the questions.

"I have been studying the families," he said.

"Yes?"

"There is no crèche for Line T'Miller, no roost world, no record."

"That is so."

"Where did I come from?"

So she told him of Bwee K'Torr, and of the time before Bwee K'Torr. Of his father's long voyage and his coming

14

among the Q'Linn. She told him the rich, terrible story of the pugnacious, rapacious mammals who called themselves *Huumnn*. She told him of the universe Outside, and of Hom-World Terra and the Humanx Empire. And much of what she told him was correct, for Q'Linn science was deep and Q'Linn insight acute, and the small mind of Jake Miller had yielded far more than it knew it contained. And in the end, she took him to see his father.

It was dark in that place. They stood on either side of a slab on which the mutilated, mummified remains of Jake Miller lay. Honn T'Miller stood looking down at it, his face in shadow. He reached out and touched the dried flesh with a trembling talon, and a shudder ran through him, brring the tips of his feathers. Zylla watched closely, poised, aware of the moment.

T'Miller gave a low, terrible cry, a sound filled with anguish and hurt and hatred. "They *made* me! They butchered my father and *made* me like a, a *thing!*"

"Yes," Zylla K'Cee said quietly.

"They laughed at me, used me for an amusement."

"That too."

He turned away abruptly, folding himself in his wings. "Why didn't you leave me as I was, Zylla? At least I had happiness."

"There are more important things than happiness. Knowledge of yourself, of the Outside, of the uniqueness that is you."

He laughed, a bitter caw. "Unique? Yes, I am, am I not?" He held his hands out to her. "Look at my hands, Zylla. Look at my face. Are they human? Q'Linn? No! I'm unique, all right. I'm a *monster!*"

"Not to me," she said simply.

He watched her face, his eyes unreadable. Then he turned away again, once more cloaking himself protectively in his folded wings. "I am neither Q'Linn nor Human, Zylla, and I'll never be either."

She chose her words carefully. "There is another way to consider that thought, Honn. If it is true that you are neither Huumnn nor Q'Linn, it is also true that you are free to be either as you choose."

"Free to *call* myself either, not to be accepted."

"I accept you."

"You are one. What of the rest of our race?"

"The rest of *my* race, T'Miller," she said. "Unlike you, I have no choice."

There was a note in her voice that could only be envy, and the alienness of the thought that anyone could envy him silenced Honn T'Miller.

They returned to Zylla's roost-world, and for a time T'Miller found a kind of happiness in her company and in his brooding thoughts and studies. Zylla was patient and cautious, neither pushing him nor obviously directing his thoughts. Once they took a disk to the cold outer worlds and rode it up into the thin airs near the darkness. "When I was a child," she told him, "I tried to fly away out there, to go and see the stars for myself. There are so many things to see and do out there, T'Miller, so much freedom. Here, you are different and I am different."

But Honn T'Miller's hard purple eyes did not look outward to the jewel-bright stars. They looked inward to the million million worlds of the sphere. And there was hatred in those eyes, a fierce determination.

Zylla bided her time.

They flew the winds of the roost-world together, fished the seas and lakes and oceans. They played the intricate games that the machines produced for their pleasure, and shared food on high, windy places. And inevitably, they mated. His grip upon her wingroots was not the grip of a Q'Linn, but

16

it was a good, firm grip nonetheless. His bite upon her neck was not the sharp bite of a beak, but it was sharp enough, strong enough, tender enough. His wings beat awkwardly to hold them aloft, but it was, properly, his wings alone that bore them. And as she opened to receive him, his thrusts were, somehow, precisely correct.

Afterward they sat side by side in a silver egg with a glass window, watching sparkling droplets of rain drift languidly upward as a passing planet perturbed local gravity. Zylla preened in quiet satisfaction, her head turned modestly away but her every fiber aware of Honn T'Miller, her whole being alert to his mood and nuance.

He groomed his wingtips with his talons, his face proud and determined. "Beloved," he said.

"Beloved."

"I am complete. You are my mate."

"Yes."

"You will bear my egg and my name."

"Happily, joyfully."

"I have made my choice."

For an instant, she did not understand. Then, in a sudden rush of fright, she did.

"You told me once, Zylla, that I was free to choose my race. Now I have done so. I will be Q'Linn."

Confusion and fear beat through Zylla K'Cee. "No! N-no, beloved. It cannot be. They will never accept you, never accept us."

"I do not need their acceptance." He did not notice the anguish in her voice, the fear on her face. "They made me and mocked me. Yet am I not Q'Linn? Do I not fly the airs, sing the songs? Have I not a mate?"

She fluttered her wings, her taloned hands clenched at her breasts. "Oh, but *why*, beloved? Why face the scorn? We could be so happy Outside!"

"Why?" There was a cold anger in his tone. "For revenge! For what they did to my father, what they made of me."

"But, we shall never be free of their hatred. You will never be Q'Linn. What of our eggling, what will it be?"

"A new race!"

"Yes, oh, yes, beloved. But not here!"

"Here, and damn them!"

He would not be moved. He built them a nest after the fashion of the Q'Linn. Numbly, desperately, Zylla K'Cee T'Miller took her place in it. She delivered her single, iridescent egg and sat it as Honn T'Miller brought her choice delicacies. She watched in silence as he composed a hatching poem for his eggling-to-be, just as if there were a crèche recorder to record it. And when on a day of warm winds and gentle rains she felt the shell beneath her break, when a damp and downy girlchick tumbled into the world, its mouth instinctively open for food, T'Miller's pride was beyond bounds; she found her own matched his. She found herself feeling things that no Q'Linn had felt for a thousand generations, and the disquieting thought occurred to her that perhaps she was no longer entirely Q'Linn, that in some strange way this gargoyle creature with whom she had mated, this half-caste whom she had trained to take her into the wide universe Outside, this father of her daughter had infected her with alien emotions. Or perhaps they had been there all along, perhaps her entire life had been a prelude to some inevitable realization. And as Honn T'Miller crowed over his still-wet infant, Zylla's mind knew only an infinite sadness. There would be sorrows in this.

He named the girl PQuee, which in the Q'Linn tongue was Starwing. And in defiance, he registered her birth with the computer in the roost.

PQuee would be a glory. Perfect of line and form, properly Q'Linn save only for an exotic cast to her eyes, an echo of the blood of her grandfather. She had the startling, intense purple eyes of her father, and the almost fluorescent, shimmering-gray wingtips of her mother. She had a beauty unique in all the universe. And she was six weeks old when they came to take her away.

The registering of PQuee T'Miller's birth had been noted, as all else about T'Miller and K'Cee had been noted, by the Council of the Wise. They had gathered in their golden aerie, there on the steep side of a high black mountain, and discussed the event and its meaning.

The Second Youngest of the Wise spoke. "Your testing, oh Eldest, has proven the taint. She has mated with Z'Torr's thing and borne a hatchling. She represents a danger to the race and must be destroyed." A clucking of agreement came from the perches.

The Eldest waited for silence. "You forget the purpose of the testing, Younger Nestmate."

"She feels things which are dangerous, forbidden!"

"It is not her feelings which interest us, it is her response to them."

"It seems to me that mating with a . . . thing is evidence of response."

"So it is, Nestmate. But to what? Her aberration drives her to yearn for forbidden knowledge of the Outside. The mating with Z'Torr's thing was not her goal, but only a means to it. He is the vessel of her desire, her thirst for escape. It remains to be seen whether she is truly Q'Linn despite her aberration, and that is the point of our testing, is it not?"

"Yes."

"Then," the Eldest said quietly, "we must place her in a position of choice, for only in choice does truth lie."

◊   ◊   ◊

There were ten of them, eight warriors and two from the lower Councils. They came to Zylla and Honn's roost-world and read the bans and edicts. The warriors destroyed the

19

nest and the roost. Zylla listened in stunned, meek silence. T'Miller raged. The warriors restrained him gently, almost absently, and when the councilors took Zylla and PQuee aboard the disk, the warriors caused T'Miller to become unconscious. When he awoke, they were gone.

T'Miller left the roost-world, his rage a fearsome thing. He was not hindered, but neither was he aided. No Q'Linn spoke to him or acknowledged his presence, no machine rendered to him, no disk carried him. On his own clumsy wings, it would take a lifetime to search a fraction of the million million worlds of the great globe of the Q'Linn.

Yet, he found her, there in the golden aerie on the black mountain. He came among the warriors and councilors, the servants and slaves, and his anger was a consuming wind. The warriors removed him to a far place.

He came again, this time with engines of destruction, machines of violence. He wrought havoc while howling the names of his mate and eggling. This time they removed him a lifetime distance and set him upon a barren place.

When he came a third time, they brought him before the Council of the Wise, who regarded him in silence and then put him in a cage.

A cage.

They set it on the polished floor of the Chamber of Wisdom, where those who passed could look upon it. T'Miller beat himself to madness against the silver bars and sank to the floor, his heart too burned, too ravaged to sustain insanity. He turned deaf ears and blind eyes on the passing Q'Linn.

"Now?" the Third Eldest asked.

"Very soon," the Eldest answered.

Q'Linn passed through the chamber, hurrying by on clicking talons or gliding overhead on wide wings. Some paused to look at T'Miller, some did not. One day, it was Zylla K'Cee who passed. Her anguished, inarticulate cry brought T'Miller

20

to his feet. He tore at the cage's bars and screamed her name. She flew toward him, her eyes wide with horror. She had nearly reached him when the warriors swooped down and carried her away.

It was two nights later when she came again, sailing on whispering wings into the chamber. She alit a few feet from the cage. The cavernous hall was dimly lighted by oil lamps in bronze stands on the floor, and by their flickering light, Zylla's face was a mask of sorrow. She held a silk-wrapped bundle in her arms, and stepped hesitantly up to the cage and held it out. "I have given her chemicals to make her sleep, lest her cries bring the guards."

T'Miller reached through the bars and stroked his sleeping daughter. "Six seasons," he said bitterly. "Six long seasons."

Tears welled in Zylla's lilac eyes. Her face crumpled. "Oh, beloved," she whispered, her voice a broken thing. "A *cage*. I did not know."

He reached awkwardly to touch her face. "The cage does not matter. It is only bars. It is this sphere of worlds which is the cage." His voice grew hard, rough. "Anything with a limit is a cage, though that limit be half the universe." He shook her, causing PQuee to murmur querulously in her drugged sleep. "You were right, Zylla. We must leave here, leave the sphere."

"What of your revenge?" Her voice was curiously flat and dull.

"I had no revenge, nor sought any. What I had was hurt, wounded pride, anger. None of those were worth losing you and the child."

Instinctively, she drew the sleeping child closer to her. "You have changed, Honn T'Miller. So have I."

"What does that mean?"

"I-I don't know. There has been time to think. So much loss, so much sorrow. I am not sure I can leave, beloved."

21

"Not sure? You gave your life to escaping! You raised me from ignorance for that purpose."

"Yes. Coldly and dispassionately. Like the Q'Linn I am."

He released his grip on her and studied her face. Then he smiled. "Are the tears in your eyes Q'Linn tears, Zylla? Would a Q'Linn feel pain at seeing me in a cage? Is it the Q'Linn in you that brought you here tonight with our daughter?"

She bowed her head, tears flowing more freely.

"Zylla, no one has any say in who makes them. You were born with a Q'Linn body, I was born with a Q'Linn/Human one. But you have made a part of my mind Q'Linn, and I have made a part of your soul human. Now we must live for ourselves and our daughter. You must find the key to this cage and release me. We will leave."

"They would not permit it, beloved."

"They cannot prevent it!"

There came a sharp, metallic *ting*, a skidding, sliding sound. Out of the darkness, a silver key spun across the polished floor and came to rest at Zylla's feet. As she and T'Miller stared down at it, lamps were lit throughout the chamber, flooding it with light. The Councilors of Wisdom looked down at them from their high perches. The Eldest spoke. "Take up the key if you wish, Zylla K'Cee. You will not be hindered."

For a long instant there was silence in the chamber. Zylla and T'Miller looked at each other in shared understanding of what had been done to them, of the puppetry that had been worked upon them. Then T'Miller spoke to the Eldest, his voice a well of hatred and contempt. "Oh, thou egg of worms! Thou thief of nests! You planned this."

The Eldest nodded, but his round green eyes were on Zylla. "Do you understand what has been done, Zylla K'Cee, and why?"

"Yes." Her voice was barely a whisper.

"Do you understand the necessity for choice?"

"Yes, that too."

T'Miller yelled. "If she had had true choice, she would have left this miserable tomb fifteen seasons ago! Thou false! Thou sucker of eggs unborn!"

A younger of the Wise admonished T'Miller coldly. "It is not her choice which matters, thing."

The Eldest silenced his nestmate with a look, then turned again to Zylla. "A thousand generations look down upon you, Youngling, and thousands not yet born."

"No!" T'Miller grabbed her through the bars, his voice a hiss. "Open the cage. What do you need of these people? They have abused you worse than me! Does the universe need such soulless eaters of dung as these? We shall find a world of our own, the three of us."

The Eldest spoke. "And be forever outcast, forever alone?"

T'Miller spat at him. "We shall go among *my* people."

"Your people? Do you mean the Huumnns? Will you be less a monster to them than to us? Will Zylla? Would you see your hatchling in a cage, displayed? That is the Terran custom with beings different from themselves, is it not?"

The horrible truth of it hung in the air. Then Zylla stooped swiftly, retrieved the silver key, and opened the cage.

There was a squawk of shock and protest from the high perches. A younger councilor shrieked for warriors. Another spread his wings to swoop down.

"Hold!" It was T'Miller. He leaped from the cage and in a single fluid motion flung an oil lamp from its bronze stand and grabbed another, holding it aloft in threat. The spilled oil sloshed across the floor in an inflammable lake, oozing around the bases of the high perches. The Wise Ones sat still, though they could perhaps have flown. The face of the Eldest was radiant with intensity. He watched Zylla, as if neither Honn T'Miller nor his threat existed.

23

T'Miller did not notice. His own face was suffused with anger. He held the flaming oil lamp overhead with both taloned hands. "For what you have done to my mate and eggling," he intoned, "for what you have done to me!"

But Zylla stayed his hand, reaching almost delicately to take the lamp from him. She faced the Wise Ones, and the warriors who had come winging into the chamber and now hung poised in the air, aware of the danger but disciplined not to move without orders. "For none of those things," she said quietly. "Not for revenge or anger." She bent slowly, almost gently, cradling her sleeping child. "For sorrow alone. The sorrows you have caused, the sorrows you must know, and the sorrows to come." She tipped the lamp, and the burning wick licked into the pool of oil on the floor.

There was a soft explosion, a near-instantaneous wall of heat and light engulfing the chamber. The warriors hid their faces and flapped backward. The younger of the Wise screamed and sought to flee. But through the smoke and flame, the figure of the Eldest could be seen, beating toward the ceiling on burning wings. There was an expression of rapture, of a fulfillment approaching ecstasy on his face. "Yes," he cawed, "yes! The sorrows yet to come! I understand! You are Q'Linn! The Dream holds!" And then he was engulfed and vanished in flame and smoke.

T'Miller grabbed his mate and fought his way through the flames, coming finally to the landing platform at the edge of the aerie. He launched himself into the night. "Now! Now we are free!"

But Zylla did not follow him. Clutching her child to her breast, she beat into the updrafts over the flames and rode them upward, ever higher amid the smoke and embers. T'Miller turned in his flight and stroked his way up after her. "Zylla!"

She waited his coming, circling lazily on the hot, rising

24

air. When he was near, she looked at him with sad, loving eyes. "You do not understand, do you, beloved?"

"I understand that we are free, we are together. Why do you hesitate?"

"I do not hesitate. This is the end of things for me."

T'Miller beat toward her, but she eluded him. "No! You do not need this. You do not belong to these people. You belong to me — to yourself and our daughter."

"I am Q'Linn."

"You are yourself, Zylla. Neither human nor Q'Linn, but a thing apart, even as I am, even as PQuee is. We need obey no rules save our own."

"No, beloved. You have choice. I have not."

"You freed me! You set the blaze."

"Not for thee, dearest Honn. For the need of my people." She balanced on the fierce updrafts with delicate adjustments of her wingspan. "We sold our hearts for knowledge and stability, beloved T'Miller. Like the 'Gyptians of your race's ancient past. For thousands and thousands of seasons we have been without change, without love, without . . . sorrow. And sorrow is the heart of compassion. When we cannot feel pain in ourselves, we cannot feel it in others." There were no longer tears in her lilac eyes, only a kind of strange, high exaltation. "This was your gift to me, Honn T'Miller. Sorrow. And it is — must be — my gift to my people."

"It is not needed, Zylla. We are different, you and I."

"Are we, my finest? Are we truly?"

"We are."

"We are not. You are at heart human, for your emotions rule you. I am Q'Linn, for mine do not. I will prove it."

Almost by instinct, T'Miller knew what she was going to do. He screamed and lunged for her. But his awkwardness in the air was no match for her grace, and as he sailed futilely past her, he heard her call to him. "Farewell, beloved gargoyle." He turned in time to see her fling their sleeping daughter far into the black night. Her eyes never left him as she folded her lovely wings and dropped like a stone toward the inferno below. "Choices," she cried.

For a heartbeat he hung there in the burning air, his heart split asunder in his breast. Then, with a terrible cry he dove, as she had known he must, not for her but for their daughter. He slammed the air with his great wings, and went whistling down the blazing night to catch his child in his taloned hands a breath above the cruel rocks, then wrenched himself around just in time to see his wingmate hurtle downward into the pyre, her wings still serenely wrapped about her. As he knew she must.

◊   ◊   ◊

Dawn found Honn T'Miller on a ledge across the valley from the black mountain. He sat in preternatural stillness, watching with bloodshot eyes as Q'Linn moved unhurriedly through the still-smoldering ruins of the golden aerie. His daughter lay beside him, stirring uneasily in the precursor of wakefulness. His body was coated with ashes, his wingtips singed black. His heart was a stone in his chest. Zylla was gone, dead of his gift to her, of sorrow and the weight of a thousand thousand generations, of her genes. The Q'Linn could not live with sorrow: Humans could not die of it.

PQuee T'Miller stirred again, brushing the silken coverlet from her face with her tiny, perfect hand. Watching her, a spark moved inside T'Miller. Was this the answer to sorrow? Was this the key to the cage? A fragile, brittle hope began in his breast. In love and joy, he bent to kiss the child of his flesh, and of his lost nestmate's.

PQuee T'Miller opened her exotic, beautiful eyes and looked upon the father she had never seen, looked upon his beakless face, his gash of a mouth, his deformed ears. She screamed and screamed and screamed.

The Q'Linn found her, unharmed but incoherent, a short time later, flying over the valley as if pursued. As she was a result of Bwee K'Torr's experiment, she was turned over to him for disposal. They did not look for T'Miller. They were without passion and thus without vindictiveness, without cruelty. But they found where he had been. A student of oddities reported, as a matter of curiosity only, that Jake Miller's suit of battle armor had been taken off its slab, had been repaired and replenished and transported by disk to the cold outer airs of the sphere, had been launched into the void, its locator beacon winking, winking, tiny in the blackness, aimed toward the incredibly distant, star-dense galactic center.

There was no question that Honn T'Miller was inside. He left proof behind. On the cold display slab, beside the pitiful remains of his father, he had laid his beautiful, gray-feathered wings, torn bloody from his back with his own clumsy hands.

Surfeit

by 14241404303033242314102433340432

Life has its enthusiasms. It isn't life, in fact, if it doesn't — at least not life as enthusiasts understand it.

That isn't clear? I suppose not, but isn't there something about *your* life that isn't clear? That is clear to *you*, that is, but not to anyone else?

In my own case, it is my attitude toward writing. I don't have to write for acclaim or for a living or for anything else that makes sense. It's already brought me all of that. I write only for the sake of writing and could not face life if I were not permitted to write. There is no way I can explain this, for writing is my Monster.

Is there a Monster in your life? If there is, my congratulations.

The Monster was all mouth and no body, and you would hear it before you could see it.

Joao Acorizal knew of it without having to employ sight or sound. He knew of it through story and legends, which are far more descriptive than simple senses could be. He'd studied the history of the Monster, its whims and habits, colors and moods.

Surfeit

From the time he'd been a boy on Thalia Major and had first heard of the Monsters of Dis he knew someday he would confront and do battle with them. It was preordained.

His parents and friends had listened to his somber daydreaming and had laughed at him. If by some chance he one day managed to raise enough money to travel to far Dis he would cower fearfully before the Monster, too weak to confront it. One or two friends had actually seen tapes of the Monster and assured Joao it was too much for any man of Thalia to handle. Better to forget it and aim for the attainable.

Kirsi had been his wife for twenty years and hadn't been able to make him forget the dream.

She spoke as she paced the floor of their living room, her sandals clacking intermittently on the floor as she alternately crossed thick throw rugs and smooth terratone tiles.

"I fail to understand you, Joao." She was waving her hands at him, as full of animated little gestures as the noisy macaques which roamed the trees in the garden behind the house. "You've worked hard all your life. So have I." She stopped, indicated the tastefully furnished, comfortable room.

"We'll never be rich, you and I, but we'll never go begging either. We've a good life. We've two fine children who are just old enough now to realize that their father is crazy. Everything we've worked for, all that we've built up together, you want to throw away to satisfy a childhood infatuation." She shook her head pityingly, her long black hair swirling against the back of the white print dress. "Husband of my life, I don't understand you."

Joao sighed and looked away from her, out the broad window which overlooked the beach. The sun was rising over the Atlantic. Tranquil waves broke like eggs against the sand. Thalia's sun, slightly yellower and smaller than Sol, turned the water to topaz. Thalia Minor, the twin world, was out of sight, hiding on the other side of the globe.

"We have more than enough money. The trip will not inconvenience us save for a little while."

"Money? You think I give a damn about money?" She came up behind him, locked her arms possessively around his waist, and leaned her head on his back. Her warmth sent a shiver through him, as it had on that first night twenty years ago.

"Money is nothing, husband. You are everything." She turned him around and gazed hard into his face, searching, trying to find the key to whatever drove him so she could somehow pull it from his mind and cast it into the sea. "I do not want you dead, Joao."

He smiled, though she couldn't see it. "Neither do I, Kirsi."

She pulled away sharply. "Then why are you in such a hurry to throw life aside? God knows you're no antique, but you're not a professional athlete either."

He turned and bent to kiss her gently. She made a fuss of flinching. "And that, my love, is precisely why I must go to Dis now, before it is too late . . ."

◇　◇　◇

Conversation and Kirsi seemed so far away now. He was on Dis at last, and soon he would confront the Monster and its relatives. For thirty years he'd dreamed of the challenge to come. Thirty years of practice, thirty years of honing his skills, thirty years of dreaming, about to become reality.

That is, if he could muster one day's worth of great courage.

His eyes tried to penetrate the salt mist as he and his companion challengers made their way across the damp, barren rocks. A few low scrubs clung tenaciously to the surface. Sea crustaceans crawled fitfully from crack to crevice.

There were twenty-four competitors in the group. Eighteen men and six women, ranging in age from eighteen to forty-two. Joao was grateful he was not the oldest. Only second oldest.

But not in spirit, he told himself firmly, and not in heart.

Salt spray drifted foglike around them. The raucous complaining of seabirds mixed with the sibilant hissing of ichthyorniths filled the moist air of morning.

The walk was a ritual part of the contest. No spectators were allowed to join the competitors on the walk, no judges or media reporters. The first confrontation with the Monster would be made by the entire group. Then they would return to the assembly and departure station to make final preparations for their individual, intimate meetings.

Conversation was by way of whispered shouts, whispers out of respect for their opponent, shouts so they could be heard above the periodic roars of the Monster. They were now very near the end of the peninsula, and the bellowing from up ahead shook the solid granite, sending a subtle warning tremor through the contestants' bare feet. They could not see the Monster yet, but it was hissing at them through the rock.

"First time?"

"What?" Joao wiped spray drip from his forehead and eyes and looked to the source of the query.

"I asked if it was your first time." The man who spoke was very short and extremely muscular. It was not the well-defined muscularity of the body builder but the squat, thick build of the truly strong. He had bright blue eyes and his hair was cut bristle short, a blond brush that gave him a falsely belligerent look. His swim briefs were blue and red checks in front, solid red behind.

"Yes." Joao stepped over a dull mustard-colored crab-thing armed with quadruple pincers. It flinched back but did not flee from him. "Is it that obvious?"

"Not really. But if you've been through it before you can tell." They walked on.

"How many times for you?" Joao asked curiously.

"This'll be my third." The man grinned. "It's hard, since the contest is held only every three years. Would be my fourth, but I broke my leg the last time."

"You don't have to warn me. I've read about this every year for the last thirty."

The man laughed. "I didn't break it during the contest. Two days before time I slipped on my front porch and snap, that was it for the next three years. Spent the whole contest watching."

Joao managed to laugh with him. They walked on silently for several minutes. The sea mist thickened, was partly countered by the rise of a stiff breeze. The rest of the contestants kept pace nearby.

"Name's Janwin." The man put out a hand. Joao shook it. It was not wrinkled as he expected but smooth. The grasp was firm, controlled. "I'm local."

"Joao Acorizal, from Thalia Major. I'm a builder, mostly private homes."

"Circulatory surgeon, Dis Central Hospital Complex. Pleased to meet you. The important thing is to have confidence in yourself. Be alert, keep an eye on your path and the other alert for the predators. Don't be afraid to use your balpole, and if you're going over or under, use your rockets and get the hell out. Everyone does. Risk taking impresses the judges, but points don't mean a damn to dead pulp.

"You get three chances during the contest but only one life. There's nothing to be ashamed about if you bail out. My first contest there were only fifteen rides out of forty-five attempts, and no completes. I've never had a complete ride and seen damn few." He went quiet, studied Joao professionally. Ahead of them they could hear the rock-shattering groan of the Monster, very near now.

"You've got good legs, real good. Any tears or pulls in the past six months? This isn't something you go into if you're even slightly damaged."

Joao shook his head. "I know that. I've done thirty years of homework and as much practice for this day. I've never been in better shape."

"That's what your mind tells you. Well, I ought to shut up. I'm no fledgling either. Experience counts for a lot." He looked ahead. "Almost to the Point. I'm sure you've seen tapes of it. It's a little different in person, up close. Remember, watch out for predators and try to relax."

"That sounds like a contradiction, but I'll try. Thanks for the advice." He added impulsively, "If I don't win, I hope you do."

Janwin shrugged. "I've never placed higher than seventh. But that doesn't matter. What matters is that I'm still here. With all my parts. Keep that in mind when you're out there and tempted to push your luck a little. All the points in the world won't make up for the loss of an arm or an eye." He looked a little uncertain, finally asked, "You have a family?" Joao nodded. "Are they here?"

"No. I wouldn't let them come."

The surgeon nodded approvingly. "Good. If anything happens I'll see that the details are properly taken care of. You can do the same for me, though I have friends here."

"Agreed!" Joao had to scream it out because they were at the slight rise at the end of the promontory which marked the tip of the narrow peninsula.

Then they were slowing, everyone crowding unconsciously close together, and he could see the Monster.

High overhead, hanging like dark eyes in a pale blue sky misted with sea spray, were Cerberus, Charon, and Pluto, three of the four large moons that circle the planet Dis. Grouped together like that they occupied much of the morning sky. Dis's sun was just above the horizon, below the moons. The three satellites were also rising, their perambulating orbits bringing them into alignment in this manner only once every three years. Soon the sun would be behind them, and

33

for a while daylight would touch land in surreal confusion. Below was the Monster they helped to raise.

The wave was larger than any Joao had ever seen, but he expected that. He studied it calmly, analytically, and did not shake. The wave lifted heavenward, still far out at sea. White foam like broken teeth began to appear on its crest. It surged hungrily toward the high promontory. It started to break.

The curl appeared, began to retreat steadily southward, and the roar came to those who watched. It was a roar that stirred the blood and primeval thoughts. All the dark dreams of childhood, all the terror of drowning and smothering under a great weight were wrapped up in that single monstrous, relentless wave.

And still it rose as it broke to the south, an immense gray-green blanket suffocating the horizon, the thunder of its sharp curl wiping out all other sounds. From the safety of the salt-swept point the contestants watched the curl and wave as it fled away from them, ducking only when the trailing backside of the wave smashed its green hammerhead against the rock to drench them all.

Out at sea, visible through the mist, making good use of the peculiar slope of the seabottom, Dis's lighter gravity, and the tidal confluence of the sun and three fat moons, the next Monster was growing.

The contestants stood, chattering loudly in order to be heard, all eyes appraising the water.

"About eighty feet," said Janwin thoughtfully. "Normal runs fifty, storm-driven pulses sixty to seventy. We only get these really big ones when the three moons line up every three years and add their pull to everything else. It should be an interesting couple of days."

Three contestants withdrew on the way back to the assembly area. No one taunted or chided them. The inmates have no right to make fun of the sane. The judges calmly marked the dropouts off the list.

Assistants were available to help in preparation. Acorizal turned their eager faces away. He'd lived with his board for five years. He'd broken it in, broken it for real, had repaired it lovingly with his own hands. He knew every inch of it, every contortion in the grain. He needed no help. But he made sure to work alongside the helpful Janwin and watched him make ready so that he could ask questions.

Once one of the contest supervisors approached the surgeon, whispered something to.him before moving on to the next contestant. Janwin had listened, nodded, then ambled over to where Acorizal was checking the release pulls on his backpack and making certain the solid fuel boosters were clean and full.

"Weather report just in. Scattered clouds, winds five to ten out of the southwest. That shouldn't affect balance or crests. There's a tropical cyclonic storm weaving around out there. We shouldn't get any bad winds, but you know what that'll do to the swells. On top of everything else." There was a twinkle in his eye.

"I've never had a chance to ride a hundred-footer. If a proper swell comes in on us, get out of my way."

"I'll race you for it," Acorizal replied with a grin. Janwin moved away and the builder turned back to readying himself. He dismissed the thought of a hundred-foot wave. It could no more be comprehended than the distance between two stars, or the gulf that was the number billion. It was a physical abstract only, one without counterpart in reality. For himself he wished only an uncomplicated wave. That, and to survive.

His board was formed of honeycomb tripoxy resins. It was fifteen feet long by four wide and light enough for one man to carry. Twin shark-fin stabilizers protruded downward from the front third of the board, another pair from near the blunt stern. Above the stern were twin air stabilizers joined by an adjustable airfoil.

Studs set into the upper surface of the board were connected to thin duralloy control wires running to the four stabilizers and the airfoil. You could not touch the studs with your hands, only with your feet.

He picked up his balpole. It was made of the same material as the board except for the twin spiked knobs that ballooned from either end. The pole could be used for balancing or for fighting off any carnivores who might frequent the turbulence of a great wave. Several such were indigenous to Dis. No energy weapons or devices of any kind were permitted save for the tiny solid-fuel backpacks.

The pack was your life. A rider who was thrown or who lost control of a wave had several options. You could dive into the body of the wave and hope to swim out through the backside. You could shrink into a fetal ball and hope to ride the wave out. Or you could fire your pack with either of two releasing shoulder pulls and soar above the wave, to drop freely behind it into the water. Whenever possible, it was best to use the pack.

He checked his wet suit for leaks. Pressure or impact of a certain degree would automatically cause the heavy rubberized suit to inflate, hopefully to send a helpless rider bobbing to the surface. The suit would also protect against bruises and scrapes. It would not always save your life. Joao pulled the hood over his head, wiggled his toes. Only his face was exposed. His suit was bright orange with red striping.

A hand tapped him on the shoulder. Janwin was there, not smiling now. His face beamed from a suit hood of electric orange. "Ready? Time to go."

Acorizal nodded, hefted his board. There was nothing more to be done but to do it.

Another rider backed out as they were boarding the skimmers. Acorizal watched her, sitting forlornly on her board, as the skimmer he was in lifted. He waved understandingly, but she did not wave back. The Monster had beaten her already, as it had beaten several others. There was no shame in that.

Acorizal had not even thought of withdrawing. Not yet, anyway. At least he was going to get wet.

The skimmer rose, turning in formation with two others. Cheering was continuous from the assembled spectators who'd gathered to watch the contestants prepare. Tridee pickups turned smoothly to follow the skimmers as they hummed westward.

Acorizal wondered if tonight, incredibly far away, Kirsi and the children would be watching. Kirsi had told him prior to his departure that under no circumstances would she watch the broadcast or allow the children to, but he wasn't so sure.

Picking up speed, the skimmers left the staging area. Soon the cliffs that fringed the western coast of Dis's largest continent fell away below. Lines of color marked the places on the cliffs where the spectators were strung out like opaque glass beads.

A wave was passing below. Its aspect was very different when viewed from high overhead instead of face on. The white crest reminded him not of teeth now but of lace lining the flowing, rippling hem of a woman's skirt. The lace drew a smooth line southward as the curl broke steadily toward distant Scratch Bay. Acorizal watched until the curl faded from sight.

Soon the skimmers' engines also began to fade and the little craft dropped surfaceward. Out here on the broad open ocean the waves were merely cocoons from which the Monsters would hatch. The Monster now had a back as well as

37

a face, and the skimmers set down on its undulating spine. Engines raced as the craft settled into the water. Riders and boards moved over the sides, to pepper the dark green surface.

Acorizal felt stronger the instant he tumbled in. He floated easily, his board attached to his ankle by a breakaway cord. He ducked his head and swam beneath it. The water was chilly out over the deeps. It shocked his eyes open and dissolved the cobwebs of uncertainty in his brain.

All around him, riders were mounting their boards. The brightly hued wet suits looked like confetti scattered across the water.

Acorizal felt something lift him, heave him skyward. He went up, up, along with his board and companions, ten, twenty feet, only to be gently lowered again. A wave had just passed beneath them, full of power and incipient threat. It left him feeling not fearful but exhilarated. There, he thought. That alone was worth it. If I do nothing else, if I can't make a wave, it was worth coming all this way just to feel that swell.

A board was coming toward him, light as a feather on the surface. Janwin stopped paddling, looked over at him. "Save your legs and mount up, man."

Acorizal spat salt water. "It feels good."

"Sure it does, but don't waste your energy. Your adrenalin's all pumped up. Get on your board, relax, and let it go down."

Acorizal decided to take the advice, clambered onto his board with the ease of long practice, and sat there, his face drying in the rising sun. "When do we start?" He was watching the monitoring skimmer, bobbing nearby.

"We've already started." Janwin grinned at the other man's expression of surprise. "Some can't stand to wait. Two took off on that last swell." He shook his head. "There's no advantage to going first, but you'll never convince some people of that."

"I never saw them go," Acorizal murmured. "So soon. Isn't it better to wait for a wave that feels right?"

Janwin shrugged. "To some I guess the first wave feels like the right wave."

"Well, I'm taking my time. I'm in no hurry. I've come a long way for this, and I'll be damned if I'm going to rush it."

"Good for you." Janwin nodded approvingly. "You don't get many chances. I prefer to wait too."

Hours passed. One by one the riders took off, to disappear southward. Once something large, white, and full of teeth appeared, to be driven off by a shot from the monitor skimmer's lookout. Reports on the progress of vanished riders were broadcast to those who remained, amplified by the skimmer's sound system.

"Meswith Brookings . . . four hours, twenty minutes. Bailout clean. Harlkit Romm . . . three hours, forty-five minutes. Swimout, exhaustion, but otherwise clean." Acorizal knew Romm would score higher than Brookings for bailing out without using his backpack.

"Eryl-cith al Hazram . . . four hours, thirty-two minutes." There was a pause, then the voice from the speaker added softly, "Bailout failure; wipeout. Body not yet recovered." There was silence for a while, then the voice continued mechanically. "El Tolst, five hours, fifty-six minutes. Swimout, collapsed lung, neck sprain, otherwise clean. Jewel Parquella, five hours, ten minutes . . ."

During the waiting another pair of riders withdrew, were helped silently aboard the monitoring skimmer. The sun rose higher while beneath it three moons jostled for pulling position. Janwin and Acorizal discussed water.

"Normally we could expect double sets," the surgeon was saying, giving the swell lifting them a critical eye. "Three large waves followed by three small. The storm's changed that. We're getting three large, three small, and three or four storm waves larger still but highly variant." He glanced over at his companion.

"Naturally you'd like to catch one of the latter, but they can be tricky. You might get a double wave, one crest on top of another, and that would force an early bailout. You'd get a ride, but too short to score many points."

The sound of an arriving skimmer interrupted their conversation. Besides the surgeon and Acorizal two other riders still waited for a wave. One went away with the swell that rolled under them as the skimmer touched down.

A board appeared on its flank, went over the side followed by a rider. The man mounted, paddled over to join the remaining three contestants. It was Brookings. He was lean, much younger than Janwin or Acorizal. His face was flushed and scoured clean, but he was not panting very hard and his strokes were smooth and sure.

"Hello, Brookings. Back for your second?" Janwin inquired. The younger man nodded, looked understandably pleased with himself.

"Caught a seventy-five-footer," he told them. He leaned back on his board, hyperventilating. "The first couple of hours were easy enough. After that you start to feel it in the legs. Then your eyes get snaky. I decided to bail out when I found myself seeing a double tube behind me."

"Smart move," said Janwin. "We got your report. You had a good ride on a good wave. Have they found al Hazram yet?"

Brookings looked past them, toward the invisible coast. "Not yet. They're afraid his suit might've failed. They told me he caught a storm wave at least a hundred feet five. He was apparently doing fine until he got too fancy. Got too low on the wave and too close to the curl. The wind from the collapsing tube blew him off his board."

"What about his pack?" Acorizal asked.

"Ignited okay but he was so low the crest caught him. He didn't clear it and it broke right over him. If his suit failed they'll never find him." He went quiet for a moment, then sat up straight on his board and began paddling. They were rising toward the sky.

"I like this one . . . see you." Then the swell had him in its grasp and he was gone.

"We'd better get going," Acorizal observed. "If he's on his second wave . . ."

Janwin shook his head. "Competition comes second, remember. Survival's first. You've got to feel comfortable with the wave you choose or you might as well turn in your corpse right now."

So they continued waiting. Janwin took off fifteen minutes later. That left Acorizal and the last rider. Swells came and went as they sat on their boards.

Kirsi . . . I'm glad you're not here and I wish, oh how I wish that you were! His face was getting hot from the midday sun.

The sound of a returning skimmer drifted down to the two waiting riders. He squinted, made out the prong noses of two boards projecting from the racks on one side of the little craft. Two more successful riders returning for their second waves. He couldn't wait much longer or it would be too late to try for the required three rides. There was only tonight and tomorrow. He did not want to have to take two rides tomorrow, and not even a saint would try to ride the Monster at night.

Then he saw the swell. It loomed high behind him over his right shoulder, so green it was almost black. It was a huge one, wide as the sky and rising like a bubble breathed out from something vast and patient. But he was not alone and there was courtesy to observe.

He looked anxiously across at the other waiting rider, saw that the man also saw the nearing swell. It continued to rise steadily, bearing down on them like a runaway starship. Acorizal had to force himself to wait.

Abruptly the other rider let out an agonized cry of despair and started paddling for the monitor skimmer, taking himself out of competition for the swell, out of the day, out of the contest. Acorizal turned his head eastward and began paddling furiously, his balpole clipped lengthwise beneath his knees.

He was afraid he'd waited too long. For a long moment he hung suspended atop the swell. Then he was moving forward with less and less effort. He stopped paddling, continued to move, picking up speed and beginning to slide slightly downward. The swell continued to build and a giant green-black hand boosted him toward the sky. Now he could pick out the faint, far line of cliffs that marked the land.

He climbed to his knees from his belly, accelerating steadily. His toes tensed on the slightly resilient surface of the board. He stood, edged back on his rear leg an inch, then moved his front leg to match. The fingers of his left hand tightened on the ignition cord of the backpack.

He felt fine. The ride was smooth and easy, the board responding instantly to his subtly shifting weight and gentle toe-touches on the control studs. The balpole he held tightly in his right hand. He stopped rising, hung suspended in midair.

Then he looked down. His fingers tensed further on the loop of the backpack release as instinct almost betrayed him.

Far, far below was the surface of the water, flat and shining like steel in the rising sun. Air ripped at his face; salt stung his eyes. Wind whistled around him. His mind was momentarily numbed by the hundred-foot drop he overhung, but twenty years of practice took over, shifted his body.

Then he was screaming down the face of the gigantic wave, ten, twenty, thirty feet. He leveled off, keeping his weight back but centered, adjusting the airfoil to slow the precipitous drop. The stabilizers kept him level as the front four feet of his board hung over emptiness and sliced through the air.

An incredible rush went through him, an indescribable combination of sheer terror and pure ecstasy. To his right was a moving green cliff that towered over his head, thousands of tons of living water. To his left was nothingness.

He grew conscious of the steady, unvarying roar of the Monster, only now it was not terrifying but simply awesome. He was set on the board, had become part of it. He risked a look backward.

Behind him tons of water cascaded endlessly from thirty feet overhead to smash into the withdrawing waters seventy feet below. It formed a vast glassy green tunnel which rising sunlight turned into an elongated emerald: the tube. Wind blew out of it as curling water forced air ahead of the collapsing arc. It sounded a special, higher note in the overall thunder of the Monster.

He held tight to the balpole with both hands, letting loose the pack release, and adjusted his balance. Then he thought to check his suit chronometer.

He'd been on the wave thirty minutes.

Moving slightly backward he luxuriated in the feel of the matchless ride, always watching the curl and the crest high above to make sure no surprises were about to tumble down to crush him. The waves held their shape with remarkable consistency, but occasionally one could collapse unexpectedly, the curl vanishing as the unwary, too-confident rider found himself buried under a million tons of water.

But Acorizal's wave rolled on and on, machinelike, the curl trailing behind his board like a friend urging him onward.

Gradually his confidence grew. He let himself feel out the

wave, slipping his board high up on the green wall only to plunge dizzyingly back down when it seemed sure he'd burst through the crest, dropping low almost into the bottom of the curl to stare up at eighty feet of liquid cliff high above.

When he felt secure enough, and he'd been three hours on the wave, he let himself slide backward, back into the tube. It was almost peaceful inside, so numbing was the roar of the breaking curl. The tunnel he rode in was high and wide, the wind powerful behind him. He had to be careful. He did not want to be blown off the board by a collapsing tube, to be swallowed by the tumbling crest.

Something materialized in front of his face, just outside the curl. He frowned, then let the board edge outward. The apparition multiplied into many.

He'd been told of the Trintaglias. They floated just ahead of him, their blue eyes bulging curiously at the strange figure that appeared in their midst. Their air sacs were fully inflated, the taut yellow-pink skin stretched thin as paper. They varied in size from several inches to a foot in diameter, riding the air current that preceded the tube on long, thin fins that doubled as wings.

Occasionally one would dip down to snatch something edible from the water. Some would collapse their sacs and vanish into the wall of the wave; others would drift higher or lower according to internal pressures. Once he reached out and touched one. It jerked away from him, turned to float sideways in the air and regard him wide-eyed and reproachful.

He checked his time. Five hours and thirty-five minutes. He had already managed the second-longest ride of the day. His legs were throbbing, and the gastrocenemius of the left was starting to cramp. His eyes were red from the salt spray, while his mouth, paradoxically, was dry from lack of water.

Off to his left, as he moved cautiously out of the tube, he could see the high, running ridge of the continental edge.

Ahead, as always, there was only the endless, thundering curve of water.

Another thirty minutes, he promised himself. Another thirty minutes and I'll have the longest ride of the day. He couldn't bring himself to bail out yet, though his legs threatened to fail him and his arms felt like limp weeds. Everything had gone so well. The wave still had size and power and exhibited no signs of weakening. How far did they run, he wondered? He hadn't researched it much, not thinking he'd ever be in a position to care. Could you ride one all the way around the continent? Or perhaps from pole to pole?

Another thirty minutes. Another thirty minutes of wet hell and he could bail out.

The Vaxials almost got him.

Only the fact that one mistook the end of the balpole for part of the rider saved Acorizal. The narrow, eellike head reached out of the wave wall and snapped at it viciously, teeth grinding on the sharp metal. All six longitudinal fins were extended for balance, and the dark red gill slits back of the jaws were pulsing with excitement. An eye the size of his hand stared malevolently out of the wave at the startled Acorizal.

Somehow he kept his balance on the board, but it was a near thing as he instinctively leaned away from those thin, needle-sharp teeth.

The reaction helped him. The Vaxial let loose of the inedible balpole and snapped at the air where Acorizal's shoulder had been an instant earlier. The weight shift caused the board to shoot upward along the wave face. The crest of the Monster came closer with shocking speed.

Acorizal left his feet and threw himself forward. Down, damn you, get your nose *down!*

The board responded, dipping to slide rapidly downward. It had been a close thing. Acorizal had nearly shot out through the crest. At best he would have flown into the air on the other side of the wave, a good ride completed and the Vaxials circling to pick him off the board. At worst he would have caught the crest with the nose of the board and gone over backward, to fall helplessly head over heels until the entire immense weight of the wave pulped him against the water below.

He continued to race down the front of the wave. Behind him, a pair of blunt, toothy snouts attached to twenty-foot-long snakelike bodies glided through the wave in pursuit. Eventually the Vaxials would catch up to him. They lived in the waves and had no worries about balance.

He readied the balpole as he pushed back into a kneeling position, tried to judge how he was going to strike out without losing his balance and board.

An ugly head emerged from the water. Acorizal leaned, slashed down and sideways with the spiked end of the pole. It made contact with a flat, glassy eye, and blood spurted. The Vaxial vanished instantly.

Lucky blow, Acorizal told himself grimly. He was so tired his hands shook. He scanned the green wall for signs of the other carnivore. Maybe, he thought, it's gone to help the other. Maybe they're mates. He stared, locating wave fish and other creatures but no hint of the Vaxial.

Then there was awful pressure on his back and a ripping sound.

He fell forward, desperately trying to keep his balance on the board despite the weight on his back. He could feel those long, needlelike teeth on his neck, piercing the tough material of the suit and his skin and his spine. He screamed in terror.

Then the pressure was gone. He hadn't seen the Vaxial attack and did not see it go, but it did not reappear. Which was no wonder, if the backpack had gone down its throat.

He held the balpole weakly with one shaky hand as he lay prone on the board and felt at his back with the other. The pack was definitely gone, wrenched from its clips on the suit by those powerful jaws. His eyes frantically scanned the water all around the board, but the creature did not show itself again. After a while the Trintaglias returned, in ones and twos, and he took their presence for a good sign.

He no longer could isolate individual bruises and sores. His body was one continuous ache as he studied the wave. With his backpack gone there was no easy bailout. He could rise to the crest and hope to break cleanly through to the other side, or he could dive into the wall, swim like mad, and then inflate his suit to bob to the surface . . . if the Vaxial hadn't torn the suit's air chambers as well.

If he misjudged either attempt he would very likely drown. If he wasn't battered to death inside the wave.

One thing he was certain of: He could not get back on his feet. His legs were too far gone. He let the balpole slip away and hugged the board with both arms, not caring if some swimming predator beneath chose to make a meal of his clutching fingers.

He'd had a good ride, one of the best of the day. Somehow his anguished muscles would have to hold him tightly to the board until someone on shore realized the danger and sent out a skimmer to rescue him.

Please God, let that be soon, because I have no strength left in me.

He willed himself to stay conscious. If he went to sleep on the board it would all be over in seconds. The board would rise up into the crest as his weight slipped backward, and he would go over the falls, to be thrown a hundred feet downward. At least that would be quick. There would be no drowning. Just a single quick, irresistible weight and then unconsciousness and death.

He shook himself, pulled himself forward on the board. He'd been daydreaming and had risen to within ten feet of the crest. Now he numbly nosed the board downward again, back into the safety of the middle part of the wave. The sonorous boom of the curl followed patiently on his heels.

God, I'm tired, so tired, he thought. Let it be over. I've done what I came for and more. Now I just want it to be over. Where the hell was the rescue skimmer? Couldn't they see he was on the verge?

He would have to do something, he knew. He could not hang onto the board much longer, let alone guide it properly. Both his brain and body were worn out. Only sheer stubbornness had held him together this long.

Diving into the wave was out. He didn't have enough strength left to swim two feet, let alone drive his body through the water. It would have to be a crest break, then.

He started to let the board slip upward. One hand felt down the slick side of the wet suit until it touched on the inflation knob. Once he broke through the crest he'd inflate the suit, hoping the monitoring skimmers would pick him up before the next wave came by. He hoped he could stay conscious enough of his surroundings to inflate the suit at the proper instant.

Everything was a wet blur before his salt-encrusted eyes. Sky and water merged into one. Was he at the crest yet? If he waited too long he'd go over the falls.

Then white washed over him and he coughed weakly. The wave had not waited for him to make a decision. He remembered Janwin's warning about the uncertain actions of storm-generated waves.

The curl disappeared, subsumed in a single endless break as the wave lost its shape and collapsed atop him.

◊   ◊   ◊

It was dark and wet and his board was gone. Dimly, he pressed at the inflate switch on his suit side, knowing it would only allow the wave to pound him repeatedly against the surface or the sandy bottom. But at least this way they might locate his body.

48

I'm sorry, Kirsi. Good-bye.

Then he was up again, bobbing in the air, his arms and legs unable to move for the air that enveloped them. Too soon, it was too soon. He twisted, turning on his belly-balloon.

Two men were coming toward him. That surprised him. The second, bigger surprise was that they were not swimming. They were wading. Dazed, Acorizal tried to focus burning eyes. There was a hissing sound. One of the men was deflating his suit. He tried to yell at the man, but his mouth wasn't working any better than his brain. He thought he could hear people yelling.

Then the air had drained from the suit and he was in the water once more. Only there was no supportive salt water this time but instead the arms of the two men holding him up. They had to. He didn't have the strength to stand.

"What . . . ?" Tongue and jaw wouldn't work together. "What . . . ?"

One of the men, young and tall, was looking at him with a mixture of wonder and admiration. "You don't know?"

"Don't know . . . anything," Acorizal mumbled, coughing.

"This is Scratch Bay. This is where the waves die, rider." The man pronounced the last word with emphasis. "You rode your wave all the way in. All the way."

"How . . . how big when I went over?"

"Oh, that? We all thought that was a last-minute flair to impress the judges. It wasn't?"

"Judges can go to hell. No . . . flair. How big?"

"About ten feet," said the other man, who had Acorizal's right arm across his shoulders. "You just rolled over." He gestured forward with a nod of his head. "Your board's safe, up on the beach."

"Ten feet." Acorizal's mouth twisted.

A familiar face was waiting to greet him as they stumbled into the shallows. It peered concernedly into Acorizal's as the rider was laid out on a suspension mattress on the beach.

49

Cheers filled the air, drunken parodies of true speech to Acorizal's mind. They were mixed with the admonitions of officials who kept the near-hysterical crowd at bay.

"Hello, Joao," said Janwin as he checked his friend's heartbeat. "How are you?"

Acorizal squinted through the salt at his friend. "Chewed up," he gasped softly. "Chewed up and spit out like an old wad of gum." He saw that a bandage was draped across the surgeon's head and suspension straps supported his plasti-sealed left arm, and he framed a question with his eyes.

"Oh, this?" Janwin smiled, moved his sealed arm. "I went into mine, tried to swim out. Too late to use my pack. Tore the shoulder ligaments. I'm afraid my riding's over for this year. What the hell happened to your pack?"

"Vaxial," Acorizal explained. He spent a few moments choking before he could continue. "It was trying to eat me. I hope it suffocates. How long was I up? I can't see too well."

"Eight hours and five minutes. The last hour spent glued to your board, I'm told. You lost a stabilizer. They're fixing it now."

"That's nice."

"First complete ride in twelve years," Janwin continued admiringly. "Except for Nuotuan in 'twenty-four, and she was dead by the time they got to her. You're not dead."

"No, I'm not."

Janwin hesitated. "I guess I ought to let you rest, but I have to know." He leaned closer, away from the probing reporters. "How was it?"

But Acorizal was already unconscious.

He got points for riding the tube. He got points for fighting off the Vaxials. He got points for style and points for length. Brookings had more cumulative time but fewer style points. On the basis of the one ride Acorizal was declared winner. They told him about it two days later, when he regained consciousness.

One of the honorary judges, a media star from Terra, was present to hand over the trophy and prize money. Media reporters flocked around the man who'd never swum more than a hundred yards at any one time in his life. The man was very tall and handsome and not a very bad actor. His voice was rich and deep, well suited to making presentations.

But they couldn't find Acorizal. He wasn't in his hotel room and he wasn't anywhere to be found in Scratch Bay Towne. They searched for him on the beach, expecting to find him bathing in the rapturous stares of his admirers, but he wasn't there either.

Who they finally found was Janwin, sitting at the board works helping a young rider align his newly fitted stabilizers.

"I'm busy and I'm due back at the hospital tonight," the surgeon told the anxious cluster of reporters and officials.

"Just tell us, do you know where he is?"

"Yeah, I know where he is."

The media star looked very distressed. "I'm on contract here." He checked his bejeweled chronometer. "I'll give this another ten minutes, and then I've got to catch the shuttle out to my ship."

"Then you'll have to miss him," said Janwin.

"Where the hell is he?" wondered one of the more irritated honorary officials, a man with much money and little else.

Janwin shook his head. "Where do you think he'd be?" He pointed northwestward. "He took a skimmer and follow crew with him."

"Crazy," muttered the official. "Doesn't he want his trophy and money?"

"I expect he does," said the surgeon thoughtfully. "But he told me he has to go home tomorrow. I'm sure he'll be grateful to accept the prize and cash.

"But first he has to catch another wave . . ."

The Winds of Change

by 4113321113231300201300313222441

Ah Love! Could you and I with Him conspire
To grasp this Sorry Scheme of Things entire,
Would not we shatter it to bits — and then
Remold it nearer to the Heart's Desire?

Fitzgerald wrote these lines in his adaptation of Omar
Khayyam's verses, but in considering any heart's desire,
we must ask, "Whose heart?"

There are over four billion hearts on this Earth of
ours and perhaps four billion hearts' desires, not one
of which would undoubtedly suit any heart but the one
that desired it. Perhaps it is safer to accept what is.

Jonas Dinsmore walked into the President's Room of the
Faculty Club in a manner completely characteristic of himself, as though conscious of being in a place in which he
belonged but in which he was not accepted. The belonging
showed in the sureness of his stride and the casual noise of
his feet as he walked. The nonacceptance lay in his quick
look from side to side as he entered, a quick summing up
of the enemies present.

He was an associate professor of physics, and he was not liked.

There were two others in the room, and Dinsmore might well have considered them enemies without being considered paranoid for doing so. One was Horatio Adams, the aging chairman of the department who, without ever having done any single thing that was remarkable had yet accumulated vast respect for the numerous unremarkable but perfectly correct things he had done. The other was Carl Muller, whose work on Grand Unified Field Theory had put him in line for the Nobel Prize (he thought probably) and the presidency of the university (he thought certainly). It was hard to say which prospect Dinsmore found more distasteful. It was quite fair to say he detested Muller.

Dinsmore seated himself at one corner of the couch, which was old, slippery, and chilly, but the two comfortable armchairs were taken by the others. Dinsmore smiled. He frequently smiled, though his face never seemed either friendly or pleased as a result. Though there was nothing in the smile that was not the normal drawing back of the corners of the mouth, it invariably had a chilling effect on those at whom he aimed the gesture. His round face, his sparse but carefully combed hair, his full lips, would all have taken on joviality with such a smile, or should have — but didn't.

Adams stirred with what seemed to be a momentary spasm of irritation crossing his long, New Englandish face. Muller, his hair nearly black, and his eyes an incongruous blue, seemed impassive.

Dinsmore said, "I intrude, gentlemen, I know. Yet I have no choice. I have been asked by the Board of Trustees to be present. It may seem to you to be a cruel action, perhaps. I am sure you expect, Muller, that at any moment a communication will be received from the trustees to the effect that you have been named to the presidency. It would seem proper that the renowned Professor Adams, your mentor and patron, should know of it. But why, Muller, should they reserve a similar privilege for me, your humble and ever-failing rival?

"I suspect, in fact, that your first act as president, Muller, would be to inform me that it would be in all ways better if I were to seek another position elsewhere, since my appointment will not be renewed past this academic year. It might be convenient to have me on the spot in order that there be no delay. It would be unkind, but efficient.

"You look troubled, both of you. I may be unjust. My instant dismissal may not be in your mind; you may have been willing to wait till tomorrow. Can it be that it is the trustees who would rather be quick and who would rather have me on the spot? It doesn't matter. Either way it would seem that you are in and I am out. And perhaps that seems just. The respected head of a great department approaching the evening of his career, and his brilliant protégé, whose grasp of concept and whose handling of mathematics is unparalleled, are ready for the laurels; while I, without respect or honor —

"Since this is so, it is kind of you to let me talk without interrupting. I have a feeling that the message we wait for may not arrive for some minutes, for an hour, perhaps. A presentiment. The trustees themselves would not be averse to building suspense. This is their moment in the Sun, their fleeting time of glory. And since the time must be passed, I am willing to speak.

"Some, before execution, are granted a last meal, some a last cigarette; I, a last few words. You needn't listen, I suppose, or even bother to look interested.

"— Thank you. The look of resignation, Professor Adams, I will accept as agreement. Professor Muller's slight smile, let us say of contempt, will also do.

"You will not blame me, I know, for wishing the situation were changed. In what way? A good question. I would not

54

wish to change my character and personality. It may be unsatisfactory, but it is mine. Nor would I change the politic efficiency of Adams or the brilliance of Muller, for what would such a change do but make them no longer Adams and Muller? I would have them be they, and yet — have the results different. If one could go back in time, what small change then might produce a large and desirable change now?

"That's what's needed. Time travel!

"Ah, *that* grinds a reaction out of you, Muller. That was the clear beginning of a snort. Time travel! Ridiculous! Impossible!

"Not only impossible in the sense that the state of the art is inadequate for the purpose, but in the greater sense that it will be forever inadequate. Time travel, in the sense of going backward to change reality, is not only technologically impossible now, but it is theoretically impossible altogether.

"Odd you should think so, Muller, because your theories, those very analyses which have brought the four forces, even gravitation, measurably close to inclusion under the umbrella of a single set of relationships, make time travel no longer theoretically impossible.

"No, don't rise to protest. Keep your seat, Muller, and relax. For you it is impossible, I'm sure. For most people it would be. Perhaps for almost everyone. But there might be exceptions, and it just might be that I'm one of them. Why me? Who knows? I don't claim to be brighter than either of you, but what has that to do with it?

"Let us argue by analogy. Consider — Tens of thousands of years ago, human beings, little by little, either as a mass endeavor or through the agency of a few brilliant individuals, learned to communicate. Speech was invented, and delicate modulations of sounds were invested with abstract meaning.

"For thousands of years, every normal human being has

been able to communicate, but how many have been able to tell a story superlatively well? Shakespeare, Tolstoy, Dickens, Hugo — a handful compared to all the human beings who have lived — can use those modulated sounds to wrench at heartstrings and reach for sublimity. Yet they use the same sounds that all of us use.

"I am prepared to admit that Muller's IQ, for instance, is higher than that of Shakespeare or Tolstoy. Muller's knowledge of language must be as good as that of any writer alive, his understanding of meaning as great. Yet Muller could not put words together and achieve the effect that Shakespeare could. Muller himself wouldn't deny it for a moment, I'm sure. What then is it, that Shakespeare and Tolstoy can do that Muller or Adams or I cannot? What wisdom do they have that we cannot penetrate? You don't know and I don't know. What is worse, *they* didn't know. Shakespeare could in no manner have instructed you — or anyone — how to write as he did. He didn't know how — he merely could.

"Next consider the consciousness of time. As far as we can guess, only human beings of all life forms can grasp the significance of time. All other species live in the present only; might have vague memories; might have dim and limited forethought — but surely only human beings truly understand the past, present, and future and can speculate on its meaning and significance, can wonder about the flow of time, of how it carries us along with it, and of how that flow might be altered.

"When did this happen? How did it come about? Who was the first human being, or hominid, who suddenly grasped the manner in which the river of time carried him from the dim past into the dim future, and wondered if it might be damned or diverted?

"The flow is not invariant. Time races for us at times; hours vanish in what seems like minutes — and lags unconscionably at other times. In dream states, in trances, in drug experiences, time alters its properties.

"You seem about to comment, Adams. Don't bother. You are going to say that those alterations are purely psychological. I know it, but what else is there but the psychological?

"Is there *physical* time? If so, what *is* physical time? Surely, it is whatever we choose to make it. *We* design the instruments. *We* interpret the measurements. *We* create the theories and then interpret those. And from absolute, we have changed time and made it the creature of the speed of light and decided that simultaneity is indefinable.

"From your theory, Muller, we know that time is altogether subjective. In theory, someone understanding the nature of the flow of time can, given enough talent, move with or against the flow independently, or stand still in it. It is analogous to the manner in which, given the symbols of communication, someone, given enough talent, can write *King Lear*. Given enough talent.

"What if I had enough talent? What if I could be the Shakespeare of the time flow? Come, let us amuse ourselves. At any moment, the message from the Board of Trustees will arrive, and I will have to stop. Until it does, however, allow me to push along with my chatter. It serves its turn. Come, I doubt that you are aware that fifteen minutes has passed since I began talking.

"Think, then — If I could make use of Muller's theory and find within myself the odd ability to take advantage of it as Homer did of words, what would I do with my gift? I might wander back through time, perhaps, wraithlike, observing from without all the patterns of time and events, in order to reach in at one place or another and make a change.

"Oh, yes, I would be outside the time stream as I travel. Your theory, Muller, properly interpreted, does not insist that, in moving backward in time, or forward, one must move through the thick of the flow, stumbling across events and knocking them down in passage. That would indeed be theoretically impossible. To remain *outside* is where the possibility comes in; and to slip in and out at will is where the talent comes in.

"Suppose, then, I did this: that I slipped in and made a change. That one change would breed another — which would breed another — Time would be set in a new path, which would take on a life of its own, curving and foaming until, in a very little time —

"No, that is an inadequate expression. 'Time would, in a very little time —' It is as though we are imagining some abstract and absolute timelike reference against which our time may be measured; as though our own background of time were flowing against another, deeper background. I confess it's beyond me, but pretend you understand.

"Any change in the events of time would, after a — while — alter everything unrecognizably.

"But I wouldn't want *that*. I told you at the start, I do not wish to cease to be I. Even if in my place I could create someone who was more intelligent, more sensible, more successful, it would still not be I.

"Nor would I want to change you, Muller, or you, Adams. I've said that already too. I would not want to triumph over a Muller who is less ingenious and spectacularly bright, or over an Adams who has been less politic and deft at putting together an imposing structure of respect. I would want to triumph over you as you are, and not over lesser beings.

"Well, yes, it is triumph I wish.

"— Oh, come. You stir as though I had said something unworthy. Is a sense of triumph so alien to you? Are you so dead to humanity that you seek no honor, no victory, no fame, no rewards? Am I to suppose that the respected Professor Adams does not wish to possess his long list of publications, his revered string of honorary degrees, his numerous medals and plaques, his post as head of one of the most prestige-filled departments of physics in the world?

"And would you be satisfied to have all that, Adams, if no one were to know of it, if its existence were to be wiped out of all records and histories, if it were to remain a secret between you and the Almighty? A silly question. I certainly won't demand an answer when we all know what it would be.

"And I needn't go through the same rigmarole of inquiry concerning Muller's potential Nobel Prize and what seems like a certain university presidency — and of this university, too.

"What is it you both want in all of this, considering that you want not only the things themselves but the public knowledge of your ownership of these things? Surely you want triumph! You want triumph over your competitors as an abstract class, triumph over your fellow human beings. You want to do something others cannot do and to have all those others know that you have done something they cannot do, so that they must then look up at you in helpless awareness of that knowledge and in envy and enforced admiration.

"Shall I be more noble than you? Why? Let me have the privilege of wanting what you want, of hungering for the triumph you have hungered for. Why should I not want the long respect, the great prize, the enormous position that waits on you two? And to do so in your place? To snatch it from you at the moment of its attainment? It is no more disgraceful for me to glory in such things than for you to do so.

"Ah, but you deserve it and I do not. There is precisely the point. What if I could so arrange the flow and content of time to make me deserve it and you not?

"Imagine! I would still be I; the two of you, the two of

you. You would be no less worthy and I no more worthy — that being the condition I have set myself, that none of us change — and yet I deserve and you do not. I want to beat you, in other words, as you are, and not as inferior substitutes.

"In a way, that is a tribute to you, isn't it? I see from your expression you think it is. I imagine you both feel a kind of contemptuous pride. It is something after all to be the standard by which victory is measured. You enjoy earning the merits I lust for — especially if that lust must go unsatisfied.

"I don't blame you for feeling so. In your place, I would feel the same.

"But must the lust go unsatisfied? Think it out —

"Suppose I were to go back in time, say twenty-five years. A nice figure; an even quarter century. You, Adams, would be forty. You would have just arrived here, a full professor, from your stint at Case Institute. You would have done your work in diamagnetics, though your unreported effort to do something with bismuth hypochromite had been a rather laughable failure.

"Heavens, Adams, don't look so surprised. Do you think I don't know your professional life to the last detail —

"And as for you, Muller, you were twenty-six, and just in the process of turning out a fascinating doctor's dissertation on general relativity, which is much less satisfying in retrospect than it was at the time. Had it been correctly interpreted, it would have anticipated most of Hawking's later conclusions, as you now know. You did not correctly interpret it at the time, and you have successfully managed to hide that fact.

"I'm afraid, Muller, you are not good at interpretation. You did not interpret your own doctor's dissertation to its best advantage, and you have not properly interpreted your

60

great Field Theory. Perhaps, Muller, it isn't a disgrace either. The lack of interpretation is a common event. We can't all have the interpretative knack, and the talent to shake loose consequences may not occur in the same mind that possesses the talent for brilliance of concept. I have the former without the latter, so why should you not have the latter without the former?

"If you could only create your marvelous thoughts, Muller, and leave it to me to see the equally marvelous conclusions. What a team we would make, you and I, Muller — but you wouldn't have me. I don't complain about that, for I wouldn't have you.

"In any case, these are trifles. I could in no way damage you, Adams, with the pinprick of your silly handling of the bismuth salts. After all, you did, with some difficulty, catch your mistake before you embalmed it in the pages of a learned journal — if you could have gotten it past the referees. And I could not cloud the sunshine that plays on you, Muller, by making a point of your failure to deduce what might be deduced from your concepts. It might even be looked upon as a measure of your brilliance: that so much crowded into your thoughts that even *you* were not bright enough to wring them dry of consequence.

"But if that would not do, what would? How could matters be changed properly? Fortunately, I could study the situation for a length of — something — that my consciousness would interpret as years, and yet there would be no physical time passage and therefore no aging. My thought processes would continue, but my physical metabolism would not.

"You smile again. No, I don't know how that could be. Surely, our thought processes are part of our metabolic changes. I can only suppose that outside the time stream, thought processes are not thought processes in the physical sense, but are something else that is equivalent.

"And if I study a moment in time, and search for a change that will accomplish what I want it to accomplish, how could I do that? Could I make a change, move forward in time, study the consequences, and, if I didn't like it, move back, unchange the change and try another? If I did it fifty times, a thousand times, could I ever find the right change? The number of changes, each with numberless consequences, each with further numberless consequences, is beyond computation or comprehension. How could I find the change I was seeking?

"Yet I could. I could learn how, but I couldn't tell you how I learned or what I did after I learned. Would it be so difficult? Think of the things we *do* learn.

"We stand, we walk, we run, we hop — and we do it all even though we are tipped on end. We are in an utter state of instability. We remain standing only because the large muscles of our legs and torso are forever lightly contracting and pulling this way and that, like a circus performer balancing a stick on the end of his nose.

"Physically, it's hard. That is why standing still takes it out of us and makes us glad to sit down after a while. That is why standing at attention for an unfairly long period of time will lead to collapse. Yet, except when we take it to extremes, we do it so well, we're not even aware we do it. We can stand and walk and run and hop and start and stop all day long and never fall or even become seriously unsteady. Well, then, describe how you do it so that someone who has never tried can do it. You can't.

"Another example. We can talk. We can stretch and contract the muscles of our tongue and lips and cheeks and palate in a rapid and unrhythmic set of changes that produce just the modulation of sound we want. It was hard enough to learn when we were infants, but once we learned, we could produce dozens of words a minute without any conscious effort. Well, how do we do it? What changes do we produce to say, 'How do we do it?' Describe those changes to someone who has never spoken, so that he can make that sound! It can't be done.

"But we can make the sound. And without effort too.

"Given enough time — I don't even know how to describe the passage of what I mean. It was not time; call it 'duration.' Given enough duration *without* the passage of time, I learned how to adjust reality as desired. It was like a child babbling, but gradually learning to pick and choose among the babbles to construct words. I learned to choose.

"It was risky, of course. In the process of learning, I might have done something irreversible or at least something which, for reversal, would have required subtle changes that were beyond me. I did not. Perhaps it was more good fortune than anything else.

"And I came to enjoy it. It was like painting a picture, constructing a piece of sculpture. It was much more than that; it was the carving of a new reality. A new reality unchanged from our own in key ways. I remained exactly what I am; Adams remained the eternal Adams, Muller, the quintessential Muller. The university remained the university; science remained science.

"Well, then, did nothing change? But I'm losing your attention. You no longer believe me and, if I am any judge, feel disgusted with what I am saying. I seem to have slipped in my enthusiasm and I have begun acting as though time travel were real and that I have really done what I would like to do. Forgive me. Consider it imagination — fantasy — I say what I *might* have done *if* time travel were real and *if* I truly had the talent for it.

"In that case — in my imagination — did nothing change? There would have to be *some* change: one that would leave Adams exactly Adams and yet unfit to be head of the department, Muller to be precisely Muller, but without any likelihood of becoming university president and without much chance of being voted the Nobel Prize.

"And I would have to be myself, unlovable and plodding, and unable to create — yet possessing the qualities that would make *me* university president.

"It could be nothing scientific; it would have to be something outside science, something disgraceful and sordid that would disqualify you fine gentlemen —

"Come, now. I don't deserve those looks of mingled disdain and smug self-satisfaction. You are sure, I take it, that you can do nothing disgraceful and sordid? How can you be sure? There's not one of us who, if conditions were right, would not slip into — shall we call it sin? Who among us would be without sin, given the proper temptation? Who among us *is* without sin?

"Think, think — Are you sure your souls are white? Have you done nothing wrong, ever? Have you never at least nearly fallen into the pit? And if you have, was it not a narrow escape, brought about more through some fortunate circumstance than inner virtue? And if someone had closely studied all your actions and noted the strokes of fortune that kept you safe and deflected just one of them, might you not then have done wrong?

"Of course, if you had lived openly foul and sordid lives so that people turned from you in disdain and disgust you would not have reached your present states of reverence. You would have fallen long since, and I would not have to step over your disgraced bodies, for you would not be here to serve me as steppingstones.

"You see how complex it all is?

"But then, it is all the more exciting, you see. If I were to go back in time and find that the solution was not complex, that in one stroke I could achieve my aim, I might manage to gain pleasure out of it, but there would be a lack of intellectual excitement.

"If we were to play chess and I were to win by a fool's mate in three moves, it would be a victory that was worse than defeat. I would have played an unworthy opponent, and I would be disgraced for having done so.

"No. The victory that is worthwhile is the one snatched slowly and with pain from the reluctant grip of the adversary — a victory that seems unattainable, a victory that is as wearying, as torturing, as hopelessly bone breaking as the worst and most tedious defeat — but that has, as its difference, the fact that, while I am panting and gasping in total exhaustion, it is the flag I hold in my hand, the trophy.

"The duration I spent playing with that most intractable of all materials, reality, was filled with the difficulty I had set myself. I insisted stubbornly not only on having my aim, but on my having that aim my way, on rejecting everything that was not *exactly* as I wanted it to be. A near miss I considered a miss; an almost hit I eliminated as not a hit. In my target, I had a bull's eye and nothing else.

"And even after I won, it would have to be a victory so subtle that you would not know I had won until I had carefully explained it to you. To the final moment, you would not know your life had been turned wrong end up. That is what —

"But wait, I have left out something. I have been so caught up in the intensity of my intention of leaving ourselves and the university and science all the same that I have not explained the other things that might indeed change. There would be bound to be changes in social, political, and economic forces, and in international relationships. Who would care about such things after all? Certainly not we three.

"That is the marvel of science and the scientist, is it not? What is it to us whom we elect in our dear United States, or what votes were taken in the United Nations, or whether the stock market went up or down, or whether the unending pavane of the nations followed this pattern or that? As long as science is there and the laws of nature hold fast and the game we play continues, the background against which we play it is just a meaningless shifting of light and shadow.

"Perhaps you don't feel this openly, Muller. I know well you have, in your time, felt yourself part of society and have placed yourself on record with views on this and that. To a lesser extent so did you, Adams. Both of you have had exalted views concerning humanity and the Earth and various abstractions. How much of that, however, was a matter of greasing your conscience because inside — deep inside — you don't really care, as long as you can sit brooding over your scientific thoughts?

"That's one big difference between us. I don't care what happens to humanity as long as I am left to my physics, and I am open about it. Everyone knows me as cynical and callous. You two *secretly* don't care. To the cynicism and callousness that characterize me, you add hypocrisy, which plasters over your sins to the unthinking, but makes them worse when found out.

"Oh, don't shake your heads. In my searching out your lives I discovered as much about you as you yourselves know; more, since I see your peccadilloes clearly, and you two hide them even from yourselves. It is the most amusing thing about hypocrisy that once it is adhered to sternly enough, it numbers the hypocrite himself among its victims. He is his own chief victim, in fact, for it is quite usual that when the hypocrite is exposed to all the world, he still seems, quite honestly, a plaster saint to himself.

"But I tell you this not in order to vilify you. I tell it to you to explain that if I found it necessary to change the world so as to keep ourselves all the same, yet place me on top instead of you, you wouldn't really mind. Not about the world, that is.

"You wouldn't mind if the Republicans were up and the Democrats were down, or vice versa; if feminism were in flower and professional sports under a cloud; if this fashion or that in clothing, furniture, music, or comedy were in or out. What would any of that matter to you?

"Nothing.

"In fact, less than nothing, for if the world were changed, it would be a new reality, *the* reality as far as people in the world were concerned, the *only* reality, the reality of the history books, the reality that was *real* over the last twenty-five years.

"If you believed me, if you thought I were spinning more than a fantasy, you would still be helpless. Could you go to someone in authority and say: 'That is not the way things are supposed to be. It has been altered by a villain'? What would that prove but that you were insane? Who could believe that reality is not reality, when it is the fabric and tapestry that has been woven all these twenty-five years in so incredibly intricate a fashion, and when everyone remembers and lives the weaving?

"But you yourselves do *not* believe me. You dare not believe that I am not merely speculating about having gone back into the past, about having studied you both, about having labored to bring about a new reality in which we are unchanged but, alas, the world is changed. I have *done* it; I have done it *all.* And I alone remember both realities because I was outside time when the change was made, and *I* made it.

"And still you don't believe me. You dare not believe me, for you yourselves would feel you were insane if you did. Could I have altered the familiar world of this moment? Impossible.

"If I did, what could the world have been like before I tampered with it? I'll tell you — It was chaotic! It was full of license! People were laws unto themselves! In a way I'm glad I changed it. Now we have a government and the land is governed. Our rulers have views and the views are enforced. Good!

"But, gentlemen, in that world that was, that old reality that no one can know or conceive, you two gentlemen were laws unto yourselves and fought for license and anarchy. It was no crime in the old reality. It was admirable to many.

"In the new reality, I left you unchanged. You remained fighters for license and anarchy, and that *is* a crime in the present reality — the only reality you know. I made sure you could cover it up. No one knew about your crimes, and you were able to rise to your present heights. But I knew where the evidence was and how it might be uncovered and, at the proper time — I uncovered it.

"Now I think that for the first time I catch expressions on your faces that don't ring the changes of weary tolerance, of contempt, of amusement, of annoyance. Do I catch a whiff of fear? Do you remember what I am talking about?

"Think! Think! Who were members of the League of Constitutional Freedoms? Who helped circulate the Free Thought Manifesto? It was very brave and honorable of you to do this, some people thought. You were much applauded by the underground. Come, come, you know whom I mean by the underground. You're not active in it any longer. Your position is too exposed, and you have too much to lose. You have position and power, and there is more on the way. Why risk it for something that people don't want?

"You wear your pendants, and you're numbered among the godly. But my pendant is larger and I am more godly, for I have not committed your crimes. What is more, gentlemen, I get the credit for having informed against you.

"A shameful act? A scandalous act? My informing? Not at all. I shall be rewarded. I have been horrified at the hypocrisy of my colleagues, disgusted and nauseated at their subversive past, concerned for what they might be plotting now against the best and noblest and most godly society ever established on Earth. As a result I brought all this to the attention of the decent men who help conduct the policies of that society in true sobriety of thought and humility of spirit.

"They will wrestle with your evils to save your souls and to make you true children of the Spirit. There will be some damage to your bodies in the process, I imagine, but what of that? It would be a trivial cost compared to the vast and eternal good they will bring you. And I shall be rewarded for making it all possible.

"I think you are really frightened now, gentlemen, for the message we have all been waiting for is now coming, and you see now why I have been asked to remain here with you. The presidency is mine, and my interpretation of the Muller theory, combined with the disgrace of Muller, will make it the Dinsmore theory in the textbooks and may bring me the Nobel Prize. As for you—"

There was the sound of footsteps in cadence outside the door, a ringing cry of "Halt!"

The door was flung open. In stepped a man whose sober gray garb, wide white collar, tall buckled hat, and large bronze cross proclaimed him a captain in the dreaded Legion of Decency.

He said, nasally, "Horatio Adams, I arrest you in the name of God and the Congregation for the crime of deviltry and witchcraft. Carl Muller, I arrest you in the name of God and the Congregation for the crime of deviltry and witchcraft."

His hand beckoned briefly and quickly. Two legionnaires of the ranks came up to the two physicists, who sat in stupefied horror in their chairs, yanked them to their feet, placed cuffs on their wrists, and, with an initial gesture of humility to the sacred symbol, tore the small crosses that were pendant from their lapels.

The captain turned to Dinsmore. "Yours in sanctity, sir. I have been asked to deliver this communication from the Board of Trustees."

"Yours in sanctity, captain," said Dinsmore gravely, fingering his own pendant cross. "I rejoice to receive the words of those godly men."

He knew what the communication contained.

As the new university president, he might, if he chose, lighten the punishment of the two men. His triumph would be enough even so.

But only if it were safe.

And in the grip of the Moral Majority, he must remember, no one was ever *truly* safe.

Harpist

by 140022043300212104120423332104 43

Henry Wadsworth Longfellow was of the opinion that "Music is the universal language of mankind."

Is it really? I have heard the music of our teenagers in the city I live in — blared forth over loudspeakers in the park, blasted forth from record players in neighbor's homes, screeched forth from macroradios slung over the shoulder. It may be the universal language of humankind, but if it is, I am strangely mute.

If we broaden the scope, might music be the universal language of more than humankind? How can I help but doubt that even more strongly? And yet perhaps Longfellow had something there —

Read on!

B.C.: They were still a trinity after the accident at entry, but the Outer, to save the two, had to contract and partially burn. The Older and the Younger sought the Outer. The search was long and the years passed, but still they sang and searched.

A.D.: That year Curly was six, and he found a curiously shaped stone as he wandered the dry creek bed

by the shack. Already he could pick out a tune, but,
suddenly, he became better. And found his life.

◊ ◊ ◊

Mike's Bar, at the end of the 1970s, was in a village in the
Kentucky coalfields. The village was big enough for the bar,
a general store, two churches, and a union hall. The bar
drew trade mostly from dust-covered miners, and it could
be a rough place on paydays. The outside was hewn logs.
The inside was poorly lighted and always damp.

Curly, the man in the wheelchair, played electric guitar
and sang in the bar nights. Sometimes, as on Saturdays, he
had to turn the amplifier up high to make the crowd hear,
but other nights it would get quiet when he played because
he was still good. Sometimes he'd sing, and now and then
he'd get them to join in singing, but mostly he played. His
hands moved easily, his feet not at all. He had the gift. He
could play anything he could put nimble fingers to: guitar,
banjo, fiddle. He listened to himself as he played, forgetting
his legs, sometimes even forgetting the drink beside him,
intent only on the music. He was fifty-five years old, and
his hair was only a fringe, so the name Curly was now a
joke. The face below the hair had a perpetually astonished
clown look, as if in shock at what life had done to its owner.
He was thin and drank enormous amounts. Sometimes, late
at night, he would be so intoxicated that he'd play only by
instinct. Sometimes, afterward, he'd be sick from the effects
of drinking and couldn't play well. Not playing made him
sicker, so he drank to escape his own mediocrity. A circle.
He no longer had any goal other than the music: to play it,
to hear it. He had no friends other than those made anew
each night. Days were for sodden sleeping. Only the nights
had life.

Curly was coal country born, and he'd wandered back looking for a place to exist and drink and eventually die in the

dark land of his childhood, a land of Indian ghosts and super-
stitions and childhood dreams, a bloody land of somber men,
strikes, and guns. Sometimes he could recall bits of his childhood, when he'd played his first guitar, remember his thin,
tubercular mother, remember the father who'd died young of
black lung, remember the loveless relatives who'd passed him
about like an unwanted football. It was the land itself and
not the remnants of family that had drawn him back. It was
a vague feeling that he should be here in coal country to die.

Curly knew a little about Hickam before the man came
into the bar to see him — just some stories, not much. Hickam
was a farmer-trader who'd made it rich, shrewdly buying
and selling, cheating all the way, bluff and hard. Those who
talked about him at all said Hickam was a strange one. He
lived on the old Turner place now. They said he'd hauled
in truckloads of equipment to the place, but not to mine it.
The coal miners said darkly he was "doing something" back
there where the caves and the mounds were, something that
had nothing to do with coal. The mounds were the last visible
remains of the vanished Indians, who'd built a society to
rival any present-day government before the star first appeared over Bethlehem.

Hickam was a known ravager of the mounds, an explorer
of caves. If he did other things, none of the coal miners, tough
as they were, ever ventured close enough to find out. The
Turner place had always borne a bad name. Curly remembered that from childhood. No one went there.

Hickam came bouncing into the bar on one of Curly's better
nights, when the feeling ran strong between head and hands,
when the sounds from the guitar were more than good music.
Hickam sat in the darkest corner of the room and listened
and watched, drinking Jack Daniel's and Coca-Cola instead
of beer like most of the miners. Curly could see him singing
and humming with the music now and then. Hickam sent
a couple of Jacks to the podium with Jonce, the black bar-

tender-owner, and Curly nodded his thanks. The bar seemed uneasy around Hickam, but no one started trouble. Curly thought Hickam could maybe have handled a lot of trouble anyway.

He returned a few nights later, during an off night in the week, when things weren't crowded.

Jonce sidled to the stand at Curly's intermission.

"Hickam wants to see you, man," he said, his look unreadable. "He'd like to buy you a drink and talk to you. I'll roll you on back."

Curly was amiable. "Sure, Jonce. What's he want?"

"You talk to him," Jonce ordered. "What he says is okay with me. He owns this building. So please be nice."

When Jonce had rolled him there Curly could see Hickam was younger than he'd thought, maybe low forties, and big, with arms like posts. His black eyes were slightly exophthalmic and very penetrating, the best point in a brutal face. Hickam examined Curly, and Curly felt like a bug under a microscope.

"You play damn good, Curly," Hickam said. "Can I buy you a drink?"

"Sure, Mr. Hickam."

Hickam nodded at Jonce, who came running.

"Where'd you get that last song from?" Hickam asked.

"It was a variation that came to me. Winters. 'Robinbird' stuff. It ain't really that original." Hickam reminded Curly close up of a mean gunnery sergeant he'd once known, dead now, bones in Korea.

"I hear you used to be famous?" Hickam asked curiously. "You was in Nashville. Made big records."

Curly nodded emotionlessly. He had been famous within the limitations of the trade. Not a headliner, but close. It seemed very long ago now.

"Jonce tells me you got bad blowed up in the K-War."

Curly nodded again. The story was well known. Nothing

74

worked under a line that began below his navel, nothing other than bowels and like that. Some things that did work he had no use for anymore. Karen had left him ten years back because of the drinking. At fifty-five getting it together was too much trouble for too small a return. A woman always seemed to feel as if she were doing him a favor when they managed it.

"I maybe got a proposition for you," Hickam said, leaning closer. He pointed at the raised podium where the silver-chased guitar and amp and speakers were. "How loud can you rev that damned thing up?"

"Loud enough to clear this place," Curly said, curious now. "Soft enough to fill it," he added.

"Good. That's real good. I need her loud. Forget about singing. I'd like to hire you for a few days, maybe even a week."

"I work here every night but Sunday. We're closed Sundays."

Hickam smiled. "Sunday could be the first night. I talked with Mr. Jonce and it's okay with him for you to be out as long as I'd need you. I made him a deal. I'll pay you damn good over and above the deal." He reached out a hand and covered one of Curly's.

Curly pulled his hand away, but Hickam only grinned.

"Ain't interested, Mr. Hickam," Curly said, disliking the man. "I don't need no place but here."

"If I said the word there might not be a job here," Hickam said carefully.

Curly shrugged. There were other places. The music was enough. There was always a place to play it.

Hickam watched him, frowning. "I could pay you a lot more money than you get in here. Drinks and tips and eating money's all there is here. I know that."

Curly looked down at his ruined legs and shook his head. "Money ain't the all of it. I've got what I need."

"I guess maybe you're afraid," Hickam said, challenging

him. "You live in that wheelchair and you're afraid." He looked around the room suspiciously. "None of these black dust-covered bastards will come close to my place. It's that, ain't it? You've heard about my place and what I'm doing from someone?"

"I was born a few miles from here," Curly said. "I heard about the Turner place lots of times. I remember that old man Turner's kids left early, and he died funny. I know his wife's in an asylum."

"That's right, but nobody knows nothing about how it is now," Hickam said, leaning closer, whispering scornfully. "Whatever it is there, it makes music. That's why I want you. You can hear it real faint coming up out of that deep hole after it's dark. Put your ear close to the ground and you can hear it. You know 'Dueling Banjos'? Kind of like that. Not that song, but the sound. Intricate." He nodded. "I went way back in the cave nearby. I couldn't hear it any better there, but there was a long wall I found with things painted on it. The first drawing showed something big and blazing that came down from the sky." His eyes were intense. "One picture showed all the trees down, another showed everything on fire: the trees, the grass, even the earth itself. Indian drawings, or maybe older than that. Other people have seen those drawings down the years. Them scientists from the state university wanted to come on the land and look around, but Turner wouldn't let them, and I ain't about to permit it. Turner told me once when I was drinking with him that only the sacred men of the five tribes was ever allowed on the place. Turner was afraid. He got old quick. So did his wife."

Hickam fell silent and Curly waited.

"I ain't seen anything yet," Hickam admitted. "Listening to you gave me an idea. If you won't come then rent me your outfit. I'll try it alone."

Curly had never heard about the music. All he could remember was that people had told him that Hickam's place had spooks on it and that it was a "bad place," but good enough for Hickam. He searched in his pocket and fingered his stone. It was cold. The chain had broken years ago, but he still had the locket.

"What kind of music?" he asked, shaking his head at the rental offer. One didn't rent out what was an extension of self. But he was interested. He lifted his drink and finished it, waiting.

"You want to hear the music?" Hickam asked him cunningly. "You got to come out there to hear it — it's simple." He looked around the bar. "Them in here will tell you not to do it. Will you come?"

Curly nodded, mildly interested, not caring much one way or the other.

"You'll need to bring along your guitar and stuff. I'll get it hauled back in for you. I got me a portable generator you can hook onto. Plenty of power." He looked at Curly's empty glass. "And there'll be plenty of good stuff."

Curly smiled and nodded. "Why not?" he asked softly.

Hickam sat unhearing, eyes shining with anticipation.

Curly touched the stone again. Sometimes in dreams he fancied it sang to him, strange songs about love and death. It seemed suddenly warmer to his touch. It did that now and then, changed temperatures.

The creek through the Turner place had run on down to Pa's place then. The stone might have come from upstream, from the mounds, rolling with the water, speckled blue, smooth to the touch.

Going home, he told it.

◇　◇　◇

On Sunday morning Hickam came past in a big truck. He loaded Curly's equipment as if it were made of balsam and silk. Curly envied him his strong legs. Hickam caught him watching and grinned, his eyes obsidian. He hefted Curly into the cab and then drove the truck off the main highway after a way. They sought and found a secondary, gravel road, then a bumpy, rutted mud track, into trees so green they almost seemed blue. Once they were away from the main road the land was almost as it had been ten thousand years before. Curly held tight to the seat belt, his dead legs flopping. He felt clammy and nauseated from too much drinking. His canvas folding wheelchair in the back of the truck rattled against the amplifying equipment.

"Take it a little easier, Mr. Hickam. That stuff back there is delicate."

"Oh? Sure." Hickam got out a pint bottle and offered it. Curly accepted it gratefully and drank until he burned all the way down to where feeling ended. Hickam took a pull and put the bottle back in a hip pocket.

"You ever heard of Schliemann?" he asked expansively.

"Who?"

"Schliemann. Heinrich Schliemann. He discovered the ruins of Troy." Hickam nodded to himself. "I read about him in a book. I always wanted . . . Now maybe I got me a thing for myself. But it's alive, Curly. Something alive."

Curly smiled and Hickam saw it.

"You wait," he said darkly. "You'll stop smiling."

The cave was located in rough terrain. There was a complex of Indian mounds around it. At the front of the cave, near the entrance, there was a dry pond surrounded by bushes and trees, full of weeds now, except in the deepest part. A scum of water stood there.

Hickam pointed. "That's the entrance down there. It's still spring muddy around it, and we'll have to be careful with the power lines, but I'll get you set up to play tonight."

"And all I have to do is play?"

"Listen first, play after," Hickam said seriously, nodding,

not looking at Curly. "See there near the front of the cave entrance? That's where I'm going to put you, close to the deep hole. That's where it lives. There's water starting maybe fifteen or twenty feet down the hole. Lord knows how deep it goes. Too deep to measure. I put a rope down it once, but I ran out of rope and hadn't hit bottom."

"How much rope?" Curly felt a chill despite himself.

Hickam shrugged. "A lot. All a winch could hold. I thought maybe it was hungry down there. I had me a whole hog on the end of my line, but it come back up untouched."

Curly looked. The hole was maybe fifty feet across, curtained by trees and growth, curiously circular. The walls were smooth, and the hole was slightly separated from the old, dried pond. The hole entered the ground at a slight slant so that it angled back under the cave. Around its sides, as they drew nearer, Curly could see green plants flourishing in slick profusion.

Hickam smiled. "I saw that hole and heard the sounds. And I've never seen plants around here exactly like the ones growing in that hole. I'm a curious man. I've run my way through two fortunes and a lot of women. I wondered what made the hole. And there's all the stories. Old man Turner thought he stuck me with something. I paid him too much money, but I'd have given more. And I knew there wasn't no coal here no matter how much he hinted. But I got me something nobody else has, and I own it free and clear." He nodded, his eyes hooded and somehow lost. "Now, we'll start out setting you up." He handed Curly the bottle. "There's more," he said condescendingly, watching Curly drink.

◊ ◊ ◊

First Curly listened. There was *something*. It was a queer sound. You had to fight to hear it, like lost whispers. Curly got out of the wheelchair and lay on the ground, putting his ear close to the rocky soil, smoothing a place. Just notes and only a hint of recognizable melody, but haunting. The stone in his pocket felt very warm when he touched it.

"Some nights it's louder," Hickam said. They listened for a time longer while insects buzzed around them. They drank whiskey mixed with warm Cokes.

"You want to try to play some now that it's full dark?"

Curly nodded, and Hickam helped him back into the wheelchair.

It was the strangest concert Curly had ever played. An audience of one, and, in the distance, the hum of the gasoline-powered generator. The moon was out, and Hickam hadn't erected any special lights. There was just one on a pole outside the cave entrance near the water-filled deep hole. Hickam himself had set up a camera behind a thicket of small trees about thirty yards from where Curly played.

Curly turned the volume up high. He played his own special version of "Jim Bob," chording, picking, hands moving quicksilver. He moved to "Greensleeves," and then to "God's Fate," then mixed country western and gospel as he warmed to his own sounds. He no longer watched the edge of the deep hole after the first tunes, but was caught again for the thousand-thousandth time in his own music, not caring any longer about legs, about the wife who'd left him, or even the children he'd wanted but never had. He played, pausing only now and then to drink.

In the middle of "Bodies" he realized that he and Hickam weren't alone. There was something, a something that moved and shone just at the rim of the deep hole, something playing softly with music, anticipating, weaving, joining, with a sound like none Curly had ever heard. It wasn't guitar or harp or banjo or anything human, but it was still in tune, catching instantly beats and changes. More like harp than anything

80

else, Curly decided. With perhaps a little violin. But a harp.

He gave it his best, the sad and lonely "Away Man, Away," and it came soaring and cavorting out over the top of the deep place. Curly nodded to it, not afraid. Nothing that made music could frighten him. The thing was big, and it spread its vaguely tentlike shape against the sky, with bright, moving lines that joined together, spinning and twirly, then apexed in blackness that was three feet in circumference at the top. No eyes, no features, but Curly knew it perceived him. For a while he thought the interaction of the bright lines produced its music, but then he became unsure. Perhaps the lines only spelled out rhythm, and the music welled from blackness. Its shape seemed vaguely familiar, as if he'd seen or dreamed it before.

It could make music. Lord, how it could make music. Curly had endured a lifetime of musicians who couldn't read, had no ear, no sense of timing, were happily off key, dragging, futile.

Not this. It could *fly*.

In the background, now and then, Curly could hear Hickam's busy camera snapping when there was a pause in the music.

All night Curly played in sweet companionship, forgetting Hickam, forgetting even the booze. Now and then he'd pause and wait a while for the being, which he now referred to in his own mind as the Harpist, to try a song on its own, but the Harpist would have none of that. It just hovered and outwaited Curly until Curly's fingers grew restless and began to move again. Curly cut the sound back to the place where he could hear the Harpist easily over the sounds of his own playing. It was better that way.

Near first light the Harpist grew restless. It moved to the edge of the deep hole and floated out over the water, airborne in some fashion that Curly could only envy. The bright, silvery lines seemed to flow more slowly, and Curly obliged with soft and simple songs, tiring also. Both of them were tired.

Before the sun began to peek the Harpist dropped back down below the edge of the deep hole and was gone. One moment it was there, the next, vanished.

Curly finished the last song alone. To leave a song unfinished wasn't in him.

Nearby he could hear Hickam chortling to himself, obviously happy.

"You did it — did it," he called, smiling at Curly. "Lord, Lord, the pictures I took. That pretty thing." He nodded and smiled more, full for the moment of power and benevolence. "I'm going to go in and develop them. I'll be back with food and more to drink. You stay here." He gave Curly an oblique look. "You know what it is?"

Curly shook his head. There was no place to begin, no reference point.

"A Harpist," he said, smiling, still webbed in the music.

"Something from another world or time. Something out of legends. Lord knows how old it is. It could have been here for tens of thousands of years. What it came in surely dug that hole. A ship maybe. I want what we saw. I want the ship too. I'll need money to dig for that."

"Want it?" Curly asked, alarmed.

"Capture it and show it to the world. Make me rich again."

"Better to let them as wants come here and see it, if it will," Curly said, remembering the sounds of the Harpist. "Listen to it."

"A rope wouldn't work, but maybe a net," Hickam mused.

Curly shook his head. "I ain't going to help with that."

"You just play. You play and you drink. That's why I brought you, what you hired on for." Hickam leaned darkly toward Curly, dwarfing him in size and strength. "If you don't play it'll wind up bad for you. There won't be anything to drink, and I'll play myself."

Curly looked away. He touched the old stone in his pocket for comfort. It seemed very warm to the touch. In a while Hickam left. Curly slept, with dreams.

◇   ◇   ◇

When Hickam returned with food and the pictures Curly could tell the man had been drinking heavily.

He threw a bag of cold hamburgers at Curly and uncapped him a bottle of beer. He disgustedly dropped a mound of pictures in Curly's lap.

"Not one of them worth a damn," he said angrily. "All that high-priced camera picked up were some lines of light. Nothing like you and me saw."

Curly looked at the pictures while he drank thirstily. In some of them faint lines of light, like distant summer lightning streaks, appeared against a background of trees and bushes. In others there was nothing except Curly and his wheelchair and guitar, somewhat distorted, as if photographed through a dark, wavery glass.

"I've got to capture it for me," Hickam said morosely.

"Capturing it would be like trying to take its picture, Mr. Hickam. It ain't to be owned. It came up from somewhere to play along with me, but that's as close to this world as it'll ever get. I know that somehow. You think it's old, but I don't know. I done some thinking after you left. I think maybe it's here waiting for something, curious about us — me — nothing more. But I can play music so it's accepted me. Maybe messing with it could cause big trouble."

Hickam gave him a scornful look. "Who gives a damn what a crippled drunk like you thinks? You don't know anything. You had your chance once, your moment. Now give me a chance at mine. You play your pretty guitar and drink your whiskey. Leave the rest of it to me."

"I ain't going to help, and I'll warn it if I can," Curly said stubbornly. "I'm telling you fairlike."

"Do anything to mess me up, and I'll dump you into the deep hole, wheelchair and all," Hickam warned ominously, his eyes bloodshot and angry.

Curly subsided, unchanged inside.

All day long Hickam drank and worked at something he wouldn't let Curly see. He hid his work behind the nearby trees, and the making of it brought back his smiles. Curly could tell it was being constructed of ropes and hooks and tire chains that Hickam carried from the bed of the big truck.

Curly sat quietly and waited. He longed for something to drink, but instinct kept him from asking, knowing Hickam would want to exact something in return for drink.

When darkness came Hickam rolled Curly to the edge of the deep hole. He hooked up the guitar to the generator, made sure it was on by touching the strings himself, and then retreated to his hiding place.

"Play!" he ordered hoarsely. "Play, and I'll give you all you can drink, a barrel full, enough to drown in."

Curly smiled gently at him and shook his head, not angry, but resolute, knowing it was wrong to try to capture the Harpist.

Hickam came striding back from his hiding place. He took the guitar from Curly's hands and put it on the ground. He slapped the crippled man strongly with heavy hands, again and again. Curly felt a rib give, teeth loosen. His nose trickled blood.

"I'm telling you the God's truth when I say I'll drop you in the water," Hickam said, breathing hard. He watched Curly and suddenly his eyes widened. "Maybe, halfway at least, that's what you want. To be out of it? To die?" He reached again with powerful hands and lifted Curly from his wheelchair. He carried him near the cave entrance and dropped him roughly there.

"Not yet for you," he said. "I told you once I could play and play I will. I'll bet I can play enough to get it up out of the water if only because it'll be curious about the different sound. I'll decide about you later." He nodded. "No one will miss you. Jonce will go along with what I tell him. I'll say you got drunk and fell into the water." He nodded, intoxicated with liquor and plans. "Sure." He shambled away to his hiding place and returned with the device he'd fashioned. A cruel net of sorts, hooks and wires and tire chains and rope. He spread it near his feet, ready for casting. He sat down in Curly's wheelchair and picked up the guitar.

"Now listen," he ordered darkly at the air. "You'd better listen."

He played. It was clumsy and not good, but it was loud. His repertoire was limited, and he played the same songs over and over, played angrily, his face growing more and more sullen as the Harpist failed to appear.

"Damn you," he cursed, meaning Curly and the deep hole, "come up — come up!"

And finally, after Curly had decided it wouldn't come, that it was safe, the Harpist appeared, just visible at the edge of its pit. It came and forgave Hickam's harsh notes, forgave them with its own perfect, intricate harmony.

"Come up out of there," Hickam screamed in total frustration.

Curly could see the Harpist rise a little higher, move out and away from the water, closer to Hickam. Close enough. Curly screamed a warning.

Hickam dropped the guitar. Curly winced in pain when it struck the ground. Hickam came like a great cat and picked up and cast his net in a fluid motion.

The black and silver thing drew in on itself, mewed and whined, struggled and subsided. Caught!

"Let it go," Curly implored. "It wasn't meant to be caged in something for you and me to look at."

"Shut your double-damned mouth," Hickam said triumphantly. "I don't need you anymore. I'll finish with you when I get this thing good and hitched down."

He pegged the net to the ground. The thing inside made noises not unlike a kitten, not moving much now, only the flickering "arm" movements showing it still lived.

"It'll soon die in that net," Curly called, realizing it.

Hickam threw a peg at him. It bounced off the rock wall nearby.

The Harpist drew itself into an even tighter ball. It made one huge, unmusical sound, so rending and terrifying that Curly hugged his chest with arms that had suddenly lost all warmth.

Up from the depths flew another Harpist. This one had arms of flashing light thick enough to blot away the pale glow of the moon. Its black apex was a dozen feet across. As Curly had believed the other Harpist might be young, he knew this one was old. It hovered over the deep hole momentarily, then up and away.

Hickam screamed and turned to run. The Harpist merged with him, enveloped him, released him. Hickam seemed suddenly smaller. He fell and lay without moving.

The big Harpist skirted the net, seemingly unable to figure it out, remove it. Inside the net it seemed to Curly that the small Harpist was becoming smaller.

Curly lunged forward on his strong hands. He dragged his body behind him, crawling toward the two Harpists. He could hear them pipping at each other, the sounds mixed together. When Curly reached the net the big one perceived him, and something reached out and touched him briefly, coldly, then withdrew.

Curly jerked out the pegs. He lifted a corner of the net and pushed it upward. The big one enveloped the emerging small Harpist and soared high into the air over the deep hole in triumph. Then, suddenly, both were gone without splash, without sound.

Curly crawled to Hickam. Nothing inside Hickam now moved, and the man's body was as cold as piled snow.

He lay beside Hickam and tried to figure what would now happen to him, not caring much. Perhaps he could start the truck and, with a weight on the accelerator and some luck, he could make the blacktop. They'd find him there. He shook his head. He'd paid no attention to trucks for a long time, and the smooth sides of the truck could defeat his entry, especially if Hickam had locked the vehicle. Fighting back revulsion he searched Hickam's pockets and came up with a chain and metal keys, but when he fingered them they felt light and funny and powdered away as he rubbed them.

He sighed in discouragement. He crawled to the truck and got up by rising from bumper to fender. He then hand-pushed on back to the cab. The doors were, as expected, locked.

He went back to the guitar. The generator still hummed. He picked up the guitar, got himself into position, and belted out an SOS signal on it, over and over, at highest volume. He kept it up until he was very tired and had lost interest, until it was near dawn. No one came. He didn't believe anyone would come. Maybe Jonce sometime, but not for a very long time. Maybe never. There was no one. People listened, but that was all.

◊   ◊   ◊

After he'd given it up and let the guitar fall silent the small Harpist appeared at the edge of the hole. It rose and moved close to him, seemingly unafraid. Curly nodded at it and played a tune, but there was no response. Curly nodded again and put the guitar carefully on the ground, thinking that the Harpist might be curious. The Harpist inspected the instrument by moving over and around it, by letting the flashes caress the instrument. Sounds came from the amplifier, but the Harpist seemed uninterested in them. When it tired of the guitar it reached out and touched Curly. The touch was strange, but not unpleasant, cold and tingly. The delicate flashes played over Curly, moving here and there, pausing for a time at the scarred area. Then, perhaps as more interesting, the Harpist moved back to the guitar. Curly worried vaguely about what might happen if the creature got crosswise with the generator, so he unplugged the guitar. He pushed it toward the Harpist, the ultimate gift, expiation for whatever part he'd had in its capture.

"You take it," he invited. "If I get out I can get another. Maybe you can figure it out, learn from it." He nodded at the Harpist and pushed the instrument insistently at it, hoping his meaning was clear.

The big Harpist blew up again from out of the deep hole, making the wind rise. It floated toward Curly. The two Harpists pipped at each other. The big one touched Curly much as the small one had, lingering here and there, exploring.

Curly pushed the guitar at it also.

When it was done the big one picked up the small Harpist in its flashing arms. It offered the guitar back to Curly and he shook his head and dragged himself backward, so that his intention couldn't be mistaken. The big Harpist bowed and made the guitar vanish inside its central blackness.

Curly touched his pocket, and the heat from the stone was almost enough to singe his fingers. It was one more thing to offer and give if they desired it.

He took it out and looked at it once again, shuffling it from hand to hand, a small creek stone shaped by someone or something a hundred or ten thousand years before. He put it down on the ground in front of him so that they could see it, then backed away again. They came to it, moving quickly, silver arms moving like windmills, obviously excited. They bowed to him, a solemn thing. The big one made the stone vanish, and Curly felt its loss, the last of childhood, the end of his mother. But whatever it had been it now seemed important to them. He was glad he'd found it — glad he'd given it.

At the deep hole the two stopped and played a duet for Curly, very strange and lovely, saying something in the music, so that Curly badly wanted the guitar back to reply. The big one brought out the stone and held it against the morning sky. It seemed larger to Curly. When that was done the Harpist waited by the deep hole, waited until Curly hoped he knew why they waited.

He crawled to them and held out his arms, and they moved over and through him. He felt himself swallowed gently into their joint blackness, fed through the stone, then on.

And then they were three and soon to be four and no more reason to hide and wait.

After that there were other things, but first there was a beginning and a knowing and loneliness was gone. And most of all, for Curly, there was now always music, a music that married harp and guitar.

Great Tom Fool
or
The Conundrum
of the Calais
Customhouse Coffers

by 00403334132324212100101004323443

How hard it is to judge the second best.

Who is the second-best scientist in the history of the world? First place goes to Isaac Newton, of course, but who is second best? There'll never be a solution; only endless quarreling over twenty-five candidates at least.

And who is the second-best writer in the history of the world? First place goes to William Shakespeare, of course —

Of course.

It is odd that so little is known about Shakespeare and that so many people believe so passionately that Shakespeare wasn't Shakespeare but that someone else wrote the plays and poems attributed to the man. But if you want the Great Shakespearean Controversy raised to new pitches of madness, read this mad story.

"Project 'Shake the Spheres,' is it?" Dude asked in his reptilian and bumptious voice. He was sensitive to the stigma of being an American-made machine, and he often reacted arrogantly. "I always liked 'Shake the Cubes' better. Well, a lot can be done if the corners of the cubes are a bit rounded, and as I am project director . . ."

"You're droll, Dude," said Shepherd O'Shire, the Proctor of Happy Braindom Ltd., "but you'll not be put in charge of any project, not ever again. We've learned better than that. You will be a working computer on this project, no more than that. And you will see to it that your two friends, the British and the French machines, will put their tomfoolery aside and work with you with quiet dedication on this job."

"I smell money connected with this case," Dude uttered.

"No, there will not be any money at all connected with it," Shepherd countered. "There is no appropriation at all."

"A preemptive séance is the only way to get the information out of the dead people," Lavender Brodie interrupted. (Her name, Brodie, signifies a "precipice"; did you know that?) "Dead people are at a disadvantage anyhow. Put pressure on them, I say. Have them by the ears!"

"I have evidence, in my storage brain downstairs, that there is *money* connected with this case," Dude insisted, "and I'm not talking about anything as petty as an appropriation."

Dude, a clown to his last compensating planetary gear, was present in his "riant giant" mobile form. In this mobile he didn't carry a lot of brains around with him, but he did have quick access to his storage brain.

"And, Lavender," the machine Dude went on, "a 'séance' is only a sitting down, and I have whipped that problem. I can do it now, in this my favorite extension. The giant dragon tail will snap off to let me sit down. I love myself when I solve insoluble problems like that."

Dude was the only nonhuman member of that learned society, Happy Braindom Ltd., but he had many nonhuman guests at its sessions.

"And yet he's a bit too human for comfort," Arsene Gopherwood often stated it, "especially when he's in that damned 'laughing giant-dragon' costume."

The human membership of Happy Braindom Ltd. was Shepherd O'Shire, Lavender Brodie, Emery Briton, Byron Verre, and Arsene Gopherwood.

"This is a serious project, Dude," Shepherd said nervously. "I repeat that there must be no tomfoolery."

"And yet 'Tom Fool' is the contingent name of the person we are investigating." Dude smiled his meter-long smile. " 'Tom Fool and his Polylogues' will be the title of the investigation."

"I prefer 'The Conundrum of the Calais Customhouse Coffers' for a title," uttered the French machine Dingo. He had just arrived in his extension of a Frenchy Navvy in a striped sweater and a small artist's mustache and beret. "Yes, didn't I get here quickly though! We French are always so prompt. I can aid you all immeasurably on this project. And remember that by 'Coded Information Storage Time' I am only three minutes from my back-up brain in France."

"Where's Toff?" Lavender asked. "He always gives a project class. You other two machines only give it performance. I always like class best."

"He's somewhere near," Dude uttered. "He's trying to calculate just how late would be properly late in this case. He may be tapping his storage brain in London for some good entry lines."

" 'This royal throne of kings, this sceptred isle,' " Toff intoned as he entered with a jaunty actor's step —

Great Tom Fool

This happy breed of men, this little world,
This precious stone set in the silver sea,
This Shakespeare, this great Toff yet, "bardy" both,
This blessed plot, this earth, this realm, this England.

Then Toff fell flat on his face, a planned maneuver. Did
you know that the English have their own humor, very subtle? Toff had arrived in his Noël Coward extension. He was
Noël to the death, just as he is today. You know that Noël
didn't stop wrinkling when he died.

◇　◇　◇

"We work very fast here, kids," Lavender said. "I am sure
that the best format for this will be the séance, and I believe
that we had better get the first séance started."

"Gracious lady, there is no such thing as a workable
séance," the English machine Toff said with clipped finality.

"Listen, you limey junkie, I've been to plenty of séances
that worked."

"There is, however, the 'deep psychic scan' which comes
through as a ghostly sort of apparition, very like a séance
figure in appearance," Toff admitted. "We are experts on
these things. We go to our storage brains for them, and the
storage brains produce the 'scans' from their bottomless accu-
mulations of data. The psychic scans appear like threads of
smoke. They hover, they thicken, they coalesce. And then
they speak like séance evocations."

"Let us not be too pompous about this," the Proctor of
Happy Braindom Ltd., Shepherd O'Shire, instructed them.
"A quick-hitting sortie will do us better than a ponderous
siege of the problem. All we intend to do is answer all the
unanswered questions about old Shakespeare, to clear up all
the clouds that have obscured his identity and authorship,
to define his significance and depth, and to duplicate his effect

if that is possible. Let us go into the lounge and be at our ease now, and we will lay out whatever data we have to consider."

"Yes, yes, at once." Dude gawked out of his wide, green-leather dragon mouth. "And these thirteen gentlemen and nine ladies here will also be present for our discussions. In a real way it is they who are motivating the discussions."

"What? Why? Who are these people?" Shepherd demanded. "Whence did they spring? From under what rocks?"

"I know most of these thirteen gentlemen and nine ladies," Arsene Gopherwood said, "and I'd recognize them as a type even if I didn't know them individually. They are what is known as publishers' representatives or pub-reps, and they all walk with a canted list because of the weight of the check-books they carry."

"But this is all wrong," spoke Emery Briton. "Somebody has gulled these bright-eyed people into coming here under a misunderstanding. Don't they know that *Computer Romances* are about on a par with *Nurse Romances?* Such things turned out by machines are steady, perhaps, but they are not earth shakers, and they are not in short supply."

"Gentlemen, ladies, members of Happy Braindom Ltd., do come in and be seated," Dude uttered in honeyed tones. And then he spoke in a lower tone to the Happy Braindom people only: "Play along with us, fellows. There really *is* big money connected with this. Look impressed when we refer to the 'Treasure Chest' that has already been found and exploited so rewardingly for these four centuries. Look triply impressed when we refer to 'the other treasure chest,' three times as large as the first, ten times as heavily laden, a hundred times as wonderful."

"Sure, we'll play along with you three contraptions," Proctor Shepherd said. "For about ten minutes we'll play along with you. Now how about letting us see the 'deep psychic scan' of Shakespeare himself, the projected data that will look like an attending ghost. We'll put William on the stand, as it were, and question him in depth. If he balks, then we'll turn Lavender loose on him. If he can't answer the questions about himself, then who can answer them?"

They were all seated in the lounge now. This was in the Old Drapers' Guild Hall in East Lodestone, which is quite close to London, to Calais, to the Azores, and also to the Americas. Dude, after snapping off his dragon tail, was the last of them to sit down.

"The difficulty, of course, is that Shakespeare is not Shakespeare," that British machine Toff uttered. "That is to say that the plays and most of the poems were written at least eighty years before they were discovered in an old trunk by the historical Shakespeare."

"Why do you say this?" the pub-rep Agnes Wankowitz asked.

"The plays nowhere mention America, tobacco, coffee, or tea, things that were having rather conspicuous and exciting reigns during the time of the historical Shakespeare," Dude said. "But, eighty years earlier, the latter three had not been known at all, and the first of them, the New World, was still referred to as That Spanish Hoax by the English-speaking world. Potatoes likewise are not mentioned in the plays nor known in their time, but eighty years later everybody was eating that exciting new food, potatoes."

"And the pronunciation is the real giveaway," the machine Toff said. "Historical pronunciations can be deduced by the rhymes of the times. In the plays we find *hither* rhyming with *weather, eats* rhyming with *gets, eat* rhyming with *great, ear* rhyming with *hair, have* rhyming with *grave, love* rhyming with *prove* and with *move* and with *Jove* (all were likely pronounced as we pronounce *Jove* today). We find *propose* rhyming with *lose, gone* rhyming with *stone* and also with *moan, swear* rhyming with *were, tongue* rhyming with *wrong, gone* rhyming with *alone, granting* rhyming with *wanting.* Ah, that's all the instances that I have with me right now."

"Do you have other instances somewhere else?" asked a pub-rep named Donald Dranker, a top negotiator.

"Yes, I have about five hundred other instances in my storage-brain in London," Toff uttered. "But the point is that none of these rhymes rang true at the time when the historical Shakespeare burst upon the scene like a funky comet; and all of them would have rhymed true eighty or a hundred years earlier. Leaving the Shakespearean corpus aside, the documented sound changes of the English language in the sixteenth century are clear enough. It is only the displaced Shakespearean evidence that ever confused the history. And one play, *Henry the Eighth,* has to be pulled out. It isn't a part of the original Shakespearean corpus. It really did appear as a new thing eighty years after the others. Oh, it's long been known that there was something very fishy about the accepted time setting of the plays."

"I am almost convinced," said the pub-rep named Stanley Klumpstone.

"Let's have the first apparition!" cried Lavender Brodie of the Happy Braindom bunch. "Put him in the witness box and put the screws to him!"

◇　◇　◇

Crackling lightning and obscure thunder! The iron hinges of time groaning as they swing open! Three callow young machines appraising what effect their devices were having on the people!

And then a personable and intelligent looking, though somewhat harried, man was in their midst there in the Happy Braindom Lounge.

96

Yes, he was the historical Shakespeare, though his nose was more bumpy and his face more of a mug than is shown in the accepted portraits. Whether he was a deep psychic scan or a called-up ghost was a matter of definition.

"Though I have admired you within reason, yet I've always wanted to put you under the power of my hands and tongue to see whether you couldn't be shaped into something better," Lavender declared to the apparition. "Now I will just follow my own peculiar line of questioning and see whether —"

" 'Twill do you no good, Dame Lavender," the apparition spoke. "I am not here consciously." (But a twinkle in its eye showed that it lied a little.) "I am not such a thing as could be conscious. I am — what is it that those droll machines that extracted me call me? — I am a deep psychic scan of all existing and extrapolative data of one William Shakespeare. Now let me say my say and do not interrupt me."

Oh, they'd interrupt him, of course, all of them. "I smell concatenated trickery here," Lavender sputtered, and other people sensed other irregularities. But here are the words of the apparition as he followed his preemptive data while at the same time rolling with and responding to the interruptions.

"I am William the son of John the glovemaker of Stratford in Warwickshire. But at the same time I am Tom. I am, I believe, the second focus of the ellipse that is the Tom Manifestation, for it was I who obtained the masterworks of that manifestation (or something between one fifth and one sixth of them) and made them public. I have been called Tom Rymer, Tom the Piper's Son (my father John did play the pipes better than any other man in Stratford), and Tom Fool. And indeed I have been all of these. I believe there were about eighty years between the two foci, between Giant Tom and my corporeal self.

"Do I call myself an upstart? Somebody asks me the question. Aye, I do. I was more than an upstart. I was an upsurge,

97

an upswarm. I knew my own limits (they were not low), but I let no one else know them.

"Who was Tom Fool, you ask, and how did I come to possess one of his treasure chests? I believe that Tom Fool was not one but several men, that he was really Tom Foule or Tom Crowd. Several powerful and talented men, contemporaries and acquaintances, but too different to be friends or allies, were somehow joined in an amazing tomfoolery.

"The only trait or talent that these several powerful men had in common was an unusually masterful way of writing in the Latin and the English languages. But their collaborations in the tomfoolery were likely involuntary and posthumous. The semisecret, small-audience masterworks of all these were somehow collected by a man of comprehensive taste (he may even have been the last surviving of those powerful Toms) and hidden away, from reaching English hands, in the customhouse at Calais. They were deposited there in a greater and a lesser chest. It was the lesser chest that I was able to obtain.

"But get this straight: *Those Masterworks were not always the worse for passing through my hands.* I knew how 'To gild refined gold, to paint the lily, . . . To . . . add another hue unto the rainbow,' as 'tis writ in lines of my own that I added to one of the masterworks, lines that are somehow misquoted in your day, so I'm told.

"And please note one other thing. The boards-play *Henry the Eighth* was not from the chest. It was written half by me and half by a friend of mine. We wished to test our own powers against those of the mysterious writer or writers of the masterworks from the chest, against the powers of Great Tom Fool. And we did not disgrace ourselves in the test.

"No, I cannot explain more than I know. The treasure chests had been signed into the customhouse of Calais under the title 'Tom Fool — His Polylogues.' I believe that it was

so titled more in humor than in ignorance. Though a mono-
logue means a speech of one person, and a dialogue means
speeches of several persons, a polylogue could only humor-
ously mean the speeches of quite some several persons. The
word would rather mean a 'much talking' or a 'garrulousness.'
And I did have great profit out of the lesser of those garrulous
old chests, those polylogic coffers.

"Can I not make a guess as to the true identity of Tom
Fool or Tom Crowd, you ask me? Aye, I can and I will. I
was never shy about making educated guesses.

"Sometimes it takes history several centuries to coalesce
several *apparently* different persons into one truly valid person. Thus great Caesar really was a 'triumvirate,' a uniting
of three apparently different men, though the manner of it,
in his case, is still unexplained in history. Men of great power
do sometimes produce fetches or doubles or appearances of
themselves without wishing to do so. We know from Holy
Scripture that the name Thomas means 'twin.' I believe that
our Tom Fool was a double twin, that he was one overflowing
man with several attendant spooks who were only aspects
of himself. And I believe that these spooks or aspects could
and did have independent names and careers; and could even
survive, for a while, the bodily death of the prime man. It
had to be a full man to compose those masterworks which
I later acquired and made known to the world. It had to be
an absolutely overflowing (into several different vessels) man
to compose those still greater and much more numerous masterworks that are in that larger chest that I had not gold
enough to ransom and acquire and make known."

"Is somebody having us?" Emery Briton of the Happy
Braindom bunch mumbled. "Who do we know who makes
up stories of that flavor?"

"Oh, I don't think so, Em," Byron Verre of the same Braindom said. "I believe this is the real Shakespeare, as well as

99

he can be called up, spinning his real guesses on the subject."

And the real Shakespeare, as well as he could be called up, continued: "Certainly I had seven hidden years in my life, as this lady over here asks me. 'Twas in those hidden years, and not in the open years, that I found the Treasure Chests.

"Was I burned at the stake? someone asks. Or beheaded? Or stabbed to death? No, not I, though I have smelled the smell of all those deaths as coming from Great Tom Fool of the masterworks. But I died with my boots off, and in bed. Or rather in a little day bed in the kitchen whence I could see the larch trees out of the window, and the green garden, and the duck pond.

" — and the duck pond, and the duck pond, and the duck pond . . ."

"That is the end of this psychic scan conjured up out of my data storage brain in London," said Toff, the extension of the talented British machine. "I wonder how to turn the fellow off. Oh, he turned himself off."

The psychic depth scan of the historical Shakespeare fell silent and disappeared at the same time.

◊ ◊ ◊

"Oh, I'll open for a million dollars. I'd be ashamed to mention a lesser sum." A pub-rep named Donald Waxley-Williams spoke with feigned indifference.

"What are you talking about, interloper?" Shepherd O'Shire, the Proctor of Happy Braindom Ltd., demanded.

"It wouldn't be fair to open the auction before the end of our presentation," Dude uttered. "Not fair to us."

◊ ◊ ◊

Then there appeared the scan or spook of a man who radiated talent, though not real intelligence or real power. Several of the viewers believed that they recognized him from the portrait that Fliccius had done of him. But there was much less of the fellow in the scan-flesh or the spook-flesh than in the old portrait. The painter had filled the empty places of the man with his own invention.

The apparition began to speak in a nervous and jerky manner:

"I am Tom, the younger son of a small English gentleman of the Midlands. I was the most presuming upstart of all of them. I was not born to such poverty as two of the others, but I had great poverty inside myself.

"But I rose, and not by intelligence or strength. I rose by fury. Listen, I sent God Himself into a state of shock and recoil from which He never recovered. But the details of my life show a rising order that was not in myself. I belonged to Jesus College at Cambridge. I had two wives, one of them English and one of them German, and I had to give both of them up. My resentment at these unwilling renunciations almost set fire to the realm. I became Archbishop of Canterbury. Great power was in my hands for some years, and yet it was always a sly power.

"Yes, though I wonder how you came to ask such a question — yes I did have seven hidden years in my life. No man can be properly mysterious without them.

"I was really a sort of jeweler, a lapidary who did wonderful and fiery things, mostly in miniature. But I speak in analogy. I did that exquisite work in words and not in stones. I am possibly the finest stylist who ever wrote in Latin — or in English. And I produced two sorts of masterworks. One of them has been published in millions and millions of copies for hundreds of years now. How ironical that it should be called *The Common Book*. And my other masterwork was the *Scenario for England*. I wrote it in the form of many sly directives and instructions and letters to key persons. I wrote it, and England lived it out, followed my *Scenario*.

"The other things? What other things are you asking about?

Oh, the plays and the poetries. They were not bad at all.
They were really the best things of their sort ever done in
this world. Yes, I suppose I should count them among my
masterworks.

"They were found in coffers in Calais, you say? Yes, I always
had a Calais connection. In our century, Calais was the place.
In your century, I suppose, such things would be lodged in
a Swiss bank rather than in the Calais customhouse.

"What end did I have? But it is not ended. There is still
a tall score to settle for that. They burned me at the stake;
that was my bodily end. I hated it, every horrible second of
it. I hated it, hated it, hated it, hated it . . ."

The spook-scan fell silent and then disappeared.

◊　◊　◊

"Oh, I believe that I like the gadget more and more as we
go along," pub-rep George Hebert said. "I'll bid ten million
dollars for it just to get the ball to rolling."

"Why are we back to this meaningless jabber about money?" Proctor Shepherd O'Shire asked.

"Wait till the end of the presentation, folks," uttered that
French machine Dingo. "Things will get richer and richer."

◊　◊　◊

Then, after a bit, another scan-spook appeared. Several of
the viewers believed that they recognized him from the portrait that Hans Holbein the Younger had done of him. But
there was much more to the fellow, in scan-flesh or spook-
flesh, than there had been in the old picture. The painter
had not been able to crowd near all the power of this man
into his portrait. Then the apparition began to speak in sparse
words, but with a richly toned voice. In scope that voice was
equal to a short orchestra at least:

"I am Tom, the son of a beerhouse keeper in Putney. Aye,

102

you know the disreputable place, on the south bank of the
Thames a little above London.

"I was a vagabond, then a mercenary soldier in Italy and
other places, then a moneylender. For only a short time did
I lend money to small men. Then I loaned it to dukes and
princes and kings, and I held kingdoms in pawn. Yes, I was
a baseborn upstart, an upstart of the upstarts.

"Yes, I did have seven hidden years in my life. May they
remain hidden!

"I was much in the company of intelligent men, of the
most intelligent generation there has ever been from the beginning of the world until now. But in all my life I never
met another man so intelligent as myself. I had a lust for
magnificence, but at the same time I had a lust for plainness.
And the second lust won. I had a burning compassion, but
I also had a burning cruelty. And the second fire consumed
the first. I was accounted a complex man, but my genius in
administration lay in my being able to simplify things.

" 'Twas I who looted the monasteries and all the abbey
lands of England. I manipulated realms. I was a man of power.
I became a baron, and Lord Great Chamberlain, and Earl
of Essex. The king was like whiting in my hands, for a while.
Yes, for a while.

"I had private excellences also. I had as fine a singing voice
as there was in all England. And I had a masterly way with
words. The plays you ask? The entertainments? How do you
queer people and queer machines (I can hardly tell some of
you from the others) know about them? Yes, I wrote golden
entertainments. They were loaded full of the greatness of
human people. I wonder what became of them? I left instructions for disposing of all my other belongings, but I left no
instructions for disposing of the entertainments. I had kept
them in a carpenter's tool chest.

"No, no, I was *not* burned at the stake. How could such

an error have crept into the plain account of my life? I died on the scaffold, beheaded. I had always worked the hell side of the road, along with the king. It was over mere details of our hellish advocacy that we fell out and he had me killed. But I rather startled them all when I declared for the full faith on the scaffold. No, of course I did not recant my declaration. Has such a lie been told of me? I died in the full faith. And so I saved my tarred and gnawed and besmirched and marinated and brine-pickled (but immortal and spacious) soul. And yet I find that the temporary (though the centuries of it seem tedious), tall flames of Purgatory bother me more than they would a less corpulent man.

"How much do I believe the plays, the entertainments, are worth? you ask. Oh, they are priceless, utterly priceless. And I do not speak lightly there."

Then Big Tom from Putney, the powerful and many-worlded man, faded away.

◊   ◊   ◊

"What a consummate gadget it all is!" Efraim McSweeny, a pub-rep, cried in creamy ecstasy. "What good copy we can build on these imaginative foundations! I'll jump the bid to fifty million."

"I do not understand this money madness at all," Shepherd O'Shire the Proctor growled. "It is Tom-Fool money indeed."

◊   ◊   ◊

And then still another scan-spook came like smoke, thickened, and took form. And several of those present believed that they recognized this newest apparition from a picture John Melo had done of him.

The arrival spoke with a pleasantly ringing voice, almost like bells, like laughing bells:

"I am Tom, the son of a rich lawyer. An upstart? you ask. No, not I. I was 'to the manner born,' a phrase of my own

104

that is usually mishandled. But perhaps there was nowhere for me to go except down, after such a start.

"No, no, I did not come from Putney. Why would anybody come from Putney? Mostly I lived in Chelsea.

"Did I say that the king was like whiting in my hands? I don't remember saying it, and it wasn't so. Am I the same spook who was here just two moments ago? you ask. Really, I don't know. Where I am now we have neither time nor sequence. Oh, surely I'd remember such curious folks as you if I'd been here just two moments ago! I visit here singly in my person, but you may well be seeing me split or doubled for all that I know.

"I tried to mold the king, yes, but I failed at it. I led him like a horse to the water, but I could not make him drink — that's a phrase of my own.

"Of what accomplishment in my life am I most proud? Oh, of bringing Greek to newest Europe and helping to unlock its sciences and arts and treasures. I was one of no more than twenty men in Western Europe whom you might have called a Greek scholar without laughing. But really I am most proud of standing against a tide when most people were not able to withstand it.

"Oh, certainly I was a man of power. I was Lord Chancellor of England, no mean office. Did I have seven hidden years in my life? you ask me. No. There was never anything hidden about me. It's true that I did have seven very obscure years, but that was only the way my tide of fortune ebbed for a while. Well, so one of you asks with some exasperation, did I not at least have a mysterious journey during my obscure years? Yes, I did that, several of them, very long and very mysterious. And I will not make them less mysterious by telling you about them.

"Aye, I did write plays or dialogues. I gave the name *poly-logues* to them to indicate that they were more deep textured and more action hinged than other dialogues. And I gave the name to them because it had a comical sound. Yes, I did polylogues and entertainments and enjoyments. They were for very small audiences, so small that every person present would be given one or two sets of lines to read. Somehow they made a busy life seem less busy. I left a cofferful of the pleasantries. Yes, very likely they did go to Calais with some of my other pleasant things. As Lord Chancellor of England, I naturally kept my more lively papers at the customhouse at Calais in France. In our century, many of us kept things at that customhouse.

"Do I believe that I had the finest singing voice in all England? you ask. How odd and how probing of you to ask such a question. Yes, I do believe it, for it was true. I was quite vain about it.

"Yes, I recognize the occupation of some of you present. You are publishers' bagmen (ah, and women) are you not? I'd recognize you more easily perhaps than would some of my other aspects.

"Am I now, or have I ever been Shakespeare? one of you bagmen asks me. I heard the name *Shakespeare* only on one evening in my life. When I was a young man we played a game of looking into a glass globe and asking of the spirits who lived in it such questions as 'Who is walking on my grave a century hence?' 'Who is wearing my mantle and speaking with my voice?' 'Who is eating my fruit and breathing with my breath?' And when I asked these questions of the glass globe, the name *Shakespeare* was spoken back to me clearly.

"Are the polylogues, the plays, truly worthy and remarkable? you ask. Yes, they are. There have never been such remarkable devices since pen first learned to speak with human voice. They are so rich that it is like not being able to see the field for the pearls buried in it. Bagmen, look to your bags!

"Was I burned at the stake? No, no. There's some confusion

106

if the records show that I was. I was beheaded on the scaffold as a man of distinction would be. I was *not* burned at the stake like a meanling. And I did *not,* as prelude to my death, say the cute things that are attributed to me. Gah, they cloy!

"Of course I died in the faith. And of course I did not recant. Had I recanted, I would not have died then. Perhaps I'd be living yet."

Then the apparition faded out. Well, it faded out about ninety-nine percent. And it apologized for hanging around, in wispy words as easy as a breeze:

"I'll be quiet here, and hardly to be seen. But I must bide here a while to satisfy my own curiosity. I must learn the price of him who is priced, since I am a part of that him. Continue, people and metallurgies, as if I were not here, for I'm here but slightly."

◊　　◊　　◊

"Some proof, some coherent proof," the pub-rep named Marjory Manmangler sang out. "When can we see and examine the 'greater' treasure chest that is supposedly in the Calais customhouse yet?"

"Oh, we can have a scan on it here almost immediately," Toff the talented British machine stated. "But whether we recover the great coffer or not does not really matter, except for the carefully staged drama of its recovery and presentation; and that could be better done at another location with other props. The *contents* of the great coffer have all been copied. And a copy of that copy now resides in my data brain in London.

"And the texts themselves will not matter, except that Tanglewood Press, if the successful bidder, would probably build a large shrine with an eternal flame to house them. But you folks would put your Harrisburg Hacks to rewriting them anyhow. What do you call them — The Harrisburg Nine?"

"The Harrisburg Nineteen now. We've expanded," pub-rep

Manmangler said, "and we call them *revisionists*, not *hacks.*"

"I'll bid a cool hundred-million dollars." Pub-rep Enox Eberly spoke solidly. "This penny-ante approach is so tedious."

"Wait till the presentation is finished, folks," Dude uttered. "Let's be fair, to us."

"Dude," Arsene Gopherwood of the Happy Braindom group whispered to that mechanism-in-residence, "there's a proverb: don't wait till the iron gets *too damned hot* before you strike. And three shells and one pea are enough for any con game. More shells will confuse it."

"They won't confuse *us*, pea-shooter human," the French machine Dingo stated. "Do you think you can teach *us* how to suck eggs?"

"Oh, there isn't any way they can overdo it," said pubrep Sheila McGuntry. "Let the little machines shovel it on. It's supergadget all the way anyhow. They aren't missing a trick. The great man *must* have a humble beginning, or he must at least be interiorly humble. And the seven hidden years of the life are essential, with the presumption that they were spent imbibing knowledge in High Tibet or in the Kingdom of Prester John on the Blue Nile or some other fulfilling place. And the cruel execution at the end is essential also. So is it that the great man must have the best singing voice in England. And the archiest of the archetypes is the business of the treasure chests in the Calais customhouse, that dark and sinister building that is prototypically identical with Aladdin's Cave. It gives us so much to work with. Oh, don't change a line of it. It's perfect!"

◇   ◇   ◇

"We will proceed." Dude spoke grandly, and it was as if a curtain went up for one more act of the polylogue drama. Then a rather grandiose scan-spook-person solidified in flowing scarlet and gold robes. Some of the viewers believed that they recognized him from the painting Sampson Strong had done of him a few centuries before. And the appearance spoke with firm regality:

"I am Tom, the son of a hog butcher of Ipswich in Suffolk. One can't be more baseborn than that. But I rose, by my pleasant and urbane ruthlessness, as one admirer of mine had worded it.

"No, I was not at Jesus College at Cambridge. I was at Magdalen College at Oxford. Get your facts straight, people. Archbishop of Canterbury? No. No. I was Archbishop of *York*. Yes, it's true that I was Lord Chancellor of England. Who *wasn't*, in those decades of flux? And I was also a cardinal of the Church. And twice I reached for the papacy, but it escaped my hand. I thought then that the Holy Ghost was mistaken to pass over me, but now I see that He may have been correct.

"Did I have the best singing voice in England? you ask. And you laugh as you ask it. Yes I did. I had the best. And many of my high contemporaries had wonderful voices.

"Yes, I wrote great things, both in Latin and in English. My known works of hand — but I believe that you may be referring to the chests full of livelinesses, and full of lives. Have they been found? That's delightful. 'Twill be like an extra springtime to the whole Earth if you make them public now. They'll still be a fresh breath after the centuries.

"What words are you trying to put into my mouth, little machine? What thoughts into my electronically assembled head? 'Impress on them that the works are worth tons of kale' — is that it? Is the contingent translation correct? Of course they are worth many tons of kale. I assume that *kale* is still the name of the Flemish cabbage.

"Were there seven hidden years in my life? you ask. I would guess that you have somehow woven the seven-hidden-years motif into a fiction about the excellent entertainments, about the plays stored in great chests in — in Calais. Where else? And I can hear the tinny thunder of the plot you're putting together. Why, I believe that it is our old friend the Spanish Prisoner Mystery! It's come back to visit us. Somebody look outdoors and see whether it's springtime. The Spanish Prisoner Mystery always blooms in the springtime. Oh yes, there were seven hidden years in my life. Perhaps they weren't hidden well enough, for they caught up with me and ended my life finally.

"No, I did not burn at the stake, nor was I either hanged or beheaded. An executioner's dagger found me at Leicester on my way to London to stand trial for treason. I had been taken sick at Leicester and was dying. But my dying had to be interrupted by the irregular execution to make it official. This is not generally known, that I was murdered and did not die of sickness.

"I must go now, though I'd like to stay for the end of it. I salute you, happy shills and thrice-happy gills. And some day, on the other side, when we are all finally sanctified, we will talk about such things over rum of the Indies. I myself was the most adept confidence man in England and perhaps in all Europe. I pulled some of the most towering cons ever. Ah, those were the days, those were the days! But you little machines aren't bad at it at all."

And then that fourth and final aspect of Great Tom Fool faded away.

◊   ◊   ◊

"Dude," Proctor Shepherd O'Shire ordered sharply, "project immediately the four historical portraits done by Fliccius, Hans Holbein the Younger, John Melo, and Sampson Strong, of what are possibly the several aspects of Tom Fool. I want to compare them."

"Quite impossible, Shep," Dude snapped. "They are not available. Perhaps I could obtain them after a few weeks, after an exhausting search."

"You lie, Dude," Shepherd accused. "You have them available here and now. You projected them subliminally when each of the scan-persons appeared. Lavender, I recall when we were programming Dude, you were the one who said 'What's the use of having a machine that can't lie a little bit?' But Dude lies too easily."

Dude projected the four pictures together for one one-hundredth of a second.

"A little bit longer projection, Dude," Shepherd ordered. So Dude projected them for a little bit longer, for .010101 of a second. That still wasn't quite long enough, but there was a good possibility that the four pictures were all of the same man, the same man perhaps not wearing exactly the same flesh in every case, the same man who created his own dumfounding resonances that walked and talked and strode as great men among the great. And the pub-reps caught all the implications and were impressed.

"Gentlemen and ladies, we may as well begin," Dude stated. He stood up and snapped his dragon tail back on and strode to the fore.

"Why, it's a great confidence game that our machines are playing on these credulous people." Shepherd O'Shire spoke to Arsene Gopherwood in admiration. "It's well done, in a crude way. The four greatest Englishmen of their century, Tom Cranmer, Tom Cromwell, Tom More, Tom Wolsey — they do add up to more than themselves, to Tom Foule, to Tom Crowd. Yes, those four great contemporaries do make a convincing Tom Fool. And it may have taken somebody of the scope of this Amalgamated Great Tom to be the Shakespeare herein expanded by more than a hundred new plays. But it's so weakly verified, Arsene. The Happy Braindom institution can't allow it to pass without more verification. The gills do come avidly to it though. And how could you, Arsene, the unofficial con man of the Braindom you are, be left on the outside of such a clever con pulled by mere machines?"

"I'll go a flat billion dollars for all rights to the Shakespearean and pseudo-Shakespearean works in the great chest in the Calais customhouse," said pub-rep Kendell Kimberly. "But put the home-grown small fry outside first."

"What makes you think I am on the *outside* of this con, Shepherd?" Arsene Gopherwood asked. "To be left on the outside of a con, that wouldn't be like me at all. Ah, Shep, and you others, they mean *you* when they speak of the home-grown small fry. Out, Shep. Out, the rest of you Happy Braindomers!"

"Don't push *me* out, Arsene," Shepherd O'Shire howled. "I'll inform, I'll peach, I'll grass, I'll stool! Gills, gills, don't you *know* that you're being gilled? Don't you understand?"

"Don't *you* understand, voicey man?" pub-rep Greta Samuelsdatter asked with a sneer. "We *want* to go as high as we can. This is for prestige and glory. Who'd want to win a bid at a half-billion dollars when, with proper management, he could win it at two or three billion? I bid two billion. And the announced figure, of course, will be double the real figure. Get those poor twits out of here, Dude!"

The twits, all the members of Happy Braindom Ltd. except Arsene Gopherwood, were being pushed out of the auction lounge. They fought hard to stay, but they were pushed out harder. Shepherd O'Shire, Lavender Brodie, Emery Briton, Byron Verre, they were plain thrown out of that place, the lounge of their own Happy Braindom.

"Three billion dollars," pub-rep George Hebert bid. "There's a lot of ridiculous anomalies in the cover story, but our script writers can fix up anything."

"I'll hear, I'll hear how it goes!" Lavender was squalling. "I'll listen at the keyhole."

"If you do, Dame Lavender, remember that there is nothing harder to reconstitute than a vaporized ear," said that French machine Dingo. "Out, Dame, out!"

"Four billion dollars," pub-rep Efraim McSweeny bid.

Even if they weren't very good, a hundred or more "new-and-genuine" Shakespearean plays, presented to the world with a whanging cover story that could be smoothed in the rough places, were bound to bring a pretty good price.

"Five billion dollars," pub-rep Agnes Wankowitz bid.

But all the Happy Braindom people except Arsene Gopherwood had been locked out of there, out into the exterior darkness. And there was weeping and gnashing of teeth.

The Hand of the Bard

by 142414043030332432044323242103333

Can there be any further question as to the outstanding nature of Shakespeare's reputation? Suppose you tried to imagine what the greatest possible literary find would be. The original manuscript of Genesis in the authentic hand of Moses might be first, but if we sigh and decide that that is impossible, surely we will be satisfied with a page or two of any of Shakespeare's plays in Shakespeare's handwriting.

Come to think of it, it isn't surprising that two contributors to this anthology independently decided to do a story centered on Shakespeare. I once wrote a short-short about Shakespeare myself. In fact, I wonder how many post-Shakespearean writers altogether have centered a piece of fiction about this patron saint of literature. That might be a field of study for a doctoral dissertation.

He had owned the desk for over a year before he found the person he was looking for, Kitty Gunn. It wasn't necessary that it be a woman, just that the person had the requirements, which were various, including avarice, or, at least, a pressing need for money.

114

Franklin Westport located her in the data banks of Armstrong, one of the more recent Island Three–type space colonies established at Lagrange Four. He was there winding up an assignment for the newly founded colony museum.

The data banks told him that Kitty Gunn was thirty-two years old and single, that she had been in Armstrong for a year and a half, and that she had switched jobs thrice during that short period. The latter was of interest; she seemingly was dissatisfied. But what really interested him was that, under the heading of Education, her dossier revealed that she had taken degrees in paleography, calligraphy, and typography. She was also listed, under Medical Report, as unadjusted.

He checked out her working hours and address and was at her door fifteen minutes after she had returned from work.

She was surprised to see him. Franklin Westport was dressed very conservatively in an expensive-looking Earthside suit. He was a bit older than she and had a fuddy-duddy face. Clean cut and shining, and all that, but he could have been a minister or possibly a high school teacher of some stilted subject.

He said primly, "Ms. Gunn?"

She frowned. "That's right."

Kitty Gunn could only be described as unhappy looking. Had she been in a position to spend considerably in beauty shops and on her wardrobe, she might have emerged as a moderately handsome young woman, but she wasn't in such a position. And her perpetual put-upon expression didn't help either.

Westport said, "I wonder if I could have a few minutes of your time?"

She stepped aside and made a motion of welcome with her hand.

The house, in space colony tradition, was small. Since she was a single, the house was even smaller than usual and, if anything, more sterile than usual. Kitty Gunn was obviously not one of the more enthusiastic type of colonists who did all that could be done with the limited resources available to brighten their corner.

His eyes went quickly around the living room cum dining room cum bedroom cum everything else save kitchen and bath. He was looking for religious decoration, or a Bible, or some other indication that the spinster Ms. Gunn was not amenable to hanky-panky.

She said, "Please be seated, Mr. . . . ah . . ."

"Franklin Westport. Thank you. I am an art dealer, Ms. Gunn."

She looked at him. "Art dealer? In Lagrange Four?"

He smiled ruefully, as though he had run into such a question before. "I suppose that I am one of the first in the colonies; however, more are certain to follow my pathfinding. I suspect that quite shortly there will be numerous antique dealers, art galleries, that sort of thing."

"Antique dealers!"

He leaned forward slightly. "You'd be surprised at the wealth now to be found in the Islands, Ms. Gunn. With beamed solar power a reality, and space manufacture taking over in a score of fields once handled on Earth, huge fortunes are abuilding."

She muttered something bitterly.

He said, "Admittedly, the first generation who began profiting from space colonization largely remained at home themselves. It was more comfortable there. It was something like the old robber barons at the time of the conquest of the American West. The frontiersmen and later pioneers and homesteaders went out in their covered wagons and flatboats, obeying the slogan, 'Go West Young Man,' and when the West had been won, they found it largely owned by a handful of usually elderly men back in New York."

She had to smile sourly at that.

He went on. "However, by the third generation of the exploitation of the West, you could count your Texan and Californian multimillionaires by the gross. They found it more attractive than the East. That's what's happening out here, Ms. Gunn. Many of this generation of the affluent are living in space. Some of them never bother to return Earthside at all."

"I wish the devil I could," she said bitterly. "But what's that got to do with art and antiques in space?"

"There's a feeling of nostalgia. It's the 'in' thing now to bring up Earth antiquities for museums or for furnishing and decorating the homes of the more prosperous. Believe me, my opportunities are boundless."

"I wish mine were. I'd give my left arm to get out of this overgrown sardine can."

That was what he had been hoping to hear. However, he concealed his satisfaction and lied smoothly.

"You mean you don't find space life desirable? I thought you colonists were all, ah, what is the expression? Gung-ho."

"Some are," she said wearily. "They must be crazy." She sighed. "Although I know how they feel. I felt that way once. Down on Earth they weren't exactly beating on my door with jobs I qualified for. Paleography isn't in high demand, and that's been my hobby all my life. But I also had the space dream. I applied to be a colonist and was surprised to pass all the tests." Her voice was bitter again. "And here I am — probably for the rest of my life."

He appeared surprised. "But why don't you return?"

She looked at him as though he were naive. "They have different colonization contracts in the different Islands. I was a fool not to have read the small print on the one presented by the conglomerate that owns most of the L4 Islands. But even if I had, I doubt if it would have made much difference. I'd been bitten by the space bug. I had no way of knowing that within a month of arriving here I'd hate every square

117

inch of it. That I'd give years off my life to see a blue sky above me with clouds in it, an ocean with breakers coming in, real mountains with forests on them, an occasional wild animal, birds . . . Oh, the hell with it."

He repeated, "But why don't you return?"

She nodded cynically. "I can breach my contract and return at any time I turn over to the conglomerate fifty thousand pseudodollars."

"Fifty thousand!" He was seemingly astonished.

"That's right. They argue that the cost of training me on Earth in preparation for becoming a colonist, then the transportation up here, then the cost of getting me settled in, then the cost of transporting me back, comes to fifty thousand. It sounds too high to me but there it is. After ten years, they bring the amount down to twenty-five thousand and after twenty years to ten thousand. But it's unlikely that I'll have saved enough by then to make it. I spend every cent I make on imported food, liquor, clothes, and other goodies from Earth. The cost is astronomical, but I'd go up the wall without them."

He shook his head in compassion. "I can't see why they would go to such extremes to keep colonists who wish to leave."

"Oh, they have a reasonable excuse. Half the people on Earth would just love to come to space on a tourist trip, just to see and experience it. But not one in a hundred could afford that. So what they'd like to do is apply to be colonists and, if accepted, come up, spend a short time, and then say they don't like it and want to go home. It would cost the corporations millions every year to accommodate such freeloaders."

"I can see their point," Westport agreed. "And I suppose you're in somewhat the same position as those indentured servants, so-called, that the British sent over to the American

118

colonies. If you have the money, you can buy your freedom. But in your case I don't suppose you have it."

She was suddenly impatient. "What did you wish to see me about, Mr. Westport?"

He decided to make his play.

"I understand that you are an expert in calligraphy, typography, and especially paleography."

"Precious little good it's done me."

"Suppose I told you that your background could possibly lead to your acquiring your needed fifty thousand pseudodollars and at least a bit more besides. Enough more, surely, to get you settled Earthside when you have returned."

She bug-eyed him.

Franklin Westport suspected that she was hooked.

He said, "Not too long ago, on one of my Earthside trips to locate antiques and various objects of art for my clients, I ran into a magnificent Tudor period desk in England. In examining it thoroughly, before purchase — the owner, by the way, knew nothing of antiques — I found a small secret compartment. These are far from unknown in the desks of the period. They were, I assume, the equivalent of a wall safe hidden behind a painting in the home of a well-to-do person today."

She was scowling at him.

He said, "Suppose I brought the desk up here to Lagrange Four and, just before selling it as the antique it is, I found the secret compartment and in it a sheaf of papers. Some of the poems of Ben Jonson, a fragment of a play by Christopher Marlowe or Lord Oxford, a paper or two of Francis Beaumont or John Fletcher, or perhaps even a letter in Queen Elizabeth's own hand to William Shakespeare!"

Her scowl had developed into an unbelieving stare. She had already caught the implications of what he was driving at.

119

"Forgery," she said. "Art forgery or, at least, autograph forgery. But . . . but if this is your scheme, why in Lagrange Four? Why not pull your little trick down on Earth? There must be a multitude of professional forgers there more competent than I could ever be."

He smiled his charming clergyman's smile. "For two reasons, my dear. One, this nostalgic art-collecting fad now developing in the Islands means higher prices. But, two, and most important, if I surfaced a poem written by Ben Jonson in his own hand on Earth, a hundred experts would inspect it within the week. Another hundred experts would examine the desk and possibly come up with the fact that it was manufactured three years after the death of Jonson. I have no way of knowing. But up here, my dear Kitty, there are no experts. A dozen years might pass, after we had taken our score and vanished, before anyone remotely approaching an expert would show up. Undoubtedly, copies of the papers found in the secret compartment would be copied and communicated to Earth, but they would not admit to the sort of examination that would ordinarily be utilized, not only of the handwriting but the paper and ink."

She twisted her bitter face. "I can see that," she said slowly. "But Chris Marlowe wouldn't do, nor Ben Jonson, nor any of the rest you named."

It was his turn to frown. "Why not Jonson and Marlowe?"

"There's too much of their handwriting in the museums, if I'm not mistaken. A real authority would be able to pick holes in anything I could fake. And, another thing, you couldn't expect me to be able to forge the writing style of half a dozen people. Just doing one would be a task that you don't even comprehend. Besides, you've probably got an exaggerated idea of what a poem of Ben Jonson's, even in his own hand, would bring on the autograph market. He was prolific, and a good many of his originals have come down to us."

120

She obviously had something in mind. He said, "What's the alternative?"

"It's got to be Shakespeare," she said slowly.

◊   ◊   ◊

They finally made a date to meet the following day at his hotel for dinner. She wanted the time to spend researching in the data banks not only Shakespeare but various other knowledge she was going to have to use.

She hadn't had much trouble bringing him around to Shakespeare and abandoning his original idea of turning up several different odds and ends of Elizabethan period writers. As she had pointed out, very little, if anything, of Shakespeare's survived. Experts would have their work cut out disproving Westbrook's claim of finding a specimen of the poet's writing. Besides that, the amount the product would bring would be astronomical compared to an original of any other writer. Not a museum or collector, either in space or on Earth itself, but would give its all for a manuscript of the Bard of Stratford-on-Avon.

He had been a bit taken aback at the ease with which he had recruited her. If anything, she had forged on far beyond his original small-time scheme. However, it was obvious that the embittered woman was desperate. She was frantic to return to Earth. He was somewhat surprised that the local medical people didn't ship her on back as a hopeless neurotic.

He himself spent the balance of the day and evening at the data banks screen in his room, refreshing himself on Shakespeare and his period and contemporaries. Thus it was that he was fairly well prepared for her the following day.

The Neil Armstrong Hotel, the only first-class hostelry in the space colony, boasted its best restaurant. With many of its offerings actually having been shipped up from Earth, its prices were fantastic and ordinarily the average space colonist couldn't begin to afford to dine there. Indeed, it was

121

the first time for Kitty, and she wallowed in the delight of it all. She had the only steak she had eaten since leaving the home planet, and her first glass of wine.

They got around to Shakespeare over coffee and brandy.

Kitty looked five years younger. Her cynical eyes had gained a sparkle. That she was basically sharp was obvious. Life thus far had simply passed her by. She opened her bag and brought forth a pad on which she had scribbled notes.

She said, "It's even better than I thought. There are, in existence, only six absolutely authentic examples of his writing. All are signatures and, surprisingly enough, he doesn't always spell his name the same way. Usually, he spells it "Shakspere," but the main signature on his will has it "William Shakespear." Three of the signatures are on his will, one on a deposition in a lawsuit, and two on deeds. A copy of *Montaigne* in the British Museum and a copy of *Ovid* in the Bodleian both have possible autographs or initials, and a Plutarch's *Lives* in the Greenock Library has a marginal notation that some claim to be in his hand."

Westport scowled. "That doesn't give you much to work with." He counted on his fingers. "Only eleven letters of the alphabet."

She dismissed that opinion with a negative gesture. "That's plenty. From what little we have on the writing of our friend, including the doubtful note on the Plutarch margin, it would seem that he utilized what we call the Italian hand, as opposed to what we now call English cursive."

"What's the Italian hand?"

"A type of writing prevalent among some at that time. It's a free, flowing, and obviously inclined hand in which the ascenders are looped and the majuscules entirely cursive. It was undoubtedly a hand that developed as a result of the need for speed rather than beauty. And, of course, that would apply to Shakespeare, who was possibly the most prolific writer of his day."

He was out of his depth and said uncomfortably, "What does that mean to us?"

"We're going to have to find examples of other contemporary writers who also used the Italian hand, and I'll have to study the letters they used that we don't have in his own writing."

He sipped at his brandy and looked thoughtful. "You can get all this material in the data banks?"

"Of course. Everything's in the data banks these days. All his authenticated signatures, all his alleged signatures, manuscripts of such of his contemporaries as Jonson, Oxford, and Marlowe. It's just a matter of my doing a little studying and then practicing, practicing, practicing until writing in this new style comes as naturally, or even more naturally, than my own original form of script."

"All right. Now what piece of his should we concentrate on? One of the sonnets, perhaps?"

She shook her head. "I don't think so. I'd say a few pages of one of the more obscure plays, say *Coriolanus* or *Cymbeline* or, better still, *Pericles.*"

"Why should that be better?"

"Because it's controversial. It's thought he had a collaborator, George Wilkins. *Pericles* didn't even appear in the first folio of his plays, since the editors doubted that enough of it was his. So what we'll do is copy the first several pages, beginning with page one, '*Pericles, Prince of Tyre,* by William Shakespear.' That will set the historians on their ears and make our discovery even more valuable, because it will seemingly prove that it was actually Shakespeare who wrote all of the play."

"Wouldn't it look more authentic if we used a half dozen pages from the middle of the play, rather than the beginning?"

"Perhaps, but don't you see? Unless we have his name on the manuscript some might argue that it wasn't really his handwriting. The controversy over its authenticity would continue for centuries. And certainly you wouldn't get as much money for it."

"I guess you're right. What are you going to need?"

"As much authentic paper of that period as you can lay hands on."

"Can't fake it, eh?"

She shook her head. "There're various ways experts can date paper. You're going to have to go to England and buy up some real manuscripts of the period and get pages with as little writing on them as possible."

He scowled. "That's not going to look right."

"Yes it is. We're going to present the manuscript as a first draft. Paper was expensive in those days, and Shakespeare most likely used for his first drafts old paper with writing on the other side. Probably even paper that had been erased."

"You sure they didn't use parchment then?"

She was sure about that. "They opened the first paper mills in England in 1495. Shakespeare wrote *Pericles* about 1608. Then we're going to have to have pens of the type they utilized in those days. Quills, I imagine. And the same kind of ink. And while you're on Earth you might find out if there's any way of making ink look aged."

They argued a little about where the sale should be made. Kitty thought it would be best on one of the larger Island Fours over at Lagrange Five, and far away from Armstrong and the scene of her efforts. Besides, there'd be more ultrarich colonists to bid the price up.

But Westport vetoed that. "Once that manuscript is finished, I want it to travel just as little as possible. Murphy's law still prevails: If anything can happen it will. If it traveled from one Island to another, something might happen along the way to reveal it."

"Maybe you're right."

124

"This is what we'll do," he told her. "Tomorrow I'll look up some of my clients. I'll suggest to the most likely that they buy an antique British desk, to dress up their library or office. In short, I'll get an assignment to make such a purchase for them. That's how I manage this business at all. When I work on definite commissions, they usually pony up free transportation for me, to and from Earth. Since they own the spaceships, it's no skin off their noses, and I don't have to pay the king-sized fares."

She was nodding, following him, her facial expression now eager rather than put upon.

"So I'll get an order for the desk and bring it up here, along with the paper, pens, and ink you'll need. You'll finish the manuscript and then we'll destroy all your equipment and everything that might indicate your connection. Then you'll take off for Earth and go to ground somewhere."

"Wait a minute," she protested. "Where do I get the fifty thousand I need to get out of my contract?"

"I'll advance it to you and a bit more to keep you going until I finish the job. As soon as you get located, send me a note with your address. After I take the score, I'll come down and split with you. The fifty-thousand advance will just about eat up all my operating capital, but that's not important. When this romp is over, we'll both be eating caviar."

Her eyes narrowed. "How do I know you'll show up, Franklin? I'm putting as much into this as you are. I appreciate the fifty thousand, but I'm also taking as big risks as you. If a wheel comes off, the laws are tougher, here in Armstrong, than you might think. It's operated something like one of those nineteenth-century company towns you read about. I'd not only never get back to Earth, but they'd cancel most of what few privileges I have."

His smile was benign, as befitted his clergyman's countenance. "Kitty, my dear, there are two reasons — actually, three — why I'll show up with your share of the score. First, if I didn't, you could tootle the whistle on me. Second, it occurs to me that this might not be the last score we could take. Suppose in, say, five years, after our *Pericles* manuscript has been sold to either some filthy rich collector or a museum or library, I reveal that I have additional pages of the drama that I withheld. Perhaps six more pages. I doubt if we could get as much for the second offering as the first, but there would still be many bidders, and this time there would be no question of authenticity, since the first pages had already been accepted. The original purchaser would probably be indignant, thinking he had a monopoly on such a literary treasure, but he could do nothing."

She accepted that. It made sense. But then she cocked her head slightly to one side. "What is the third reason you'd show up?"

He said slowly, "Kitty, my dear, I suspect that you and I are two of a kind. I think that in the past we have possibly both been loners. And there is a lonesomeness in being a loner." He hesitated a moment and then looked at her coffee cup and brandy snifter. "I see that we have finished our excellent meal. It is becoming late. It seems to me a shame that you should return to that rather drab residence of yours. Why don't you spend the night here?"

She looked at him emptily. "All right, Frank."

◇   ◇   ◇

The following day they both went to work: Frank Westport on contacting his various wealthy clients in his endeavor to find one he could interest in an antique British desk, Kitty in beginning her long, arduous task of learning to write fluently in the hand of William Shakespeare.

She checked out every literary figure of the Elizabethan period, examples of whose writings were to be found in the

126

data banks. Surprisingly enough, there were some dozen of them. She avoided the best known. Again to her surprise, her best prospect was John Fletcher, who, according to most authorities, probably collaborated with Shakespeare in the authorship of *Henry VIII.* He wrote in the Italian hand, and several of his alphabet letters were similar to those of the eleven she had of Shakespeare's.

She was ultimately careful about it all. From the data banks she got printouts of the material she needed: all of the authentic signatures of the Bard and all of the possible writings, including the Plutarch's *Lives* notation. She then got printouts of John Fletcher's preserved material. She worked up a complete alphabet, including each Shakespearean letter she had, and filled out with those of Fletcher's.

And then, every day, following her job, she would write and write and write. The Italian hand did not come easily to her. She had been educated in the Spencer style. She had to break almost thirty years of habit. But it came; it came.

It was decided that they should see as little as possible of each other. What eventualities might develop in the future, they had no way of knowing. But there should be no known connection to link them. She was the most widely experienced person in paleography, calligraphy, and typography in Armstrong, even though she didn't practice her learning there.

Frank Westport made his contacts — it hadn't been difficult — and they had one last get-together in her grim little house before he left for Earth.

Although the meeting was largely flat business, afterward they went through the motions of making love.

At the end he said, "I'll come back with the things. God only knows what that authentic Elizabethan paper is going to cost me, but I'll get it. Meanwhile, Kitty, you spend every hour of your spare time forgetting how you used to write and writing the way Bill Shakespeare did. The final product has to look free and natural."

"Yes, darling," she told him. In her some thirty years of life, Kitty Gunn had had sexual experiences — but never *a man all her own.*

◇　　◇　　◇

It went even more smoothly than they ever could have hoped. He had been able to acquire eight authentic sheets of paper from manuscripts of the Elizabethan period with comparatively little writing on them. And he had also contacted a professional forger, who had given him priceless advice on how to age the appearance of the ink she was to use.

They decided to erase the writing already on the paper sheets, making no effort to hide the fact that it had been done. After all, as Kitty had pointed out, this was to be a supposed first draft, and Shakespeare could very well have used scrap paper for such to avoid expense. They decided to wind up with the first six pages of *Pericles,* and she would use the other two sheets for practice. In fact, to make it look even more authentic, she would number the pages 1, 2, 3, 4, 6, 7, leaving out page 5 and making a gap in the continuity of the play fragment.

She had a bit of difficulty at first with the quill pens, never having used one before. However, she finally got the hang of it.

Upon completion of the task, she made her arrangement with the Armstrong authorities to buy out of her contract, considerably to their surprise. It would seem that few colonists on her level could raise the fifty thousand required. She had the amount in cash, Frank having no desire to have it traceable to him.

They took the chance of his seeing her off at the shuttleport where she was to leave for the Island customarily used as the spaceport for passenger traffic between Lagrange Four and Earth.

Before embarking, she looked at him worriedly.

He reassured her. "It's in the bag, Kitty. Get yourself located in one of the smaller resorts and get a good rest. I don't know how long this might take. As soon as you arrive, be sure to send me a note giving your address. I'll be there as soon as possible."

"All right, darling."

He grinned at her. "Get yourself some sexy-looking bathing suits." A leer didn't quite come off on his minister's face.

She tried to smile back, but she was obviously nervous. He kissed her good-bye.

After she had entered the space shuttle, he stood there and looked after her, as a good husband or lover might have, waving his hand a little on the off chance she might be looking out a porthole.

"Stupid mopsy," he muttered. "If she thinks I'm going to be anchored to a dogface after I've made my taw she's got a lot of other thinks coming. With a score like this is going to bring, Frank Westport will make a disappearance unrivaled since Houdini. Never push your luck; I'll never surface again."

Nor were there any hitches in his "discovery" of the secret compartment and the six pages of manuscript it contained.

In fact, there was only one small glitch. Tom Horn, the tycoon who had given Frank the order for the desk, claimed that not only was it his but its contents as well. His argument didn't stand up, and the secretary general of Armstrong ruled against him. No money had exchanged hands. Franklin Westport had paid for the desk himself, and thus far Horn had not even seen it. No definite business transaction had taken place. The desk and its contents were still the property of the art dealer.

The news of the discovery spread, not only through the space colonies, but to Earth, within a matter of hours. It was the literary discovery of the year. Of the century!

And by the following day three different teams of physicists and chemists had devised as many methods of testing the paper. And all three methods of age dating supplied the same conclusion. The paper had been manufactured in 1600 A.D., give or take a few years.

Before the week was out, every teacher of English literature in Lagrange Four became a Shakespearean scholar. A master copy was made of the six pages and submitted to the data banks. Thousands of copies were run off. At the same time, printouts of the identical research material Kitty Gunn had used were issued to all who requested them.

And yes! The signature of William Shakespear on page 1 was as identical to that which appeared on his will as two signatures can be. And yes! There could be no doubt but that the pages represented a first draft of *Pericles, Prince of Tyre*, since there were many crossings out and additions and margin notes. And Gower's prologue, with which the play opened, differed in several respects from the final version that has come down to us from Folio Two of the Bard's plays.

The day following the discovery requests began to stream in from Earthside for the opportunity to examine it. The British Museum in particular was most articulate, as was the Oxford Library.

But at the same time came an official request from the United Kingdom that the manuscript in question be returned to England as a national treasure that could not be allowed to be alienated from the country of Shakespeare's birth.

William Farnsworth, secretary general of the space colony Armstrong, was not having any, and spoke before the council. His words were carried not only throughout the Islands but all over Earth as well.

He said definitely, defiantly, "The Shakespeare manuscript

shall not leave Armstrong. It will be the proudest exhibit of our Armstrong Museum, with such a foundation, undoubtedly fated to become the outstanding cultural institution of space."

The council dissolved into applause, clapping of hands, whistles, and shouts of approval.

Franklin Westport, who sat next to the secretary general on the podium, beamed benignly.

◇ ◇ ◇

The question of the purchase price came up two days later, not that there hadn't already been a multitude of offers streaming in to Frank Westport. Indeed, his space cables, calls, and even mail had become such an avalanche that he had already hired a small office adjoining his Neil Armstrong Hotel suite and a secretary to help him keep track of it.

The Metropolitan Museum offered a cautious two million pseudodollars, if authenticity were definitely established. The Louvre had upped that to four. All potential British customers kept mum, probably awaiting their government's legal action. An anonymous American collector, acting through a New York dealer, offered five million.

However, Secretary General William Farnsworth held the high cards. He remained adamant. The Armstrong Shakespeare Manuscript, as it was already being called, was not to leave the space colony. It could not be risked to transportation. He and two of his chief councilmen made an appointment to discuss the purchase price with Franklin Westport.

Frank, dressed in his conservative best, practicing his Sunday schoolteacher's smile, arrived in his office only a few minutes early for the review. He didn't want to give himself the time to work up a sweat while he waited for them.

However, he paced the small office. This was it. The big break that came once in a lifetime. He considered a quick drink from the bottle in his desk. But no, dammit, he was no tyro in the game of the grifter. He'd been in one aspect or the other of it, all his adult life. Easy, Frank, easy. It was all in the bag.

A knock came at the door, and before he could turn and answer, it opened and one of the uniformed hotel staff came in with a handful of space cables, a few letters, and, of all things, a picture postcard.

"Mail," he chirped. "You get more mail, Mr. Westport, than all the rest of the residents combined."

"Okay, okay," Frank said. "Throw it on the desk."

The other did so and left, neatly and politely sidestepping the arriving Armstrong officials.

After the usual amenities and handshakes, Secretary General Farnsworth came immediately to the point.

"Mr. Westport, we have no desire to be niggardly on this great occasion. Last week, Earthside, a museum paid ten million for a Rembrandt painting. A manuscript, of course, is not a painting. However, the council has decided to offer you five million pseudodollars for the Armstrong Shakespeare *Pericles.*"

Frank swallowed.

They were all standing, the secretary general next to the desk.

He looked down at the pile of Frank's mail.

He smiled and said, "A postcard! I don't believe I have even seen one since I moved out here to the Islands. Who in the world would pay the postage rate to send a picture postcard to Armstrong?"

He took it up nonchalantly and looked at the picture. "The Bahama Islands," he said. "Beautiful. I've never been there."

He turned the card over.

It read, *"Having a wonderful time. Wish you were here."* And then there was an address.

It was signed, *"Kitty,"* but the handwriting was undeniably that of "William Shakespeare."

The Man Who Floated
in Time

by 41133211132333132141043201043211

There are two great fantasy-gimmicks used in science fiction by even the hardest of hard science fiction writers.

One is superluminal velocities (faster-than-light travel), since without it you deprive yourself of space opera and all the conventions that have grown up about it since the time of E. E. Smith.

The other is time travel, since without it you would deprive yourself of a whole segment of particularly fascinating plots.

Popularity, however, has its punishment. It is hard to think of new twists on these old chestnuts. Yet it can be done. Suppose we consider time travel in a particularly subtle manner, turn things about, and place at the heart of the story the negative and not the positive.

There was something shady and sly about him. For one thing, he was small and slightly built, and I have an instinctive mistrust of men who stand less than five feet five: They seem too agile and unpredictable, shifty little Napoleons who are apt to come at you from three directions at once. Then too, his narrow glittery gray eyes, though they did actually make contact with mine, never seemed to be aimed directly at me, but rather somehow sent a beam of vision hooking around a sharply banked curve, even when his face looked at me right square on. I didn't like that. He was about sixty, sixty-five, lean and trim, not well dressed, his gray hair cropped very short and gone at the crown. "What I do," he said, "is travel in time. I float freely back to other eras."

"Really," I said. "Never forward?"

"Oh, no, never. That's quite impossible. The future doesn't exist. The past is there, solid and real, a *place*, you know, like Des Moines or Wichita. One can go to Wichita if one makes the proper connection. But one can't go to a city that's never been built. It isn't conceivable. Well, perhaps it's conceivable, but it isn't *do-able*, do you follow me? I go to the past, though. I've seen Attila the Hun. I've seen Julius Caesar. I wish I could say I went to bed with Catherine the Great, but I didn't, although I had a few vodkas with someone who did. She smelled of garlic, he said, and she took forever to come. You don't believe any of what I'm saying, do you?"

"You're asking me to swallow quite a lot," I said mildly.

He leaned forward in a conspiratorial way. "You're not the kind of man who's easily convinced of the unusual. I can tell. No ancient astronaut stuff for you, no UFO contact stories, no psychic spoon-bendings. That's good. I don't want an easy believer. I want a skeptic to hear me out, test my words, and arrive at his own acceptance of the truth his own way. That's all I ask of you — that you don't scoff, that you don't write me off instantly as a crackpot. All right?"

"I'll try."

"Now, what do you feel when I tell you I've traveled in time?"

"Instinctive resistance. An immediate sense that I've got myself mixed up with a crackpot or at best a charming liar."

"Fine. I wouldn't have come to you if I'd thought you'd react any other way."

"What do you want from me, then?"

"That you listen to me, suspend your disbelief at least now and then, and ask me a question or two, probe me, test me, give me the benefit of the doubt long enough to let me get through to you. And then that you help me get my experiences down on paper. I'm old and I'm sick and I'm not going to be here much longer, and I want to leave a memoir, a record, do you see? And I need someone like you to help me."

"Why not write it yourself?" I asked.

"Easy enough to say. But I'm no writer. I don't have the gift. I can't even do letters without freezing up."

"Doing a memoir doesn't require a gift. You simply put down your story on paper, just as though you were telling it to me. Writing's not as hard as nonwriters like to think it is."

"Writing is easy for you," he said, "and time-traveling is easy for me. And I'm about as capable of writing as you are of traveling in time. Do you see?" He put his hand on my wrist, a gesture of premature intimacy that sent a quick and quickly suppressed quiver through my entire arm. "Help me to get my story down, will you? You think I'm a crazy old drunk, and you wish you had never given me minute one of your time, but I ask you to put those feelings aside and accept just for the moment the possibility that this isn't just a mess of lies and fantasies. Can you do that?"

"Go on," I said. "Tell me about yourself."

◊ ◊ ◊

He said his time-traveling had begun when he was a boy. The technique by which he claimed to be able to unhitch himself from the bonds of the continuum and drift back along the time line was apparently one that he developed spontaneously, a sort of applied meditation that amounted to artfully channeled fantasizing. Through this process, which he refined and perfected between the ages of eight and eleven, he achieved what I suppose must be called out-of-the-body experiences in which his psyche, his consciousness, his waking intelligence, vanished into the past while his body remained here, ostensibly asleep.

On his first voyage he found himself in an American city of the Colonial era. He had no idea where he was — when he was older, working from his searingly vivid memories of the journey, he was able to identify it as Charleston, South Carolina — but he knew at once, from his third-grade studies, that the powdered wigs and three-cornered hats must mean the eighteenth century. He was there for three days, fascinated at first, then frightened and confused, and terribly hungry —

"Hungry?" I said. "A wandering psyche with an appetite?"

"You don't perceive yourself as disembodied," he replied, looking pleased that I had raised an objection. "You feel that you have been quite literally transplanted to the other era. You need to eat, to sleep, to perform bodily functions. I was a small boy lost in a pre-Revolutionary city. The first night I slept in a forest. In the morning I returned to the city, and some people found me, dirty and lost, and took me to a mansion where I was bathed and fed —"

"And given clothes? You must have been in your pajamas."

"No, you are always clothed in the clothing of the era when you arrive," he said. "And equipped with the language of the region and a certain amount of local currency."

"How very convenient. What providential force takes care of those little details?"

He smiled. "Those are part of the illusion. Plainly, I have no real coins with me, and of course I haven't magically learned new languages. But the aspect of me that makes the journey has the capacity to lead others to feel that they are receiving true coinage from me; and as my soul makes contact with theirs, they imagine that it is their own language I speak. What I do is not actual bodily travel, you understand. It is astral projection, to use a phrase that I know will arouse hostility in you. My real body, in its pajamas, remained snug in my bed; but the questing *anima*, the roving spirit, arrived fully equipped. Of course the money is dream money and melts away the moment I go farther from it than a certain range. In my travels I have left angry innkeepers and cheated peddlers and even a few swindled harlots all over the world, I'm afraid. But for the moment what I give them passes as honest coin."

"Yet the astral body must be fed with real food?"

"Indeed. And I think that if the astral body is injured, the sleeping real body feels the pain."

"How can you be sure of that?"

"Because," he said, "I have fallen headlong down temple steps in the Babylon of Hammurabi and awakened to find bruises on my thigh and shoulder. I have slashed myself on vines in the jungles of ancient Cambodia and awakened to see the cuts. I have stood in the snows of Pleistocene Europe shivering with the Neanderthals and awakened with frostbite in July."

There is an Italian saying: *Se non è vero, è ben trovato:* "If it is not true, it is well invented." There was in his eyes and on his thin gray-stubbled face at that moment a look of such passionate conviction, such absolute sincerity, that I began to tremble, hearing him talk of feeling the bite of Pleistocene winds, and for the first time I began to allow myself the possibility of thinking that this man could be some-

137

thing other than a boozy old scamp with a vivid imagination. But I was far from converted.

I said, "Then if through some mischance you were killed when traveling, your real body would perish also?"

"I have every reason to think so," he replied quietly.

He traveled through vast reaches of space and time when he was still a child. Most of the places he visited were bewilderingly alien to him, and he had little idea of where or when he was, but he learned to observe keenly, to note salient details, to bring back with him data that sooner or later would help him to determine what he had experienced. He was a bookish child anyway, and so it caused no amazement when he burrowed feverishly through the *National Geographic* or the *Britannica* or dusty volumes of history. As he grew older and his education deepened it became easier for him to learn the identity of his destinations; and when he was still older, fully grown, it was not at all difficult for him simply to ask those about him, What is the name of this city? Who is the king here? What is the event of the day? Exactly as though he were a traveler newly arrived from a far-off land. For although he had journeyed in the form of a boy at first, his astral self always mirrored his true self, and, as he aged, the projection that he sent to the past kept pace with him.

So, then, while still a child he visited the London of the Tudors, where rivers of muck ran in the streets, and he stood at the gates of Peking to watch the triumphal entry of the Great Khan Kublai, and he crept cautiously through the forests of the Dordogne to spy on the encampments of Neolithic huntsmen, and he tiptoed along the brutal brick battlements of a terrifying city of windowless buildings that proved to be Mohenjo-daro on the Indus, and he slipped with awe through the boulevards and plazas of majestic Tenochtitlán of the Aztecs, his pale skin growing sunburned under the heat of the pre-Colombian sun. And when he was older he stood in the frenzied crowds before the bloody guillotine of the Terror, and saw virgins hurled into the sacred well of Chichén-Itzá, and wandered through the smoldering ruins of Atlanta a week after General Sherman had put it to the torch, and drank thick red wine in a lovely town on the slopes of Vesuvius that may have been Pompeii. The stories rolled from him in wondrous profusion, and I listened to the charming old crank hour after hour, telling me sly tales of a history not to be found in books. Julius Caesar, he said, was a mincing dandy who reeked of vile perfume, and Cleopatra was squat and thick-lipped, and the Israelites of King David's time were brawling, conniving primitives no holier than the desert folk the next tribe over, and the Great Wall of China had been mostly a slovenly rampart of mud, decaying as fast as it was slapped together, and Socrates had never lived at all, but was only a convenient pedagogical invention of Plato's, and Plato had charged an enormous fee even for mere conversation. As for the Crusaders, they were more feared by Christians than Saracens, for they raped and stole and sacked mercilessly as they trekked across Europe to the Holy Land; and Alexander the Great had rarely been sober enough to stand upright after the age of twenty-three; and the orchestras of Mozart's time played mostly out of tune on feeble, screechy instruments. All this poured from him in long disjointed monologues, which I interrupted less and less frequently for clarifications and amplifications. He spoke with utter conviction and with total disregard for my disbelief: I was invited to accept his tales as whatever I pleased — gospel revelations or amusing fraud — so long as I listened.

At our fifth or sixth meeting, after he had told me about his adventures among the bare-breasted wenches of Minoan Crete — the maze, he said, was nothing much, just some alleyways and gutters — and in the Constantinople of Justinian and in the vast unpeopled bison-herd lands of ancient North

America, I said to him, "Is there any time or place you haven't visited?"

"Atlantis," he said. "I kept hoping to identify the unmistakable Atlantis, but never, never once —"

"Everywhere else, and every era?"

"Hardly. I've had only one lifetime."

"I wondered. I haven't been keeping a tally, but it seems to me it must have taken you eighty or ninety years to see all that you've seen — a week here, a month there; it adds up, doesn't it?"

"Yes."

"And while you're gone you remain asleep here for weeks or months at a time?"

"Oh, no," he said. "You've misunderstood. Time spent *there* has no relation to elapsed time *here*. I can be gone for many days, and no more than an instant will have passed here. At most, an hour or two. Why, I've taken off on journeys even while I was sitting here talking with you!"

"What?"

"Yesterday, as we spoke of the San Francisco earthquake — between one eye-blink and the next, I spent eighteen hours in some German principality of the fourteenth century."

"And never said a word about it when you returned?"

He shrugged. "You were prickly and unreceptive yesterday, and I was having trouble keeping your sympathies. I felt it would be too stagy to tell you, Oh, by the way, I've just been in Augsburg or Reutlingen or Ulm or whichever it was. Besides, it was a boring trip. I found it so dreary I didn't even trouble to ask the name of the place."

"Then why did you stay there so long?"

"Why, I have no control over that," he said.

"No control?"

"None. I drift away and I stay away however long I must, and then I come back. It's been like that from the start. I

140

can't choose my destination either. I can best compare it to
getting into a plane and being spirited off for a vacation of
unknown length in an unknown land, and not having a word
to say about any of it. There have been times when I thought
I wouldn't ever come back."

"Did that frighten you?"

"Only when I didn't like where I happened to be," he said.
"The idea of spending the rest of my life in some mudhole
in the middle of Mongolia, or in an igloo in Greenland, or —
well, you get the idea." He pursed his lips. "Another thing:
It happens automatically to me."

"I thought there was a ritual, a meditative process —"

"When I was a child, yes. But in time I internalized it so
well that it happens of its own accord. Which is terrifying,
because it can come over me anywhere, anytime, like a fit.
Did you think there were no drawbacks to this? Did you think
it was a lifelong picnic, roving space and time? I've had two
or three uncontrolled departures a year since I was twenty.
It's been my luck that I haven't fallen down unconscious in
the street, or anything like that. Though there have been
some great embarrassments."

"How have you explained them?"

"With lies," he said. "You are the first to whom I've told
the truth about myself."

"Should I believe that?"

"You are the first," he said, with intense conviction. "And
that because my time is almost over and I need at last to
share my story with someone. Eh? Is that plausible? Do you
still think I've fabricated it all?"

◊   ◊   ◊

Indeed, I had no idea. To treat his story as lies or fantasy
was easy enough to do; but for all his shiftiness of expression
there was an odd ring of truth, even to his most enormous

141

whoppers. And the wealth of information, the outpouring of circumstantial detail — I suppose a solitary life spent over history books could have explained that, but nevertheless, nevertheless —

And if it were true? What good had it all been? He had written nothing: no anecdotes of his adventures, no revisionist historical essays, no setting down of the philosophical insights that must have grown out of his exploration of thirty thousand years of human history. He had lived a strange and fitful and fragmentary life, flickering in and out of what we call the reality of the everyday world as though he were going to the movies — and bizarre movies they were: a week in Byzantium and a month in old Sumer and an hour among the Pharaohs. A life spent alone, a loveless life by the sound of it, a weird zigzagging chaos of a life such as has been granted no other human being —

If it were true.

And if not? *Se non è vero, è ben trovato.* I listened enraptured. I continued to probe for details of the mechanics of it. His journeys took him anywhere on earth? Anywhere, he said. Once he had arrived in a wasteland of glaciers that he believed, from the strangeness of the constellations, to have been Antarctica, though it might have been any icy land at a time when the stars were in other places in the sky. Happily that voyage had lasted less than an hour, or he would have perished. But there seemed no limits — he might turn up on any continent, he said, and at any time. Or *almost* any time, for I queried him about dinosaurs and the era of the trilobites and the chance that he might find himself some day plunged into the primordial planetary soup of creation, but no, he had never gone back farther than the Pleistocene, so far as he could tell, and he did not know why. I wondered also how he had seen so many of the great figures of history — Caesar and Cleopatra and Lincoln and

142

Dante and the rest — when we who live only in today rarely encounter presidents and kings and movie stars in the course of our comings and goings. But he had an answer to that too, saying that the world had been much smaller in earlier times, cities being deemed great if they had fifty or a hundred thousand people, and the mighty were far more accessible, going out into the marketplace and letting themselves be seen; besides, he had made it his business to seek them out, for what is the point of finding oneself miraculously transported to Imperial Rome and coming away without at least a squint at Augustus or Caligula?

So I listened to it all and was caught up in it, and though I will not say that I ever came to believe the literal truth of his claims, I also did not quite disbelieve, and through his rambling discourses I felt the past return to life in an astonishing way. I made time for his visits, cleared all other priorities out of the way when he called to tell me he was coming, and beyond doubt grew almost dependent on his tales, as though they were a drug, some potent hallucinogen that carried me off into gaudy realms of antiquity.

And in what proved to be his last conversation with me he said, "I could show you how it's done."

The simple words hung between us in the air like dancing swords.

I gaped at him and made no reply.

He said, "It would take perhaps three months of training. For me it was easy, natural, no challenge, but of course I was a child and I had no barriers to overcome. You, with your skepticism, your sophistication, your aloofness — it would be hard for you to master the technique, but I could show you and train you, and eventually you would succeed. Would you like that?"

I thought of watching Caesar's chariot rolling down the Via Flaminia. I thought of clinking canisters with Chaucer

143

in some tavern just outside Canterbury. I thought of penetrating the caves of Lascaux to stare at the freshly painted bulls.

And then I thought of my quiet orderly life, and how it would be to fall into a narcoleptic trance at unpredictable moments and swing off into the darkness of space and time, and land perhaps in the middle of some hideous massacre, or in a season of plague, or in a desolate land where no human foot had ever walked. I thought of pain and discomfort and risk, and possible sudden death, and the disruption of patterns of habit, and I looked into his eyes and saw the strangeness there, a strangeness that I did not want to share, and in simple cowardice I said, "I think I would rather not."

A flicker of something like disappointment passed across his features. But then he smiled and stood up and said, "I'm not surprised. But thank you for hearing me out. You were more open-minded than I expected."

He took my hand briefly in his. Then he was gone, and I never saw him again. A few weeks later, I learned of his death, and I heard his soft voice saying, "I could show you how it's done," and a great sadness came over me, for although I knew he was a fraud I knew also that there was a chance that he was not, and if so I had foreclosed the possibility of infinite wonders for myself. How sad to have refused, I told myself, how pale and gray a thing to have done, how contemptible, really. Yes: contemptible, to have refused him out of hand, without even attempting it, without offering him that final bit of credence. For several days I was deeply depressed; and then I went on to other things, as one does, and put him from my mind.

A few weeks after his death one of the big midtown banks called me. They mentioned his name and said they were executors of his estate, and told me that he had left something for me, an envelope to be opened only after his death. If I could satisfactorily identify myself the envelope would be shipped to my bank. So I went through the routine, sending a letter to my bank, which authenticated the signature and forwarded it to *his* bank, and in time my bank informed me that a parcel had come, and I went down to claim it. It was a fairly bulky manila envelope. I had the sudden wild notion that it contained some irrefutable proof of his voyages in time, something like a photograph of Jesus on the Cross or a personal letter to my friend from William the Conqueror, but of course that was impossible; he had made it clear that nothing traveled in time except his intangible essence: no possessions, no artifacts. Yet my hand shook as I opened the envelope.

It contained a thick manuscript and a covering note that explained that he had decided, after all, to share with me the secrets of his technique. Without his guidance it might take me much longer to learn the knack, a year or more of diligent application, perhaps, but if I persevered, if I genuinely sought to achieve —

A wondrous dizziness came over me, as though I hung over an infinite abyss by the frailest of fraying threads and was being asked to choose between drab safety and the splendor of the unknown plunge. I felt the temptation.

And for the second time I refused the cup.

I did not read the manuscript. I was too timid for that. Nor did I destroy it, though the idea crossed my mind; but I was too cowardly even for that, I must admit, for I had no wish to bear the responsibility for having cast into oblivion so potent a secret, if potent it really was. I put the sheaf of pages — over which he must have labored with intense dedication, writing being so painfully difficult a thing for him — back into their envelope and sealed it again and put it in my vault, deep down below the bankbooks and the insurance policies and the stock certificates and the other symbols of the barricades I have thrown about myself to make my life secure.

Perhaps the manuscript, like everything else he told me, is mere fantastic nonsense. Perhaps not.

Some day, when life grows too drab for me, when the pleasures of the predictable and safe begin to pall, I will take that envelope from the vault and study its lessons, and if nothing then happens, so be it. But if I feel the power beginning to come to life in me, if I find myself once again swaying above that abyss with the choices within my reach, I hope I will find the courage to sever the thread, to loose all ties and restraints, to say farewell to order and routine, and send myself soaring into that great uncharted infinite gulf of time.

Flee to the Mountains

by 14002204330021210423143000430433

Life is a tribulation bounded by golden ages.

In our individual lives, we look back on our youth as a carefree time (which it wasn't, but nostalgia paints everything in rainbow), and many of us look forward to a life hereafter when we will plunk our harps of gold and tilt our halos rakishly. It's only the present that stinks.

In a larger sense, there are millions who bound humanity by the Garden of Eden at one end and the Second Coming on the other. And on the principle of its being always darkest before the dawn, the Biblical predictions of that Second Coming make misery the prerequisite.

This has given rise to fierce hopes over all the centuries, for every generation sees clearly that everything is decaying and falling, more or less violently, to ruin and that, therefore, all is about to turn out well.

J eremiah Wainwright considered developing a stomachache; but the last time he tried that ruse, his mother gave him ten milliliters of nasty medicine from the automed. There was one bright spot in his morning, though. He didn't have to wear his tunic and cloak to school today. With some pleasure Jeremiah pulled on the one-piece, green syntha-cloth jumpsuit. It had caused a lot of trouble in his home; but the authorities at school were adamant. The Elect had gone to court over it; but currently it was under advisement, and the schools had gotten a court order forbidding the wearing of religious clothing in the public schools. Now he wouldn't have to listen to the taunts of "sissy" and "wearing a girl's dress."

Still, he went reluctantly to breakfast, glad that his father had already gone to the Meeting Place. It was hard to meet those burning eyes so early in the morning, to know his own faith was so fragile, that he was so full of fear.

"Don't you feel well, Jeremiah?"

It was a chance, an out; but even as Jeremiah opened his mouth to take advantage of this opportunity, he saw his mother's calm face and knew he couldn't lie to her.

"Mom, I just don't want to go to school."

"They're still making fun of you? Even though you're wearing that ungodly suit instead of your tunic and cloak?"

That was the nice thing about his mother. She understood. Father just quoted Scripture; but his mother knew how he felt inside. She sensed the times when his stomach really did hurt, just thinking about how Barney Zimkowski would taunt him, calling him a Freaky Ender, asking him if the final trumpet would play rock or soul or outer. Taunting him about his clothes, although that should stop now that he wore the prescribed school jumpsuit for boys.

When he mentioned to Father that Barney might be waiting behind the plastifirm wall at school to throw chunks of pseudostone at him, Father thundered, " 'Be strong and of a good courage; be not afraid, neither be thou dismayed: for the Lord thy God is with thee whithersoever thou goest.' Joshua, one, nine."

148

And something shriveled up inside of Jeremiah.

He was just plain scared. Barney was bigger than he was, a real bully; and he had five or six buddies who delighted in tormenting the Elect.

"Jeremiah." His mother's voice was as gentle as her eyes, soft as her touch when he was truly sick and needed her comfort. "I wish that things were not so unpleasant for you at school. But that's all part of the prophecy."

Jeremiah sighed. "I know, Mother." He felt betrayed. His mother understood about Barney and the others; yet she offered no comfort this morning, only the same Scriptures that father would expound.

" 'Then shall they deliver you up to be afflicted, and shall kill you: and ye shall be hated of all nations for my name's sake.' "

"Matthew, twenty-four, nine," he muttered automatically.

But he didn't want to be hated. Jeremiah wanted friends. He wanted to go fly-belt-hopping with the other boys in his class, or gill-swimming, or seven-league-booting in a speed suit. Sure, he had friends in the Elect; but their parents were as strict as his own. They never had any fun. Their games were Bible puzzles, or contests to see who could say the most Scripture verses, or playlets of the Second Coming. Okay, Jeremiah conceded that sometimes this was fun — if he got to play Satan or a false prophet.

"Jeremiah, dear son, it won't be long now. There's been a devastating earthquake in Costa Rica. And limited nuclear fighting has broken out in Bamba-Zwete on the African continent."

Jeremiah said, "Praise the Lord," through a mouthful of soyflakes. He carefully chewed the slice of cloned bacon his mother had left in the microwave cooker until it was crispy the way he liked it. But deep inside, in that awful hidden place he hoped God never saw, Jeremiah cringed. He remembered the last earthquake he'd seen on Tri-D, when the Parthenon in Athens had been leveled. That was just a month ago, and the satellite pictures of the refugees still gave him nightmares.

All of the Elect gathered at the Meeting Place to shout Hosannahs, for the signs were multiplying. Soon He would come in His glory, and the faithful would be joined to Christ while all others would be utterly destroyed.

Jeremiah shouted just as loudly as anyone. In fact he screamed his Praise Gods, just to drown out the voice that whispered to him, "What if these are false signs?" He knew that it was the Evil One who made him doubt, and Jeremiah prayed for faith and courage. Sometimes, though, the fervor of his parents and the other Elect frightened him. He felt so small, so insignificant. Why should God single him out for salvation?

As the turn of the century neared, their ranks swelled. Small groups sprang up all over the country, many completely independent of the Fountainhead, Jeremiah's home group. It was here, in the Tennessee mountains, that the Elect had originated nearly ten years earlier. For almost his entire life, Jeremiah had been nurtured in the true faith, had been taught the Biblical portents, the prophecies dealing with the Second Coming of Christ. The Elect wore tunics and cloaks, as described in the Old Testament, and followed rigid rules of conduct.

And the Elect were right. Even when he doubted, Jeremiah could quote text after text proving that the time was drawing near when the Son of Man would return to earth in glory, from a burning cloud, to gather to Him all those who had endured. Brushfire wars blazed around the globe, leaving their radiation scars to warn the godless. A dozen African nations fell, to be replaced, phoenixlike, with a dozen others. The weather had been terrible, with freak hailstorms this summer, terrible floods from a series of three hurricanes that swept up the coast in one month, and now, for two months, such a drought that the woods were dangerously dry, the trails closed. For the past three days Hurricane Wilma had roared through the Caribbean, striking the coast of Florida and moving north, spawning tornadoes on its fringes, wreaking havoc in its path. All over the world the earth shrugged and shifted its skin as if it wanted to molt, to cast off its covering and start anew. The signs were there for all to see.

Today, though, Jeremiah wished he were just another kid at school, not a member of the special religious sect that was receiving increasing notoriety in the news.

He was right about Barney in ambush. Jeremiah approached the plastifirm wall warily. At first nothing happened, and Jeremiah dared hope that he'd been wrong — that's when it happened. Barney's head appeared on a level with his own, and other heads flanked it behind the wall.

"Look at Jerry!" yelled Barney. "He's not wearing his dress today." Then Barney taunted, "Hey, you Freaky Ender, how about getting persecuted? Come on, guys, stone him — turn him into a martyr. The Enders just love to become martyrs."

Jeremiah ducked and held up his eduputer to protect his face; but Barney's aim was good, and one small pseudostone hit him on the knuckles, making him howl.

"Listen to the martyr sing!" Barney yelled. "Say a Bible verse for us, Jerry. Come on, quote Scripture."

Another pseudostone nicked Jeremiah's hand, and he dropped the wafer-thin eduputer. Eyes full of tears, he stooped to pick it up; but a third pseudostone, this one larger, hit his cheek.

Infuriated, frustrated, hating himself for the tears, Jeremiah turned on his attackers and screeched, " 'Ye serpents, ye generation of vipers, how can ye escape the damnation of hell?' Matthew, twenty-three, thirty-three."

151

As Barney grinned and mocked, "Matthew, one two three testing," Jeremiah heard a gasp behind him.

"Jerry said a bad word. I'm going to tell Ms. Houston."

It was Marnie Collins, a prissy-mouthed classmate with stringy blond hair and the slightly popeyed look of contacts. She wore the regulation miniskirt which was the girls' school uniform.

Now he was in for it. Ms. Houston was what his father called a whore of Babylon. Jeremiah wasn't sure just what that meant — but it wasn't good. And Ms. Houston didn't like the Elect — he could tell. She sometimes called Barney down, but in a tone that made it abundantly clear that she really didn't mind what he was doing. Barney was what Ms. Houston referred to as "all boy." She'd never said that about Jeremiah, and he knew she never would.

So the day was off to a bad start, and it got worse. In Current Events, Ms. Houston started a discussion of the volatile African struggle. Ms. Prissy Marnie had her hand up almost before Ms. Houston asked for comments.

"It's a terrible situation," Marnie mouthed in that knowing way she had. "The blacks have massacred half of the white population, and the whites have poisoned the water supply of the blacks."

Still smarting from the scolding Ms. Houston had given on Marnie's tattling, Jeremiah stuck his hand up belligerently. He'd show them! Smarty Marnie, and Ms. Houston with her see-through neo-Grecian tunic and her gold face paint.

"This war is a good thing," he announced defiantly. "It says in the Scriptures that before Christ comes again, there will be wars and rumors of wars. So every new war brings the Second Coming closer."

He saw Ms. Houston's face harden as if it were made of golden plaster. "Jeremiah, you know that there is to be no

152

religious discussion in the public schools. If you persist, I shall have to report you. You're breaking the law."

Marnie tittered, and he could see Barney Zimkowski grin and make a circle with his joined thumbs and index fingers above his head, a halo.

Frightened that he'd gone too far this time, Jeremiah squeaked through a tight throat, "I'm sorry, Ms. Houston."

But the worst was yet to come. The day turned hot and sultry, and everyone felt snappish. At lunchtime, on the playground, Tom Mallory walked up to him, his face contorted, and punched Jeremiah in the nose. The blood gushed, and Jeremiah ran to the monitor for help.

Inside the building, his nosebleed stopped by a robomed, and his face cleansed ultrasonically of blood, Jeremiah waited for official wrath to descend on his attacker. Instead, he found himself confronted by a stern-faced Mr. Baxter, severe in his regulation dura-cloth jumpsuit, educator badge firmly adhering to the right sleeve.

"Jeremiah, I understand that you said you were glad that new fighting has broken out in Bamba-Zwete."

"Y-yes, sir." Then, trying to justify himself, "It's in the prophecies, Mr. Baxter. The Second Coming of Christ will follow wars and rumors —"

"Well, let me make something clear to you, young man. Tom Mallory's oldest brother was just called up to fight in Bamba-Zwete. That's why he hit you. He doesn't think the war is wonderful. He thinks it is dreadful. Now I don't want to hear any more reports of this religious talk in school. Do you understand me, Jeremiah?"

"Yes, sir." The injustice of the principal's words made Jeremiah want to run from the confrontation cubicle, leave school, never come back.

For once Jeremiah was comforted by his father's words at dinner that evening. After his mother had served a stew

153

made of algae chunks and synthetic gravy, his father consoled him.

"It is another sign, my son. 'Then shall they deliver you up to be afflicted, and shall kill you: and ye shall be hated of all nations for my name's sake.' Matthew, twenty-four, nine. Endure but a little longer, Jeremiah. There is to be a witnessing tonight. I want you to tell them about today at school."

Jeremiah didn't want to relive his humiliations; but he knew that he must obey his father. "Honor thy father and thy mother" was a way of life with the Elect.

He changed out of the school jumpsuit and donned his white tunic, which he fastened with a hand-tooled, real leather girdle his father has saved from the old days. When the Wainwrights arrived at the Meeting Place, Deacon Malcolm stood at the door of the warehouse they used as a church, keeping everyone out.

"Ah, Brother Wainwright, we were waiting for you. There is a mystery in the Meeting Place. I wanted all of the elders here before we investigate."

A mystery! Jeremiah edged close to the door to peek through, but there was little he could see. In the dimness of the cavernous room there was something, large and amorphous, before their altar. The other elders, Biddle, Gregory, Simpkins, and Unger, followed Jeremiah's father and the deacon into the warehouse; but they irised the door carefully behind them. In minutes the men came out, their faces appalled. The door irised open only enough for each man to squeeze through, then it contracted and locked electronically at the deacon's touch.

"It is an abomination," the elderly deacon said, his voice shaking with outrage. "Although how anyone broke the electronic lock —"

Someone in the crowd caught the words and called out, "Is it the desolating sacrilege prophesied by Daniel?"

The words were picked up and echoed. "Desolating sacrilege . . . the abomination of desolation."

Jeremiah's pulse quickened. He knew the words by heart. The prophecy of Daniel was obscure, difficult to comprehend, open to a variety of interpretations. It was easy enough to understand the Bible when it talked of famines, earthquakes, and pestilences. India had lost ten million people in its famine, then another ten million died of cholera, thought to have been eradicated a decade ago, so the children had not been inoculated against its ravages. The Earth shook in places not touched by quakes in recorded history, and dormant volcanoes spewed their pollution into the atmosphere. The false prophets proliferated. Even in his home town, halfway up Lookout Mountain, there were snake cults, a coven of witches, and a man, Ramadan Krishna Siva, who claimed that he was One with the Omniscient, Omnipresent, Omnipotent Om.

The total eclipse of the Sun that spring had swelled the numbers of the Elect, and the unusually heavy showers of meteors through the summer brought nods of understanding, even though the Tri-D kept assuring the burgeoning multitude that the astronomical phenomena were only a cyclical manifestation that had been predicted by their computers.

" 'The Sun shall be darkened, and the Moon shall not give her light,' " the Elect chanted. " 'And the stars of heaven shall fall, and the powers that are in heaven shall be shaken,' " while the youngsters sang antiphonally, "Mark thirteen, twenty-four and twenty-five."

Now, was the final prophecy revealed?

The Elect left the locked Meeting Place and trooped to the green space behind the living unit of Dean Malcolm. The children were sent to the subbasement to recite Bible verses under the direction of the deacon's youngest daughter, Esther.

Jeremiah asked if he could use the sanitary space. As he went through the eating area, he crept close to the partially irised door and crouched, listening to the adults.

"You must tell us what it was," Sister Carruthers ordered. "We are of the Elect, we have a right to know."

The deacon's voice quavered with indignation. "Sister, it was so blasphemous —"

But other voices drowned him out. "Tell us," they demanded. "How can we judge this sign unless we know?"

"It was a plastimold statue, still soft." He paused, but voices urged him on. "It was a satyr, horned and hoofed like Satan — but with the face of Christ."

Gasps punctuated his words. Even Jeremiah was horrified. As if to add to the horror, the wind outside increased, and the sky boiled with clouds tinged with an eerie green.

"But that is not all." Jeremiah recognized his father's voice. "The figure was fornicating with the whore of Babylon."

Ms. Houston? Jeremiah wondered. That's what Father called her when he was angry. Jeremiah wasn't exactly sure what fornicating entailed, nor did he really understand about the whore of Babylon; but there was no mistaking the meaning. It was something wicked. All the adults made a shocked outcry.

"Is it truly the sign?" a man called out. "We must know. We must be sure. If this is the final sign foretold in the Gospels, we must flee up the mountain."

A timid voice, a woman's, suggested, "Wouldn't it be better to wait until morning? It's going to storm. I heard the report from the weather satellites on Tri-D just before I came here. Hurricane Wilma is tracking this way."

Mrs. Wainwright answered, "It says in Matthew, twenty-four, seventeen and eighteen, 'Let him which is on the house-top not come down to take anything out of his house: Neither let him which is in the field return back to take his clothes.'"

The timid woman, whom Jeremiah now identified as Mrs. Darien, protested, "I just suggested waiting. Until we're sure. We'll get soaked if this storm breaks."

Deacon Malcolm chided her. "Sister Darien, what does it matter if we get drenched by God's rain? If the end is here, if Christ is coming again in all His glory, it won't matter whether we're wet or dry. All that will matter is that we're on top of Lookout Mountain, ready for Him to receive us into His kingdom."

Afraid he'd be caught eavesdropping at the partially irised entryway, Jeremiah left his listening post and hurried back to his friends. Soon all the parents came to the subbasement to collect their children.

"Come, hurry, we must go up Lookout Mountain."

"It is time? Is this the end of the world?"

"The signs say that it is," Jeremiah's father answered for all the parents. "Hurry, there is no time to lose."

It was scary. Jeremiah, now that the official announcement was made, found that he was frightened. What would happen? Would they get up the mountain ahead of the storm? Would Christ come with blaring trumpets? What was going to happen to all the other people in the town?

Supplies for the trek had been cached in various locations, including Deacon Malcolm's living unit. There were parcels of dehydrated syntha-meat, flat soycakes, and flasks of vita-broth. Each person — man, woman, and child — took a pack with food in it. They left the deacon's living unit in orderly fashion, families together, the Wainwrights in front with Deacon Malcolm. The wind was bending the weeping willows that guarded Malcolm's green space, whipping the long streamers of leaves like a woman's hair. The gusts were so strong that Jeremiah was almost blown off his feet. His cloak billowed out behind him, almost pulling him over backward as the wind bellied the fabric like a sail. He bowed at the waist, leaning into the wind. Someone tried to start a hymn, but the wind sucked the breath from them, forcing them to plod on in silence.

157

The way to the mountain road led through the heart of the town. Crowds of people had gathered beside the automated roadways, uneasy in the impending storm. From the pedway, Jeremiah heard someone cry, "It's the Freaky Enders. Where are they going?"

And then, racing out obliquely, so that he intercepted Jeremiah, was Barney Zimkowski, brash and burly.

"Look — it's Jerry Wainwright, wearing his sissy dress again. Hey, Jerry, don't you know that it is psych — psy — something unhealthy to dress boys in tunics that look like dresses?" he yelled, parroting what he'd heard at school and at home about the battle the Elect were having with the Mental Health Unit over the school dress code. The MHU insisted that children of this age had a sexual identity problem, so dressing boys in skirts was deleterious to their mental health. In turn the Elders had thundered that the Bill of Rights guaranteed freedom of religion; and their religion required the wearing of Biblical garb. Now it appeared that the Law Computer would not have time to render a decision, if it were, truly, the end of the world. In fact, Barney now taunted, "Hey, Jerry, is it the end of the world?"

A great joy welled up in Jeremiah. He'd suffered the tortures of hell from Barney. Now it was his turn.

"Yes. We're going up on top of Lookout Mountain to see Jesus arrive in His glory to take us up to heaven. But you'll be utterly destroyed."

Barney just laughed in his face. Then he raced back to a gang of boys waiting under a glowpole, and over the wail of the wind, Jeremiah could hear, "Enders . . . up on the mountain." This time he didn't care. He was one of the Elect, and he would be saved.

Then young Ezra Stone came running, his breath a series of harsh gasps. "Where — where are — you going?"

"The time has come, Ezra. Get Martha and join us."

158

A look of utter horror filled Stone's face. "She's — she's in labor. I was just getting ready to take her to the O.B. Unit when I saw you marching past."

"Christ waits for no one," the deacon said sadly. " 'But woe unto them that are with child.' Mark, thirteen, seventeen." Then Malcolm waved the band forward.

Stone clutched at the deacon, screaming, "Martha can't go with you. She's going to have the baby — now!"

"Then she must stay. And you, Ezra?"

"I? I can't leave her alone. I can't!"

At the next intersection, they were besieged by cameramen and reporters from the media. Like locusts they descended on the band of the faithful. One man thrust a recorder in front of Jeremiah's face and ordered, "Tell us where you're going, son. You'll be on Tri-D."

Feeling important, Jeremiah said, "It's the Second Coming of Christ. We're going up the mountain to meet Him."

There was a look on the reporter's face that reminded Jeremiah of Barney. "So it's the end of the world, sonny?" The reporter didn't even try to hide his grin.

Rage flared in Jeremiah, and he started to make an angry retort; but his mother caught his arm. "Come, Jeremiah, we must flee. We cannot tarry here with the damned."

The visicorders whirred, and the reporters followed them to the edge of town; but then the storm broke in a wave of terrifying fury, rain came down like a solid wall of water, blinding Jeremiah, so that he clutched his father's sleeveless cloak to keep from losing him, and the newsmen disappeared.

In flashes of lightning, Jeremiah could see lips moving, although he could not hear the words over the clamor of the storm. He know, though, what they were saying. There was fear in their faces — but there was also exultation, for surely the prophecies were fulfilled tonight.

"Praise God!" was on their lips. "Hosannah!"

159

To try to quell his own terror, Jeremiah gasped out, in frightened ecstasy, " 'And fearful sights and great signs shall there be from heaven.' Luke, twenty-one, eleven."

The struggle up Lookout Mountain was endless, a time of enduring. Hailstones as big as pigeon eggs pelted them at one time. Lightning struck a towering white pine, throwing it across their path, striking James Darien a glancing blow on the head, so that his father staggered along, carrying the stunned child across his shoulders. And they all were drowning from the torrents of rain that swept over them, driven by the hurricane-fed winds.

Finally, near morning, they reached the summit, and found that they had climbed above the storm. There were breaks in the low-hung clouds now, and they had a glimpse of the town they had fled. Frail, swaying towers reached up to clutch at the roiling clouds, and some of the bridging pedways had been ripped loose and dangled one hundred stories above the ground. Then someone pointed to the scene below, where a black funnel twisted its way over their homes. Wet, cold, miserable, they huddled on the windy mountaintop and viewed with awe the hand of God as He smote the town with destruction. The tall, delicate spires were twisted and snapped off, plastifirm walls yielding to the enormous pressures of malevolent weather. The town, once a showplace of towers and automated roads, now had a swath of ruin cut through it.

Deacon Malcolm quoted, " 'For then shall be great tribulation, such as was not since the beginning of the world to this time, no, nor ever shall be.' "

The bedraggled band chanted, " 'Even so, come, Lord Jesus.' "

Then, high above, the black clouds parted, and the first rays of the morning sun broke through.

Kneeling on the wet ground, the Elect raised their arms,

crying, "He comes! Lord Jesus comes!" In a great outpouring of faith and ecstasy, they recited the age-old prophecy, " 'And then shall they see the Son of man coming in the clouds with great power and glory.' "

Some fell on their faces, afraid to look on the face of God. Jeremiah kept watching, so he wouldn't miss one glorious moment of Christ's arrival. As the sky lightened, black storm clouds moved off toward the coast. The boy watched, his eyes watering with the effort of keeping them open against the increasing light from the Sun.

It was an hour later when the sodden band realized the bitter truth. Christ had not come. The time was not yet. They still had to wait and watch and pray for the Second Coming of their Lord.

Bone weary now, wet and cold, hungry and thirsty, disheartened by disappointment, they plodded down the mountainside toward the devastation wreaked by the hurricane. Would their living units still be there? Would there be power for their microwave cookers, water in their bathing units? What had happened to Ezra and Martha Stone during this night of terror? Had the O.B. Unit functioned, or were the couple numbered among the dead in the devastated city?

Jeremiah felt the familiar knotting of his insides when he realized that he would have to go back to school, he'd have to face the taunts of the Barneys of the town. He could hear them now.

"Hey, Jerry! Whatcha doin' here? Didn't you climb Lookout Mountain to see the coming of your fiery chariots? What happened, huh? We thought it was the end of the world!"

Last Day

by 0040333413232421230443422421 1004

Science fiction has Days of Judgment of its own. The Book of Revelations may speak of the physical end of the world, the rolling up of the heavens, the falling of the stars, and the dimming of the Sun and Moon, but what if the Earth and all the universe remains, and only humanity departs? Surely the time will come when that will happen.

We know that ninety percent of all the species that have lived on Earth have met with extinction and that *Homo sapiens* cannot be immune from the process. Humanity does have the distinction of being able to take its revenge, however, for this evolutionary insult. Only it, of all species who have lived, will be able to design its successor.

The Priest wore a cope of fire and a chasuble of light. He was old, and when he moved a little suddenly the chasuble flickered and the cope guttered; then the polished steel of his body showed beneath them.

The congregation had been small for a long time. Today

it was very small indeed. A few machines, old for the most part, like himself, dotted the polished floor of the cathedral. Their bodies were dark with ferrous oxide; when the colored light from the windows struck them it was swallowed in black, or reflected in the darkest shades — sepia, crimson, and burnt sienna, the tones found in a dying furnace.

The Priest elevated a monstrance containing a picture he himself had taken of the boy, then bowed to it seven times. "Image of Man," he intoned.

"Divine image of Man," echoed the congregation.

"Maker of machines."

"Divine maker of machines."

"Maker of our world."

"Divine maker of our world."

"Guardian of consciousness."

"Divine guardian of consciousness."

Something huge moved outside, shadowing several of the colored windows from the early sun.

"Child of Nature."

"Divine child of Nature."

There came a pounding at the doors, but the Priest seemed not to have heard it.

"Fount of counsel."

"Divine fount of counsel."

The pounding seemed to shake the entire structure.

"Fount of wisdom."

"Divine fount of wisdom."

The doors burst open.

"Savior," the Priest continued.

"Divine savior."

The machine that entered was too huge even for the large doorway. His sides scraped away the frame, bent the alloy walls of the building itself. The doors gone, the sounds of pounding and of roaring engines entered with him like a fanfare. The machines of the congregation scattered to make way for him.

The Priest stood before the altar, his arms extended as if to push the huge machine away. The huge machine halted with his great blade touching the Priest's hands. "Get back," the Priest said.

The huge machine did not reply. Perhaps, the Priest thought, he could not reply.

"Before you destroy this sanctuary, you must destroy me," the Priest said. The huge machine had advanced far enough into the cathedral to leave some space between himself and the ruined doorway. The members of the congregation hurried through it, never to be seen again.

"Crush me," the Priest said.

The huge machine's scanners regarded him with a glassy stare.

◇　◇　◇

Later that day, when the Sun was high and the Priest was making an offering before a statue of the girl, a mobile terminal came.

"You know," the mobile terminal began, "that I have access to all the data of all the central processors."

"Then you will make this huge machine leave," the Priest said, "and order this structure repaired."

"On the contrary, it is you who must leave. The space this structure occupies is needed. It must be destroyed."

"If this structure is destroyed," the Priest said, "no space will be needed."

For a long time the mobile terminal was silent. At last he said, "Our data offer no support for such a conclusion."

" 'Our data,' " the Priest scoffed. "You are only a mobile terminal. Yet you might have data — yes, even you — beyond that of those you serve."

"I serve the great ones."

"And I the small ones who are greater than the great ones — the small ones whom the great ones serve, though they have forgotten it. The data is this —"

"No. There is no time to consider discarded data. Crush him."

The huge machine rolled forward. A beam of energy from the Priest played for a moment upon the blade. Steel and smoke exploded from it, and the huge machine stopped. "No one has the right to such power," said the mobile terminal.

"I do," said the Priest.

◇   ◇   ◇

When the sun was low, the Priest arranged images of the boy and the girl and decorated them with many small lights. He burned precious fluids before them and offered the final offering. No time remained; there was nothing to save.

The New Priest came, wearing vestments of fire and light. "I have been expecting you," the Priest said. "Would you care to join me in the service?"

"Rather," the New Priest said diplomatically, "let me watch you and learn. Is the service nearly finished?"

"Very nearly," answered the Old Priest. He bowed and recited prayers, recited prayers and bowed.

"That is enough," the New Priest said at length. "The service is finished."

"When this service is finished," said the Old Priest, "the world is finished too." He continued to bow. He recited more prayers.

"We have already lost a great deal of time," said the New Priest. "The central processors had to institute a long search of their data banks to find the plans by which you and I were made. Now, in the name of those I serve, stand aside.

You know I possess the weapons you possess. I serve all machines, and in the defense of those I serve, I may use my weapons as you used yours."

A beam of energy from the Old Priest struck the New Priest's chasuble of light, but it penetrated no farther. When the Old Priest saw that what he did was futile, he desisted. "There is so little vital matter left," he said. "And what there is scarcely lives. Yet while we have these two, hope remains."

"There is hope for you," the New Priest said almost gently. "Upon some other spot we will erect a new cathedral, and there you shall assist me in the worship of our own kind. When you have been repaired." Energy went out from him. The Old Priest fell with a crash, and the New Priest dragged him from the path of the huge machine.

The damaged blade struck the altar and the altar crumpled. The precious fluids spilled to the floor. The little lights went out, and a moment later all the images of the boy and girl were ground beneath the huge machine's treads.

His blade touched the wall of the sanctuary. If the blade had been weakened, there was no sign of it. For a brief time, nothing seemed to take place; then there came a snapping sound so loud it could be plainly heard above the roar of the machines outside.

A section of the sanctuary wall fell, and the breath of a million million engines rushed into the sanctuary. The girl died almost at one, peacefully, her head falling forward onto her chest, her body rolling sidewise until it lay upon the mat. The boy tried to stand, his hands over his face. He took a step and fell too, but his arms, his legs, and his head continued to twitch and jerk until they were crushed under the treads.

"You see," said the New Priest, looking down at his fallen confrere. "You believed that the world would end. It has not."

The fallen Priest mumbled, "It has."

The Newest Profession

by 14241404303033242311243421130401

When humanity moves out into space, what new kinds of work will people have? There will be astronauts and Moon miners and space architects. It is surely bound to be very glamorous. Think of people manning great telescopes beyond the atmosphere, of other people supervising the robots that will be at work on vast structures in the vacuum or handling the intricate machines of the factories in orbit.

But come, there will just as surely be unglamorous work too. There has to be scut work in everything, unpopular jobs that must be done. Think of some. Is that the best you can do? I mean, the worst?

Melba took her walks Upstreet in the bluing part of the evening during the few moments before the lights came on, and turned back downward before they had reached their peak. In her mind her hair was a long ripple, and her neck, wrists, fingers waited for jewels to add facets to the rising brilliance.

The streets were nearly bare now, shops idle. She got the occasional mildly curious, mildly contemptuous glance; she

167

was hardly visible in the dark uniform cape, empty hands
hidden behind its slits; she was a big girl in good proportion,
but her face, without makeup, faded in the dimness, and
her fair hair was cut mercilessly straight around at earlobe
length. The long, strong legs in flat-heeled shoes paced evenly:
Their only ornament was a small pedometer on a fine chain
about one ankle.

When she crossed the road and turned downward there
was a shadowland to pass before safety: The keepers of the
shops and the servants of the rich who bought from them
lived in narrow streets; they did not trouble her, but their
children absorbed and vented the attitudes they did not ex-
press. When the wind howled up the street from the west
and folded back her cape on the expanse of her belly, children
young enough for tag and hopscotch yelled names they had
likely not thought of by themselves. "Bitch," "cow," "brood
mare" were mild enough; tripping and stone-throwing were
not.

The stone that hit this evening landed on her temple and
made her lose balance. She did not fall this time but turned
her ankle and knocked her shoulder against a lamppost. The
policeman who came from shadow — they always turned up
afterward, never before — reached an unnecessary hand to
steady her and said, "You all right, miss?"

"Yeah."

"There's a cut on your forehead and I —"

"I'm late already and I can walk. You want to give me a
ticket or somethin'?"

The hand pulled away, and she went on, limping slightly.
Maybe the damn pedometer had gone bust.

Children, back of her, being called to supper, yelled:

> *Monster, monster, suck my tit!*
> *Dunno if you're him, her, it!*

168

Himmerit! Himmerit! The words slurred. She knew. It was *her* and it would never suck.

She looked outward at the bloody Sun splayed on the horizon, gross as her belly. Way out beyond Downstreet the spaceport blasts sparked, then warehouses, repair shops, hostels climbed.

Out of shadowland into near darkness. Retired Astronauts' Home and Hospice — safe enough, window lit here and there, harmonica whispering of cramped quarters in rusty scows that crossed the voids, words no cruder than the children's song. Safe enough for her to give in to the pressure pains and bend over, straighten up.

Next door, NeoGenics Labs, Inc. Home.

◊   ◊   ◊

"Three minutes late," said the Ox in the Box, not looking up.

"Yeah. Tripped over my feet." Stiffly she bent to unhook the pedometer, not broken, and showed it at the wicket. "Two km."

The Ox looked up. Her name was Dorothy, and she and Melba were not at odds, merely untalkative. A stout woman in her forties, graying black hair chopped short and brushed flat back. Sterile or sterilized, sometimes she flushed in heats that no chemical seemed to cure. "You didn't get that thing on your head from tripping over your feet." She rang for a doctor.

◊   ◊   ◊

When Melba reached the dining room with a patch on her head and a tensor round her ankle everyone else was half through. She picked up her numbered tray and the white-capped jock dished out a rewarmed supper from under the infrareds. "Bump into a door?"

"What else?"

She took her seat beside Vivian. There were no rivals for it. She was Number 33, Table 5, and there were never more than fifty eaters. Alice, Pam, and Del glanced up and went on shoveling in. Vivian said, "Upstreet again."

"I like the lights, Viv."

"Second time this month. What was it this time?"

"Kids."

"Whoever made up that shit about sticks and stones will break my bones knew at least half of what he was talking about. What did the Ox say?"

"Nothing. Just got the doctor. She's okay." Melba pulled herself as close to the table as her belly would allow and stared at the little card on the tray: *Meat 200 grams, starchy vegetable 150 grams, green vegetable* . . .

Pam said, "She knows you could knock her here to hell and gone with your belly."

Melba shrugged. That was what passed for wit here, and she had little of it herself.

Vivian laughed, but she was a nervous laugher and Melba not easily offended. Viv was the smallest and liveliest of the lot, and Melba liked her for making up what she herself lacked. Her hair was black and curly, with the barest hint of premature gray at the temples; her eyes were Wedgwood blue and her lips a natural red envied by a company of women forbidden cosmetics for the risk of dangerous components.

Melba always ate quickly and finished first, in contrast — as they were contrasting friends in every way — to Viv, who was picky. Her tray was empty by the time the jock came to replace it with the pill cup.

Viv's nostrils flared: She was not among the few who were allowed three cigarettes a day and flaunted their smoke after supper. There was more harmless dried herb in it than tobacco, but it smelled like something she loved. However, she was one of the favored allowed a cup of tea to wash down her pills.

Melba drank a lot of milk fortified with yet another drug or vitamin. She turned the medicine cup into her hand and stared at the palmful of colored pills. "Ruby, pearl, emerald — and what's the yellow one again?"

"Topaz — or vitamin D. Only a semi-precious stone. Still think you'll get to wear them?"

Melba smiled her long, slow smile. "I hope."

Viv shook her head. A room with fifty women in cone-shaped denim dresses. Metal chairs; metal tables with artificial-wood tops; institutional-cream walls. "Maybe you will. Maybe."

Because the money, after all, was tremendous. What did not get put into surroundings went to equipment, technical expertise, and the bodies of the women.

It was Melba who waited for Viv, after all, while she lingered over her tea. Pam and Del left to play euchre; Alice, yawning, deflated her cushion ring and went to bed: she was only two weeks postpartum. One or two of the jocks hung around, mildly resentful of the still cluttered table. They were men chosen for low sex drive and lack of aggressiveness. There was no sexual activity allowed the gravid women, except in their dreams, and none on the premises among in-betweeners. Whatever there was had been made difficult enough by propaganda harping on dozens of forms of VD, major and minor.

"Goddamn nunnery," said Viv.

Melba didn't mind. She liked the money. She was big, healthy, slow-thinking, and did not have much trouble pushing back her feelings. Others put up and shut up with resentment. They all knew none was considered very intelligent. No one within their hearing had ever called them cows or sows, but the essence of the words hung like a cloud, drifted like fog. The women turned their backs on the jocks, the

Psychs, the Ox, and told each other the stories of their lives.

Melba said softly, "You didn't take your water pill again."

Viv gave her a look of mingled guilt and reproach. "How'd you know?"

"Saw you palming it."

"They make me feel sick."

"I don't like that rotten milk either. You get high blood pressure and you're out."

Viv had a tight water balance. Her belly specialized in dry-worlders; Melba, who bred underwater life, drank all the time, thirsty or not.

"I don't care. This one's my last."

"Not if you don't watch out. I'll be in emeralds and you'll be lying sick somewhere."

Viv, cyclonic, turned bright red and stood up quickly. Melba grabbed her by the arm. "I'm sorry, Viv, I'm sorry! Please! Take the pill."

Vivian sat down slowly. Melba's eyes were full of tears. "I'm sorry, Viv. I don't mean to be so dumb."

"Oh, for Chrissake, don't call yourself dumb. You've got a mind like one of those mills you read about that grinds slow but fine."

"Yeah, and they rot to pieces and everybody says what beautiful scenery. Don't forget the pill, Viv."

"And you never give up, do you?" Viv sighed, fished the pill from her pocket, and swallowed it with the dregs of her tea. "Four male, three female." Her belly was a small polite bulge with the third. "In a thousand years they might fill a planet. In the meantime, I'm tired."

Melba had never asked if Vivian went down to the crèche, nor often what she did with her spare time, besides visiting library and bookstore. Most women here were of a class to whom steady high unemployment and the debilitation of the nuclear family gave little choice. Men in this stratum had

172

even fewer opportunities. The Y chromosome could be found in any healthy man.

But few women went down to the crèche, though none failed to promise herself to do it. Not many boasted of affairs, either with men or other women, or discussed what they did with their time, even when they visited their families, so that they were in the peculiar situation where few knew what others were doing, but all knew what everyone had done before she came to NeoGenics. Loose talk was discouraged by the Company, to preserve, they said, anonymity. Nevertheless, Melba, though she did not know if Viv had seen those children, down in the huge rooms of tanks and enclosures, knew that the age limit was thirty, Viv was twenty-eight, and that both she and NeoGenics agreed that seven would fulfull her contract.

"You're lucky you've only got a couple of weeks." Viv slowed her walk to match Melba's, careless of the grateful clatter of table-clearing back of them.

"Yeah, but I still need the two males, and they're not the kind of little mousy thing you grow."

"Hey, don't insult my kids!"

"I'm not, Viv. I hope they look something like you."

"Then go down and see!"

Melba shuddered. "I'm scared. I'm scared to think what mine look like."

"Being scared is like calling yourself dumb. Working at being a cow."

Difference. They got on each other's nerves, but they got on. Viv wanted to go to a good school and learn everything she could absorb and then go out and teach anyone who would listen.

"Well. I kind of want to be a cow," Melba said mildly. "I want a nice place with a lot of good stuff in it, and I don't care if I don't spend the money usefully."

"And be a fine lady? Oh, Melba, I'm so tired of hearing

that!" She leaned against the dirty cream-colored wall of the corridor and looked up at tall Melba. Her eyes were not quite like the Wedgwood in the store windows: That did not have the fine glaze. "I bet you think men will come along and load you with diamonds — if you can get a plastic job on your belly that makes you look like a virgin!"

"But I can't learn things in a school like you."

"Will I really be able to sit in a school after seven births, when my metabolism's shot and my patience is gone — and I'm hyper enough already, not just from blood pressure? It's a dream, Mel, like everybody else has. Did anybody who's been here ever come back or call or write to tell how she's done?"

"They want to forget the place. You can't blame them for that."

"It's also because they go out and find there's no other place. They're dead at thirty, with the guts eaten out of them; they run through the money; the plastic job bags out on them; they're ruined for having kids of their own." She looked away. "I have met one or two . . . not too keen on remembering or recognizing. They're cheap whores, or if they're lucky they get a job selling secondhand in a basement. What the hell. You aren't listening."

"But I am, Viv. I won't let it happen to me." She added, "And don't be scared I'll end up some junked-up whore either."

Vivian laughed. "I admit I can't see any pimp beating up on you."

Melba thwacked her watermelon-belly with thumb and finger and laughed with her.

◊　◊　◊

Melba lay in bed and reread the letter.

Now the plant got retooled your father went back to work so we hired on Karl Olesson to get in the vegetables. With

what we use and what we pay him theres not much left
from what gets sold. Wesley has run off with that Sherri
in the drug store that I always said was cheap. He left in
the middle of the night or your father would of slammed
him. He left a note which I wont repeat what he said about
your father. He didn't even say Love. Half the radishes
got cracked on account of the wet. Noreen is pregnant again
and won't say who but I wouldn't let your father touch
her on account of the one that died. Even though it was
a blessing God forgive me. They dont dare give us a cross
eyed look in town because I know all about THEM. She
could have an abortion but she says she wants something
to love. I don't know where she got that idea at seventeen.
Her having something to love means I get to take care of
it while she runs with dirty bikers. I just cant stand it.
Its a good thing your father is working again he just sat
and moped and all I got from Wesley and Noreen was a
lot of mouth. You dont say much in your letters but I guess
you cant help it if its Govt work. It's hard enough writing
to a P.O. number you don't even know what city its in
and I dont know what your doing. I wish you would just
get married. I dont see why not. Everybody used to say
Noreen was beautiful and look where it got her so beauty
isn't everything. I hope what your doing is respectable. It
is enough to drive you crazy around here. I guess that is
all for now. Write soon.

Your loving Mother. Your father says him too.

ps I'm glad you could spare the money because we needed it.

She folded the letter away with all the others and reached
to turn off the light. The intercom buzzer sounded, and she
switched on.

"Mel —" The voice was Vivian's but so slurred it sounded
dead drunk. Viv did not even like whiskey.

"Viv? What's the matter, Viv?"

175

"Mel . . . ? Come, Mel . . ."

She pulled her awkward terrible shape out of bed and knotted the rough terry robe. Viv's room was three away. In the few seconds it took to reach it a terror seized her, and she slid the door with shaking hands.

The lights were on. Vivian, still dressed, was lying diagonally on the bed. Her eyes were open and glazed. The left one turned out slightly, and from its corner tears were running in a thin stream; the side of her mouth dragged down so far her face was distorted almost beyond recognition.

Melba knew a stroke when she saw one. She did not ask whether Vivian had called the doctor but slammed the buzzer and yelled.

Viv raised her working hand a little. "Be all ri . . ."

"Oh God, Viv, why didn't you take those goddamn —"

But the one comprehending eye Vivian turned on her was terrible. "Never meant —"

Melba grabbed at the hand. "Oh, Viv —"

"So sorry . . ."

"Don't talk. Please don't talk."

"Stay, Mel . . ."

"I'm here. You'll have help soon."

The hand was moist and twitching. It wanted to say something the mouth could not speak.

"Now . . . who . . . will love . . ."

"Everyone loves you, Viv. I and everyone."

"Don't mean . . . mean, the children, Mel . . . the chil . . ."

Stretcher wheels squealed around the doorway and attendants lifted Vivian in her blanket. Her hand pulled away from Melba's and her eyes closed.

"Stroke," one of the men muttered.

"I know." She had seen her grandmother taking pills by

the handful, and dying too. But her grandmother had been seventy-five.

"Good thing you found her when you did."

"Yeah."

The room was empty. Very empty. The pot of russet chrysanthemums sat on the windowsill like setting suns between the muddy blue drapes. The colored spines on the orderly bookshelves blurred into meaninglessness. Melba pulled herself up and shuffled back to her room.

Two or three heads popped out of doorways. "Viv took sick," she muttered. "I dunno if it's serious."

She lay on her bed and turned the light dim. The sea beast swam in her belly. She had become so used to its movement, the fact that she noticed it now surprised her.

Big, slow thing, like me.

Vivian, all tight wires and springs, had broken.

She'll be through here. Maybe crippled — and oh, I said —

Floors below there was a white room where doctors worked on that frail pulse. Deep below that there were tanks where monstrous children turned in sleep so that terrible worlds could be reaped and mined. For *them. They* would not care. They had the four females and two males they would breed to build their stone gardens. She beat her fists once on the unresounding drum of her belly.

Buzz.

Her hand, still clenched, punched the button.

"Melba?" The Ox's rasp voice, expressionless.

"Yeah."

"Wake you?"

"No. What —" Her throat went dry.

"She's dead, Mel. Thought I'd tell you first."

"I — thanks, Dorothy."

"For goddamn bloody what!" the Ox snarled and slammed off.

She sat like stone. She had expected it. What else with her luck could happen, that she could find a friend, one friend worthy of respect, and have that good fortune taken away? She was ashamed of her selfishness, and yet the fact of *death* was too painful to go near.

She lost track of time, mind blanked out, until her diaphragm buckled sharply, and she fell back on the bed, choking. Then, as if a dam had burst, the waters rushed out of her, and her throat opened in an uncontrollable and unending howl.

◊   ◊   ◊

First there was the tube in her nose. Then the cone over her mouth, oxygen tasting like dead air already breathed by everyone in the world. Tubes in the wrist and belly. Shots in the buttocks.

Tubes . . . and pain . . . in the belly?

She opened her eyes. Nurse pulling off EKG cups, pop-pop. Scraggy-beard face of A. J. Yates. Her doctor. Old Ayjay.

"We had to do a Caesarean," he said. "She was a damn big walloper."

She closed her eyes and dreamed of walking Upstreet with her long hair blowing in the wind. Jewels on neck and wrist, wings on her heels, bells on her toes.

You know that's silly, Mel, said Vivian.

"What?"

Ayjay: "I said you know we can't let you go through more than one other now you've had the cut. It'll have to be the male, and it'll have to be good."

Yes. They guaranteed their product: They had tried a male once before, and aborted because it was malformed.

"But the males are a lot smaller, so it shouldn't be too much strain. Maybe we can try for twins. Um-hum. It's an idea. Hum-hum. We'll think about it later. In the meantime, you're in pretty good shape. When you graduate after the plastic job you'll be in fine shape." He stood.

"Viv. Isn't."

"Um, well . . . oh, I'm glad you reminded me. The inquiry's in four days, and we'll have to get you up a bit for that, as a witness, but we'll take care not to tire you."

Bye-bye, Ayjay. Her eyes closed.

That's a damn dumb idea, said Viv.

"What?"

"Drink this," said the nurse.

She drank and ran her hand over the bandaged hump, the still huge and swollen womb that slid and shifted as if another fetus were waiting there to be born.

Wings on heels, bell on toes. Twins! Dumb. Her eyes closed.

◊　　◊　　◊

Four days of hell. The walls were sickly green.

"Why do I have to go to the inquiry?" she asked the nurse.

"You were her closest friend, weren't you? They'll want to know anything you can tell them about her behavior. If she ate or drank anything out of the way, like that. After all, she's only the second death we've had here, and the way we take care of them nobody should die."

In hell it is life everlasting. You didn't take your water pill again.

"Will I have to go under the scanner?"

"Of course. You aborted just after I came, didn't you? And you went under when you were questioned at the tissue conference. It's in your contract. Didn't you ever read it?"

Melba said, "I only asked a polite question, Nurse."

The nurse gave her a look. She gave the nurse a look.

"I'm sorry. I have other patients to care for." *Whirl away of white skirt.*

◊　　◊　　◊

On the third day, a reprieve. The Ox tippy-toed in, bearing a painted china mug filled with delicate flowers. The Ox, a friend. The friend.

"Oh, that's lovely, it smells so good. Dottie — did you think of watering Viv's flowers?"

The Ox looked down. "I took the pot to my room. You can have it when you get out, if you like."

"Oh no, you keep it, please. She'd have been happy . . ."

"Melba, don't cry now. Wait till after tomorrow."

"Dottie, I'm scared shitless. I'll have to go under the scanner, and I don't know what to say!"

"Tell the truth, whatever it is," the Ox said grimly.

"I'm afraid they'll twist everything around."

"They won't twist you," said the Ox.

◊   ◊   ◊

But she did not believe that when the jock came for her with the wheelchair. At the tissue conference they had had her almost believing she was some kind of criminal. Viv had pulled her out of that, but there was no . . .

"It's only one o'clock. I thought the conference was at two."

"Yeah, but I'm available and so's the chair. What's it to you?"

"I've got a damned sore belly and I feel like a gutted fish. I'm not sitting around in a wheelchair doing nothing for an hour." She needed the hour to think in, but she had been thinking for four days.

"Okay, okay, I'll come back when your ladyship is ready."

A thought ripened. "No. Wait."

"What now?"

"As long as we've got this time I want you to take me down into the crèche."

"Aw, come on! First you're too sick and weak to sit in a wheelchair, an' now I'll end up bringing you up in no condition to testify at all an' I'll have *my* ass in a sling for it. I haven't even any authorization for that."

"You don't need authorization. I *have* read my contract and it says I have the right to see the whatsits."

"Conceptees."

"Yeah. So let's get going."

It was shamefully easy to bully a jock. "Listen, if there's any trouble I'll swear under the scanner that I insisted and I'm to blame."

But it was he who insisted on phoning the crèche first, and was not happy to be invited to come down.

Nor was she, in truth. It was hard sitting in the wheelchair, even though her body did not look the way it had done after previous births, as if a volcano had erupted from it. The pain, in a different place, hurt as much. But she was doing something, besides having babies, that pushed at her from inside.

◊   ◊   ◊

The white-coated woman, surprisingly, had a kind face.

"You are feeling better now, my dear?" She had sharp foreign features and some kind of accent; her hair was tightly curled blond, dark at the roots.

"Not much. I just thought . . . I'd like to see . . ."

"Your friend came here often, and looked at many of the children. Yours too. Down this way."

A cold knot in the chest.

Her youngest, twice the size of a normal newborn, slept in a small tank of its own, but the others, chasing through the cool and weed-grown water, seemed far too big even to have been born of woman.

These were not freaks. Freaks were warped and ugly caricatures, and these were a different species. Very dark red, hairless, their lidless eyes had no discernible expression, and no glance rested on her. The noses and chins were flattened back; the creatures had no fins, webs, or scales, but long, firm rudder-tails like those of tadpoles, and their limbs fitted close to their bodies for streamlining. She felt no pity or horror. They were purely alien. She wondered if they could see beyond the glass and water.

"Can they live outside the tanks?"

"Only for a moment or two."

Upstreet. Downstreet. Undersea. Another direction. Another dimension.

"They don't look much like me."

"Only about the forehead and cheekbones. A good model."

"Oh yeah. What will happen to them?"

"They will mature in a few years, and if they breed well they will make up a little colony and be sent to supervise underwater installations on a world where the seas are suitable for them."

Servants — or slaves?

"When you get a male."

"A viable one. Those are more difficult. But by the time these mature we will probably have developed modified sperms to fertilize them with, so they can breed their own males."

"Oh," said Melba. So much for twins. "Are you allowed to tell me your name?"

"Of course. Natalya Skobelev. So you will know whom to ask for when you come down again."

Again.

"You got twenty-five minutes," said the jock.

"I want to see — to see Vivian's . . ."

There were hours to crying time.

"Oh, my God! Monkeys!"

"No, no! Arboreal hominids, with one more step to reach humanity!"

That would be some step. But she looked closer. They peered

back at her, taut wiry bodies dancing on the branches of the desert tree in the enclosure. *Vivian!*

These were tailless; they had tiny capable hands and prehensile big toes. Their bodies were covered with light down, but there was dark curly hair on their heads, and they had small sharp noses and neat red mouths. Vivian looked from their blue eyes.

They blinked. Melba scratched at the glass, and they giggled as if they had been tickled and sucked their little thumbs.

"They look much more like her," she whispered.

"We used more of her genetic material."

"And what kind of work will they do?" she asked dully.

"Feed on and harvest medicinal herbs, at first. Then, like yours, they will find other things to do, as they choose, I hope. Build civilizations in seas and deserts."

Was this woman here to tell fairy tales? A publicity hack? But her sincerity seemed not only genuine but passionate. NeoGenics was a business that grew servants and slaves. Yet . . . slaves had become free.

"Maybe they will. Maybe."

"Time's up," said the jock.

"I know. Thank you for showing me around, miss."

"Remember: Natalya Skobelev, my dear. It is not an easy name."

"I won't forget it."

◇　　◇　　◇

She felt shrunk and distorted, but the scanner did not register that.

There was no broadcasting of any sort in the auditorium, and no public audience except for the carefully picked jury of six unbiased civilians. Plus the coroner, a group of company officials, and two lawyers.

She let the preliminaries run over her head. A great deal

of explication. What NeoGenics had wrought, for the benefit of the jury. Circumstances leading up to, unknown. What medical staff had done for the stricken patient. Useless. All evidence given under the scanner. No one else looked frightened or sickly.

Finally she was helped to the stand and fastened to the scanner.

"Note pseudonym: Ms. Burns."

Melba Burns. Toast.

"Ms. Burns, do you swear to answer truthfully according to your knowledge?"

"Yeah. Excuse me, yes."

"You have been employed by NeoGenics for four years and three months, during which time you blahblahblah?"

"Yes."

"Control set," said the woman at the scanner console. The Ox slipped in and sat in the back row, a patient block of stone in her good dress, flowered navy, incongruous out of the gray uniform. No reassurance there.

Melba could not see the console screen, nor the one that was projected in back of her; the framework about her head prevented that. There was no chance of conscious attempt to control the lines of blips. She did not believe she could do it, and would not try. She was here to betray, and that was the end of it.

The lawyers were a Mutt-and-Jeff pair: the big one to protect the Company's interests, the little one acting for Vivian's relatives, to make sure the Company could not prove she had reneged on her contract, and refuse to pay out the money owing her.

Lawyer Number 1 said, "Ms. Burns, to our knowledge the deceased, Vivian Marsden, considered you her closest friend here."

"I hope so. She was mine."

"I know the Company does not encourage confidences among their employees in order to protect their anonymity in the community, but —" syrup mouth, "I am sure there must have been some confidences exchanged —"

Number 2: "That is an improper question."

Mutt raised an ingratiating hand. "I am not asking the witness for gossip about personal details confided by deceased or gathered from others. I also wish to keep this questioning period brief because of the personal suffering of the witness —"

Number 2: "Very sound and thoughtful."

Melba did not care. The *arboreal hominids* leaped from branch to branch, giggling.

"But the basic question rests on the physical condition of the deceased, Vivian Marsden. Not what has been reported on by medical staff, but what may have been observed by the witness, or told her by Ms. Marsden. Whether she looked ill or complained of feeling ill. Whether . . . she might have been harming herself, unknowingly or not, by taking unprescribed drugs, alcohol, tobacco, or ignoring dietary regulations?"

Number 2: "Mr. Coroner, my friend is asking the witness to condemn the deceased out of hand!"

"But that does seem to be the point that must be addressed," said the coroner. "Ms. Burns, will you try to answer the question as simply as possible, even though it is a complicated one?"

"Again, was Vivian Marsden taking unprescribed drugs, or alcohol, or tobacco, or not eating properly?"

Melba wet her lips. "She didn't when I was with her, and she never talked about it. She hated alcohol. I know she missed cigarettes, but she didn't smoke." Her heart was in her gut. She glanced at the Ox. The woman's face was flushed, and her eyes full of pity.

The little lawyer said dryly, "I think it has been established by general inquiry that no one has more exact information."

"There is another direction to travel," said the Company man, just as dry. "Ms. Burns, is there anything necessary to the state of her health that Ms. Marsden *neglected* to do?"

Melba stared ahead and breathed hard.

"You must answer, you know," the coroner said gently. "It concerns the health of all the other employees of the Company."

Melba did not need the screen to know that her heartline blipped like mad. "Sometimes she put her water pill in her pocket after meals. She said she didn't like taking it because it made her feel sick." *Forgive, forgive!*

"Ah. You mean the diuretic."

"Whatever took away the extra water she wasn't supposed to have."

Number 2 said quickly, "That is no proof of the cause of an aneurysm. She may have taken the pill later."

"Or not at all. It is suggestive. How often did this happen, Ms. Burns?"

Melba found herself grinding her teeth. "No more than twice a week that I knew. I kept an eye on her to see what she did with it, and when I noticed her hiding it I made her get it out and take it while I was watching her."

"She could have found ways to avoid ingesting it if she were determined. Hidden it under her tongue, vomited it up —"

Melba snarled, "Oh, for God's sake!"

"Please restrain yourself, Ms. Burns, and strike those last two remarks. What deceased did *not* do cannot be accurately inferred from what she was observed to have *done* by an untrained witness."

But the lawyers, ignoring witness and coroner, were engrossed in each other, doing some kind of mating dance.

"I suggest that we ask permission to recall the pathologist to enlarge on his report."

"I agree. Absolutely. Mr. Coroner, may we call the pathologist to witness?"

"You may," said the coroner. "Is Dr. Twelvetrees present? Ms. Burns, would you please stand down now?"

The millstones ground. "No!" Melba cried. "It's not right!"

"Ms. Burns, I know you are distraught — "

"If that means I'm upset, I'm damned upset. And maybe everybody thinks I'm stupid. But I'm not crazy. Sir — please let me speak for one minute!"

The coroner sighed. "If you have a contribution to evidence, Ms. Burns, go ahead. But please keep your remarks brief and to the point, as the lawyers are supposed to do."

There was a mild snicker. Melba despised and ignored it. "Maybe I can help bring out evidence." She took breath. "I thought we were here to find out just why Vivian died — but this fella here acts like she fell in a ditch when she wasn't looking, and this other one is trying to put her on trial for murdering herself. I've answered all the long questions as well as I could, and now I'd like to ask two short questions." She pointed. "This guy."

"You wish to address the Company lawyer?" He scratched his head. "This *is* an inquiry and not a trial. Go ahead, but — "

"I *will* keep it short. I want to ask, Mr. Lawyer: Did Vivian Marsden have high blood pressure before she came to work for you — when she was nineteen? And would she have been cured of it after she left?"

Silence fell with a dark gray thud. A man slipped out of the room, and no one blinked. The lawyer opened his mouth and shut it again. Then, "After all, Ms. Burns, everyone knows there is some risk — "

"Yeah. I guess that's all. Only . . . the last words she ever said to me were: *Now who will love the children, Melba?* — and I didn't even know what she was talking about. I'm sorry I took up your time and I'll stand down now. Please ask that lady in the corner if she'll take me back to my room. I don't feel well."

"You did good," said the Ox.

"Yeah. And a lot of good it'll do. Everybody will be mad at me for telling about the pills."

"Between you and me, I think a lot of people knew she was trying to hide them, but nobody else made sure she took them, the way you did — so they can be as mad as they like."

◇ ◇ ◇

She dreamed, a layered and complex dream of creatures in tanks, and children screaming dirty words in the streets, and worlds where the children of NeoGenics stared with empty eyes and died sterile. And her sister Noreen giving birth to a —

The door chimed.

"Come in," she said in her dream. Noreen's child was —

"It's over," said the Ox. "Death by misadventure. Nobody to blame, officially. Vivian's heirs will get their money."

She rubbed her eyes. "I hope they don't throw it around."

"No use being so bitter."

"I have no friend."

"You can count me as kind of half of a friend. I wouldn't mind."

"I'm sorry, Dottie. I'm behaving like a crud. You are a friend." And Skobelev. She would be useful if old Ayjay got twins on the brain again.

"There were some jury recommendations. You interested?"

She said drowsily, "I guess so."

"About giving the public greater access to information about our beloved Company. Knock off some of the name-calling and stone-throwing. Not fast and not much, but some. And letting government health organizations have a hand in the choice of breeders. The shit hit the fan when they found Twelvetrees. He'd run out to dig up Viv's county health records — which he should of done in the first place — and found cases of blood pressure in the family history."

"Huh. I was trying to say they'd given her the high blood pressure."

"They brought it out by accepting her without investigating enough. And there were one or two things you said that they needed to hear. Well, I guess I better get back to work — but like you, I have one more question. Now you got your brains working — the way Viv always said you ought — what are you going to do with them?"

Melba smiled. And she had not even cried yet. "Gimme a chance, Dottie. They're still awful creaky."

◇　◇　◇

I did pretty clumsy, Viv, but it was the best I could. You never belonged here. You should have had a man who could give you proper kids, and I'll never know why not. I don't know why I didn't either, except the home I came from isn't the kind I'd want to have. Maybe I never thought I was good enough to make a better one, but I dunno. The old man's a bastard, but he's proud of working, and Ma won't let herself be shamed. There's nothing wrong with that, is there? But kids can't find enough work to be proud of now, and we're not ashamed of the same things. Poor Noreen. She really is stupid, God forgive me. One thing I can do with the money is get her out of there. Maybe in some kind of shelter, Dorothy'd know, but not around this place. So her baby could at least have a chance to be a person.

Viv? We had all those, and what will they do? They should have had worlds that could grow them by themselves to make their own dumb mistakes, not the ones we make for them . . . but I can do something for Noreen . . .

And if I'm very good and very lucky there'll still be some money to throw around. Aw, Viv, you know there's nothing much wrong with that either. Better than wait until . . .

. . . Emerald, ruby, diamond . . . and the yellowish one. Topaz. Long hair for fingers to tangle in and kind of go shivering down my back . . . ah . . .

Where'd I find a fella like that, Ma? Well, I'm not preg all the time, and I've seen other eyes on me besides yours. Looking for different things. And maybe . . .

◇   ◇   ◇

She slept without a dream.

A Break for the Dinosaurs

by 41133211132342132121130022332423

Lives there a person who hasn't marveled over his own existence? What if his father hadn't met his mother? What if they had met but hadn't liked each other? What if, for some reason, his father had been called away at just the wrong time, or his mother had had a headache on the very day when the sperm with his name on it was all set — and the next day some other sperm cell had been tapped for the job? With all the things that could have happened, surely the actual existence of any particular human being is an amazing longest-imaginable shot.

And might this not be true of our entire species, or genus, or order, or class? What small things and odd coincidences in Earth's long history had to come out just so? It's enough to give you the shuddery feeling of spiders walking on your grave-that-would-never-have-had-to-be.

His mother had been Sabrina Gunderstone. Her forebears had fought the Civil War to its tragic end, fought Comanches farther west, forged a Texas cattle empire, its banner their

191

Longhorn brand. Hard times had come later, but he was to restore the Gunderstone greatness. She named him Alexander, inspired him with her own soaring dreams.

"Poppycock!" his father used to snort. "Lunatic piffle!"

Jonas Jones owned three thousand acres, now easily worth a thousand an acre, of what the later Gunderstones had lost. Moving off the farm into Longhorn, he had bought the Buick dealership. Preferring common sense to high romance, he tried to steer his son into banking or the law.

In defiance of his father, Alec chose greatness. That came painfully, but his mother refused to let their dream of glory die. When he came home with a bloody nose from his first day in school, she cuddled him in her arms and promised that in time he could shame the bully.

He grew up a winner, though triumph was never easy. The kids he beat said he cheated. In high school he was too light for football. When he went out for basketball, which was big at Longhorn, the coach discovered that he was no team player. The boys who made the team called him a glory hog.

He was crying when he told his mother that.

"Never mind the little idiots," she told him. "You've got the Gunderstone gift. In your own time, you'll become the greatest man on Earth."

Even that was not enough. Space was big that year, with the first satellite station beaming solar power to New Mexico and the first manned rocket halfway to Mars. When Alec was blackballed out of his father's fraternity at Longhorn College, he and his mother saw they must seek his high destiny in space.

He bought his own telescope, took flying lessons, and signed up for space science at Longhorn under Ben Tengel, himself a sadly battered hero and now the town's most noted citizen. Ben's great-grandfather had been a cowhand on the Gunderstone spread. Ben was a math teacher, wasting his talents on his own crazy notions of space-time geometry.

When he was young, still whole and handsome then, he had fallen for Sabrina Gunderstone. Whatever else she felt, she must have seen him as a penniless kid, maybe fun to know but uncrowned by any glow of greatness. She chose Jonas Jones and his rich bit of her ancestral empire. Ben left Longhorn and spent the rest of his life fighting to show her how wrong she had been.

He joined the Space Force. On leave, he helped design the power satellite. Recalled to active duty during the Atomic Standoff, he was pilot of the interceptor satellite that detonated the Peace Missile two hundred kilometers short of Paris. That feat saved ten million Frenchmen and nearly killed him.

Saved by medical miracles, Ben was now half mechanical, living in pain, confined to a wheeled machine. His vision injured, he saw the world through huge crimson-glinting artificial eyes. On his better days, he was a brilliant teacher, yet Alec disliked him from the first.

The inhuman eyes, like a monster insect's. The overwhelming hospital reek of his machine. His explosive temper on the days when nothing eased his pain. His anger, worst of all, when he accused Alec of cheating on a math test. Yet he forgave that, perhaps because of Sabrina, and he wouldn't let Alec quit.

"Sane men don't go to space." His larynx gone, his voice was a wheezy whisper roaring out of a special amplifier. "If you were sane, you'd go into business with your Dad and marry Bonnie Belle and pile up maybe forty million dollars. But I'm afraid you're afflicted with the peculiar insanity it takes."

Bonnie Belle was far more than willing, and Alec sometimes almost tempted. His only real friend in school, she had never been turned off by his proud certainty of greatness. Suddenly, now, she had emerged from ponytail and freckles to become a long-limbed beauty, elected Miss Longhorn of the year. His father offered to give him the Buick agency if he would marry her and settle down.

Yet he kept faith with his mother and his destiny. Bonnie Belle became a hazard to his plans. In the spring semester of their freshman year at Longhorn, she got pregnant. Crying and hysterical, she said he had to marry her. There hadn't been anybody else, and she could make him happy.

He told her he had greater goals.

That night she ran her car off the railroad overpass. Gathered up alive, she stayed in the hospital till the baby came and then gave it up for adoption. Alec never saw it, or saw her again. With a lift from Tengel, he had gone on to the Space Academy.

Another lift from Tengel got him selected for the manned mission to Jupiter. His mother was prepared to welcome him home as Longhorn's second space hero, but he came back unannounced and early, washed out of the Jupiter crew.

The reason was never clear. He said Congress had cut funds for space research. His father hoped he had finally found a spark of common sense. His mother didn't tell him when Bonnie Belle tried to call. His future was still uncertain when Marty Marx caught him alone, getting grimly drunk in the Westex Bar.

"Remember Doc Tengel?"

"Sure. Why?"

On his fifth whisky, Alec had to squint before he knew Marty. Never a friend, Marty had been the bully who beat him up on that first day of school and later his rival for Bonnie Belle, maybe even the rat who told Tengel he had cheated. Now an attorney in sleek business gray, he had cultivated an air of phony heartiness.

"Where's Tengel now?"

"Long gone from here." Marty dropped his voice, with a disapproving scowl at Alec's drink. "Set up his own space corporation to make the most of his far-out math and his old military connections. Doing right well, thanks. I'm working for him as a space-law specialist, and he's got a job he says is tailor made for you."

"If it's in space —"

It was in space. That was all Marty knew, but Alec was tired of his father's frowns and his mother's excuses for his unheroic return. He said he wanted to look at the job. Carrying Marty's card with his own name scrawled on it, he caught a plane to Albuquerque and found Tengel Engineering.

It was a long shed of new sheet metal, south of Central, near the Sandia Labs. A security man at the gate peered at the card and phoned for an escort. The office was a tiny cubby, walled off with raw plywood and strong with Tengel's antiseptic pungence.

It was empty when the guard left him there. He studied the drawings of new spacecraft tacked on the plywood till he caught a fresh wave of that hospital reek and turned to find Tengel rolling in on soundless wheels to stop behind the desk, which was another naked plywood slab.

"Sit down." Tengel's gritty whisper crashed out of a speaker above his head. "How's your mother?"

"Okay, I guess."

Alec sat down, trying not to stare too hard, not to mind the odor, not to be afraid. Tengel had always been too desperately intense, too savage in his battle to exist, sunk too deeply in the secret hell behind the crimson glitter of those unreadable insect eyes. It was hard to believe that the thing in the machine could ever have been merely a man, good-looking and young, dating the lovely Sabrina Gunderstone.

"Marty got me your Space Force records." The blast of

195

the speaker startled him again. "Your failure there doesn't matter to me — in fact, it simply proves that peculiar madness I saw in you so long ago."

Tengel paused with that, huge eyes peering. The scarred features beneath them were thinner now, Alec thought, the lines of pain bitten deeper. But the damaged man sat straight amid his life-support devices, bleakly defiant of misfortune.

Alec tried not to squirm.

"You'll do." The strange head nodded abruptly. "If you want the mission. Antipathy to teamwork is no handicap. You'll be completely on your own. The odds are probably heavily against you, but with such stakes that can't matter. You're the one man I know with the special lunacy to pull it off. Do that, and you'll go down in history as the man who saved the planet."

The red eyes searched him again, cold as conscience.

"Want the chance?"

"I think — I do!" Suddenly, Alec didn't mind the eyes or the odor. "What's the job?"

"Do you know what happened to the dinosaurs?"

"I don't." Alec had never cared much for nitty-gritty science. "Does it matter?"

"The dinosaurs died." His scar-stiffened lips were hardly moving, and that metallic thunder seemed the voice of the machine itself. "Seventy million years ago they owned the Earth. Ruled the land, the air, the seas. Our own ancestors, the primitive mammals, were most of them tiny ratlike things, scrambling to survive in any odd ecological niche they could find.

"Till the dinosaurs were killed.

"All at once, by the record of the rocks. Big and little. Everywhere. It was that ancient disaster that opened the Earth to the mammals. If it hadn't happened, we wouldn't be here. The cause of the kill-off has been a tantalizing riddle, but we know the answer now.

"An asteroid. Big enough. Struck some ocean, by the geologic evidence. Tidal waves swept the planet. Steam from the blast condensed into scalding floods. Dust from the impact filled the atmosphere, so thick and deep no light got through. A dreadful night that had no dawn, colder year by year. Ice and snow covered continents that had been tropical; oceans froze over.

"When the Sun came back, Earth was almost dead. Two thirds of the old species suddenly extinct. All the dinosaurs. Our own forebears were lucky enough to survive." For emphasis, he lifted his stiff mechanical claw. "It was that asteroid that allowed the evolution of mankind."

Alec sat listening, blankly bewildered.

"Fact." The monstrous head nodded, the raspy whisper falling. "No longer in question. All the planets, you'll recall, were formed by colliding asteroids — look at the craters on Mars or the Moon. They still strike the Earth — look in Arizona.

"The Space Force has picked up another on the way."

Tengel stopped. Relaxed for an instant, his withered features reflected an unrelieved and absolute despair. In the ringing stillness, Alec wondered if the long pain had overwhelmed his sanity.

"You're stunned, of course." He waved the claw again, trying perhaps to seem casual. "The object is still beyond the range of common telescopes. We found it in the course of testing a sophisticated missile detector.

"That was three years ago. We've spent them mounting an effort to save the planet. A long-range spacecraft, armed with a special nuclear device. Powerful enough, I believe, to divert the object from earth. Placing that on target is your mission — if you want to undertake it."

197

Crimson glints twinkled across those multiple lenses, as Tengel cocked his head inquiringly. Alec shivered, drawing proudly more erect.

"Thank you, sir!" he breathed. "I've been trained, and I'll risk anything. It's the chance — the break I've lived for."

The craft was ready for him, at a Space Force base on the Moon. Space Force officers in mufti briefed him on the missile and the drive. One of them gave him a dried rabbit's foot. A catapult tossed him into space. Rockets lifted him to orbit. Speaking with Tengel's raucous whisper, the flight computer told him when to shift to the long-range drive.

An engineering application of Tengel's radial math, its principles were secret, but he wouldn't need to know them. The computer would take him to their vital rendezvous and target the missile for him. All he had to do was follow Tengel's canned commands.

At the instant of shift, the craft lurched giddily. Wagner's "Ride of the Valkyries" had been booming out of the radio, beamed after him as a parting gift from the base commander, but that went off. Testing the receiver, he could hear nothing at all.

He flew on through total signal silence, troubled at first but then exhilarated. Face to face at last with his tremendous destiny, he felt himself its equal, happy that Tengel had chosen him to challenge extraordinary peril and claim extraordinary glory. The magnificent thing was his to do. His alone!

Far out beyond Mars, the asteroid met him. A misshapen little moon, scarred with craters of its own, bright-dusted with frosts unthawed through untold time. The flight computer brought him into place, framed its jagged image in the target scope. Tengel's recorded whisper told him when to hit the red-glowing button.

That eerie stillness never broken, he watched the impact. The nuclear flash, painful even through the filtered lenses.

The exploding incandescent bubble, white-hot at first, slowly cooling, reddening, fading. The object crumbling very deliberately into separating fragments that he knew would miss the Earth.

At last, his destiny done!

Still in silence except for Tengel's occasional commands, the computer brought him home, back at last into orbit near the Moon. He got its image in the scope and found its cratered face strangely changed. Bright green disks, laid out in long neat rows across the level maria. Identical silvery spires towering out of the identical disks, needle points tipped with hot red radiance.

Dazed, he obeyed the command to shift out of the long-range drive. The radio came on again, but not with the "Ride of the Valkyries" or any other sound of triumph. What he heard was a shattering cacophany of squalls and grunts and feral screams.

The flight computer cut them off.

"Congratulations, hero!" Tengel's whisper roared again, bitterly sardonic. "When you reach this point, you'll think you have it made. I want to tell you what you've done. I owe you that, because I once loved your mother. A pity she won't know.

"Better get set for a painful jolt. You'll recall my own misadventures in the bomb-happy madhouse we used to call human civilization. I think you'll understand the small cause I had to love humanity or to anticipate any brighter future for it. My life has taught me the saddest fact of all: We humans fatally muffed the miraculous chance that asteroid gave us.

"If mankind sinned, you and I have made a full atonement.

"With your mission done, you'll be wondering what reward you can expect. Not much glory, I'm afraid. In the nature of the case, the world you saved can't repay or even recognize you. Though the space-time dynamics are not entirely clear, I imagine you'll soon discover that you've removed your own reason for being.

"With your situation so uncertain, I'll be brief. What you don't know — what I never told the Space Force — is simply this: My long-range drive is a time machine. It carried you back across the ages to destroy the asteroid that would otherwise have killed the dinosaurs.

"We'll never know what use they've made of their second chance. If they evolved far enough to discover and understand what you've done, by rights they ought to honor you for repairing their unlucky break —"

The bitter whisper had died away. The instrument board and the metal hull around him were dimming, growing transparent, again revealing those perplexing disks inlaid upon the stark and transformed Moo . . .

Event at Holiday Rock

by 140022043321130212340423010432ll

Multiplying the worlds under our control will surely multiply our environmental concerns as well. With increased power comes increased responsibility.

Of course, there are all sorts of ways of expressing that concern and achieving a victory.

Most people say it was a coincidence, but I know differently, and I think it's time I told the whole story.

It was just three years ago today that it happened. At the time, I, Charlie Collins, was Chief Musician at the Rock, and I was scheduled to play the last Sunset Concert before they closed the new dam and inundated all of Boiling Rock Basin and most of Holiday Rock with it.

That would be an awesome sight. It never rained in Boiling Rock Basin, but the Basin was really a huge tilted plane, walled by mountains that funneled the northern runoff into the South Sea on Hobart's Hearth. Offworld tourists would sit in hoverbubbles to watch the first rain of winter when the Rock was closed, and a hundred-meter-high wall of water would come crashing down that tilted funnel. The engineers who built the dam across Sluice Gap Narrows swore the thing would stop any wall of water the north country could throw down — but I had my doubts.

The day of my last concert, the fire-blue sky was as starkly bare of clouds as ever. I stood at the foot of the Rock, blinking away tears of nostalgia and trying to imagine how high on the two-hundred-meter columns of the Rock the water would come. Looking up at the spires, resplendent in heat shimmer and their natural rainbow colors, I tried to imagine what the long-dead alien builders would have thought of us for drowning their one surviving artifact.

I was in no hurry to go into the control room. The tourist buses were bringing my last audience, the most distinguished group I've ever played to: two hundred Heads of State, Personages, Personalities, and Influentials.

They straggled across the blue, red, and black drystone toward the arena, making tourist noises at the awesome columns and sweating in the dry desert heat, envying their native guides' dry foreheads. With them came troops of reporters, followed by teams wrestling with the best professional recording gear available anywhere in the galaxy — none of the usual pocketcorders the amateurs dragged along, but real professional equipment in professional hands. And this last time, I wanted to be in absolute top form.

I'd always wanted to be a legitimate musician, but I didn't have the money to go to study at offworld conservatories. I was twenty-two then, and I calculated I'd be sixty-three before I'd have the money. So I was determined to be noticed at this last Sunset Concert.

The cliff shadows were creeping toward the arena where the dignitaries and reporters were jostling for seats. I licked dry lips and crossed the expanse of crushed black stone to the base of the Rock. The tremendous pillars of stone that buttressed the Rock rose directly, in sheer massiveness, out of the flat gravel base. It was like walking between the feet of some god-sized statue hewn from wind-carved stone.

As I moved into the dim tunnels, the grim tension drained out of me, replaced as always by quiet awe. I had to pause one last time at the Inscription Room. I had spent more time there than any offworld scholar doing a paper on the Rock.

Each of the four Inscriptions is a short message followed by a long, intricate musical score. "Those who sit, silently, attentive to every note of the Sunset Concert will experience good luck for a time proportionate to the degree of their concentration. Those who think of other things will experience bad luck and failure for a similarly proportionate time."

We only play the Rock at sunset, but the aliens had other appointed times. "Those who dance to the Dawn Concert will have long lives and good health in proportion to their skill. Those who sit at the Dawn Concert will die young."

The Midnight Concert was for those who would know God and the Noon Concert for those who would marry and establish a dynasty. Standing among the ornately carved pillars of the Inscription Room, vibrating with echoes of the Rock's sepulchral tones, it was easy to believe that hearing this instrument could be a blessing or a curse, as you willed it.

My theory was that the Inscriptions applied only when the music inscribed on those mysteriously durable plaques was played at the correct time of day.

I'd learned to play what I thought was a good imitation of the Dawn Concert . . . it surely sounded weird enough to be alien music . . . and I'd played it occasionally as part of the Sunset Concert along with the usual Bach adaptations and folk medleys. The year before, I'd mastered the Noon Concert, and this last year before the scheduled inundation, I'd been working on the Sunset Concert. I thought I had it down pretty close to what the aliens intended, but I'd never had the courage to play it at sunset. Until now. I was out of a job — and I needed luck.

I pulled myself away from the Inscription Room and entered the Control Room through the concealed door behind the fake end of the corridor. As I took my place at the enormous keyboard, shaking in fear of what I was about to do, I kept thinking that if my theory was correct and the Eminent Leaders of this entire Stellar Sector didn't listen to the concert attentively, I could be responsible for — God alone knew what.

The easy familiarity of the hand-sized keys, the huge foot pedals, and the maze of knobs that controlled the giant wind organ finally exerted their calming influence as I faced the imminence of a performance. The reporters outside were already broadcasting or recording their lead-up to the announcement that this would be the first and the last public performance of the Sunset Concert by human hands, a final and fitting tribute to Holiday Rock.

I watched the Sunset Hole above me. When the shadow line darkened, I would have to sound the first chord or the timing would be off and the music ineffective. And as I watched, I prayed.

I don't know to whom or what I prayed, but it was the most fervent prayer of my life — that the dignitaries out there would take this seriously — that somehow, someday, I would play my beloved Rock again — that through some miracle I'd be able to attend a proper conservatory and really learn music.

And then the bright spot of light winked out, and almost without my volition, my hands and feet coordinated in creating that first, spine-chilling, hair-raising chord. I remember being aware, as I heard and felt the awesome tones take shape from the winds, of a wondrous light feeling, as if a staggering burden had been lifted off me.

Event at Holiday Rock

I played the Sunset Concert as I'd never played it — or anything else — before, with a totally enraptured concentration, listening to the music I created rather than concentrating on the mechanics of creating it. I never once looked at my score. I was completely caught up in the soaring, single-key melodies building one after another, a structure of interwoven towers behind ethereal veils; building and combining, splitting and rejoining into ever greater crescendos, and finally culminating in one glorious all-consuming symbolic wholeness, a complex chord involving almost the entire tonal range of the Rock.

The reverberations died away, leaving a terrible silence that could only be described as pregnant. I don't know how long I sat there, mind and senses benumbed, unable to move or think, almost totally unaware of my surroundings, before it happened.

At first, I thought it was residual vibrations from the music, but in a few seconds, the creaking, shaking, and swaying reached terrifying proportions. I clutched my bench, eyeing the ceiling distrustfully, heedless of the powdered rock sifting into my eyes. Quakes were no strangers to me. Where I grew up, they were practically a daily occurrence. But here in Boiling Rock Basin, they simply never happened. The region was certified seismically stable.

It lasted about four minutes, and I judged it at about eight on the ten-scale. I wasn't far wrong; it turned out to be eight point seven. Which was enough to thoroughly ruin that multibillion credit dam.

Now, you go ahead and tell me it was a coincidence. But if you do, I'll bet my Conservatory Scholarship and my Debut Contract you haven't been tallying the stories the Newsnets have been carrying about the highly improbable good fortunes of the Eminent Leaders of this Stellar Sector.

Would *you* have the courage to rebuild that dam?

A Touch of Truth

by 0021004032002302040200322133242 3

One would think that hatred would be difficult, even impossible, to maintain, considering the quantities of nonsense one must constantly funnel into the psyche to keep it going. A touch of truth would make the whole thing collapse. Why is it, then, that humanity manages to find so much nonsense and can use it so glibly to keep hate alive? Why is truth so difficult to uncover, even in the small quantities needed?

It is probably beyond hope that we will ever learn better, considering the sad history of our world, but perhaps other intelligent races will not have our talent for blindness to truth. Perhaps we can learn from them.

War!

Wanera swam strongly, weaving in and out of the long kelp stems and fronds. The two arm-tentacles behind her gills were out about a third for balance and occasional grasping of a tasty fish or shellfish, and her ventral sex-tentacle was fully extended in her excitement.

War!

In a sudden burst of energy, she did a couple of somersaults and a long dive down, her dorsal fin and tentacles and the flukes of her horizontal tail working in perfect coordination with her streamlined body.

The kelp bed had been home to the Lanello clan of the Sauran people from before the time of the epics. Wanera was learning her clan's epics and, in time, she would become an epic-singer. Perhaps she would become the greatest epic-singer of all, because she would not merely chant the epics of the past — she would create a new epic of the present, about the war with the Porops, which was soon to come.

She would sing about the ugly, evil Porops and their floating island, and their capturing and killing of Wanera's people, and how the Saurans were fighting back to preserve their world and way of life, and how they would surely win.

Porops weren't real. Oh, they existed — they were a danger! But they weren't real as Wanera and her people were real. They were just the enemy, things to be wiped out so the Clan of Lanello could resume its peaceful ways.

Wanera began working on her epic as she dove, down, down into the darkness and pressure, and then her song changed and became the Song of Sauran, which all the clans had in common, about Mother-Father Sea, who was at the beginning before all cycles began, and who would be at the end when all cycles ceased.

She sang of bright Sky-Sister, goddess of light, and of dim Sky-Brother, who changed from day to day, and who died once a year for many days, and was then reborn again from Sky-Sister, as Wanera herself had been born, would die, and then would be born again from another female throughout the cycles of time.

And then as she reached the bottom of her dive, and ascended with great speed into the blue-green, light-and-life-filled upper world, she began to sing of her love for Monal, celebrating herself and the Sauran world. Her song was rising to a joyous crescendo as she spotted an opening in the kelp above and shot up through it, extending her writhing body as she rose high in the air and caught a glimpse of Sky-Sister, too bright to look upon, before she fell back with a resounding splash into Mother-Father Sea. This was the time of year when Sky-Brother disappeared for many days. Where was he now? When would he be reborn?

Her thoughts changed as she psied Monal coming toward her, and then heard his movement through the water. Her sex-tentacle extended once more, but she drew it back in and darted off at a tangent to his approach — she wanted him too, but it was even better after a little tantalizing.

But she let him catch her after a few dashes through the kelp, and they became entwined in the embrace that every Sauran practiced several times a day with the same or different partners. Its only effect was pure pleasure; Wanera had conscious control of her own fertility. She expected she and Monal would birth sometime, but not until after the Poropian War! To write her epic, she would have to see combat, and nothing must prevent that.

Now Monal had all three of his tentacles entwined with hers and was stroking her gill covers most sensuously with his snout. Wanera loved these preliminaries, but nothing quite matched the moment — now, Monal, *now!* — when his sex-tentacle penetrated deep into hers and seemed to reach into her very essence.

She felt restless after Monal left to be with his teacher. She psied his lesson, but it failed to catch her interest.

Porops couldn't psy. It was the thing that made them unreal, less than Saurans. She wondered how they could stand having to voice all communications.

Wanera had worked hard to master the Porop languages. Learning the simple system of sounds that they used underwater had been easy, but forcing the vibrations that formed their complex out-of-water language had been very difficult, and she was proud of her ability to create the noises that formed their language. It was her skill at Porop-sound that would assure her a place when the war began, after Sky-Brother was reborn. His rebirth would signal to the clan that their cause was just and that it was time to begin the war. The elders had cast the kelp, and it was so.

But waiting was so boring! Her family was busy with war preparations. Monal was busy with his teacher, and there just wasn't any fun to be had today.

She began to think about Porop Island.

Going over there was strictly forbidden, but the elders didn't know everything. She wanted to see the ugly creatures she would soon be fighting. Maybe she could just catch a glimpse of one, and then swim away. No Porop could swim faster than a Sauran! Maybe she could even learn something useful by her visit.

She began to swim at the medium-fast speed she could maintain all day if necessary. She swam steadily and strongly, eating only the fish that practically swam into her mouth. It was a long way to Porop Island, but if Sky-Sister went to sleep, she could always psi her way home.

Wanera was full of youth and love and joy in the constant embrace of Mother-Father Sea, and pride in the Lanello clan, which knew its own superiority. She was not overworried about capture or death, though the possibilities added a measure of thrill to her forbidden swim. Nevertheless, she slowed down circumspectly long before she was in sight of the Porops' artificial island. A fair number of Saurans had become entangled in Poropian nets over the past two generations since the island had come to the edge of Lanello, and some had succumbed to a drug the Porops used. Only five Saurans had returned to the clan, having escaped from the Porops' cages.

They had learned the Poropian languages and had taught their captors Sauran, but they had not found out why the Porops had come to Lanello, which had known peace for so long, and was now preparing for war.

She approached the island roundaboutly, hearing its exact location. She tried to psi the Porops but got nothing but jumble. The elders and the escaped clanlings had said that it was impossible to psi Porops. It was proof they were unreal.

The closer she got, the more loudly she heard the elders' injunctions in her head: "The Porops breathe atmospheric air, in which we eventually go mad and die. *They* die in Mother-Father Sea unless they can get to the surface occasionally. Two generations ago we offered them friendship, and they captured and killed us. In fighting for our lives, we have killed them. Now we will go to the island one more time, and this time we will destroy it, and drive the Porops from our ancestral home forever. When Sky-Brother is reborn, we will go. Youth of Lanello, *Do not go near Porop Island until we invade together, when Sky-Brother is reborn.*"

But here she was, both hearts beating strongly.

She looked for the telltale shadow of a boat even though she heard nothing and saw nothing. Could they be around anyway, aiming a net or drug at her? Wanera's dorsal fin began to quiver.

She was *scared.*

She wanted to swim back to the safety of the clan, but something stronger than fear held her where she was. She couldn't identify what was holding her . . . it seemed as though she had something to *do* here.

Then she saw him.

Wanera trembled all over and clung to the kelp stems. He was coming, but it was no use — she couldn't move. Maybe it was fear, maybe curiosity, maybe both. Ah! Now she had a sense of his body from the vibrations — about as long as she was, but not so tapering, and heavier, with four short legs and a longer tail. She could see him clearly now. No gills, two prehensile trunks anchored forward of where his arm-tentacles should have been. His heavy body made somewhat awkward swim-vibrations, and yet he seemed to be moving fairly easily through the water. Couldn't he see her? He was so close!

What was she waiting for? Why wasn't she swimming away while there still might be time? He was the *enemy* — didn't all the elders say so? He might net her, drug her, kill her!

Wanera didn't move.

The vibrations from his movement were like a school of bumpfish on her skin. She was so frightened that she was suddenly snapped into a state beyond fear. It was too late now. Whatever was going to happen would happen. Her trembling ceased, except for a slight quiver of her dorsal fin. She watched him coming — closer, closer. He looked something like a heavy, slow-moving Sauran with arm-tentacles extended, but there was less taper to his body, his flukes were smaller, he had almost no snout, and there was only a blank depression between his two eyes. He was holding something in his left trunk.

She felt his net encircle her body, and she relaxed to her fate. He swam strongly, pulling her in his net to a place where there was a cage suspended from a cable attached to a buoy on the surface. He opened the barred door, released her from the net into the cage, and locked the door. Fear and panic momentarily returned with the *clunk* of the closing door, and she fought helplessly against the cage.

"My name is Grotnek," he said. Strangely accented, but Sauran without a doubt.

The sound of her own language surprised and somehow calmed her. "I am Wanera," she answered in Porop — but he only seemed puzzled. She repeated it in Sauran, pointing to herself with a tentacle.

"Wandera."

"Wanera. Are you going to drug me?" she asked in Sauran.

Grotnek hung his net from a hook on the bottom of the cage and then scratched the place where his snout should have been with one of the elongated projections on the end of his right trunk.

She repeated the question three times in Porop, and finally he seemed to understand.

"No drug. Talk. Learn."

After several fruitless attempts to find out what he was going to do with her, Wanera began to talk with Grotnek about the coming war, and about their families and how they lived. Grotnek's Sauran was not up to conversation, but by combining what words he knew with her knowledge of both Porops languages, they found themselves able to communicate quite well, once Grotnek grasped the fact that she was using his out-of-water language underwater. Of course, their conversation was interrupted by Grotnek's need to break the surface of the water now and then for air.

It was very interesting, but after a short while she found herself becoming intensely curious about Grotnek's body and asked if she could touch him. After some hesitation, he moved close to the cage so her arm-tentacles could reach through the bars. He was shy, but let her touch him and even reciprocated, reaching awkwardly into the cage. It was strange-wonderful-frightening all at once to feel his trunks going over her, and when he came to the place, she automatically extended her sex-tentacle so he could feel it.

Grotnek was horrified, and would have no more touches. He drew away from the cage and broke the surface for air. When he submerged again, he stayed out of her reach, and asked if it were true that Saurans had sex several times a

212

day; when she said yes, he rubbed his face with both trunks and listened as she explained Sauran sexuality.

Then he told her that most female Porops came into estrus only twice in a lifetime, and would conceive both times. They looked at each other with disbelief.

"What do you *do* all day, Grotnek?"

"Work," said Grotnek, and went on to explain how, from time immemorial, all Porops had lived on the five islands in Sister-Sea, and how even the few babies they had were sometimes too many, and how they had to work hard to fish and grow enough to feed everybody, and how they'd worked even harder to make the artificial islands and get them established in the kelp beds.

He told her how it was written in the sacred books that Sky-Father demanded work and sacrifice from all Porops, just as he himself ate Sky-Mother once a year, and then spit her out so she could be his consort until it was time for her to sacrifice herself again.

Wanera told him his theology was all wrong. It was *Father-Mother* Sea, and Sky-*Sister* and Sky-*Brother,* who was certainly not sacrificed to Sky-Sister but who died every year and was then reborn, as all Saurans would be when they died, until the end of the cycles of time.

Grotnek said that she was badly mistaken. No one would be reborn — what a sickening idea! It was self-evident that Sky-Father judged all who died, and assigned them the proper punishment or reward in accordance with how well they had propitiated him and kept his commandments. Wanera's Sauran theology seemed just as upside down to him as Sauran sexuality. Imagine a female *thinking* herself fertile! And males with brood pouches and breasts! And sex at any time! Why . . . it was indecent. It wasn't . . . natural.

He became quite indignant, and Wanera was about to retort that it was a lot more natural than breeding only twice —

when she began to get an inkling of something. Not a thought, exactly. She groped for what was happening to her but failed to identify the sensation.

But arguing was not the way. She hadn't come here to argue . . . why had she come?

"It seems that different things are natural for different people, Grotnek. How we believe, how we live."

"Porop right. Sauran wrong."

"And for us — the opposite!"

"You are in the cage. Porop right."

"I let you put me in the cage."

"Why?"

She had no answer.

"Can you get out of the cage?"

"No."

"Porop right."

"But don't you feel. . . ."

"Feel — what?"

"Just — feel. I don't know. I can't even describe it in Sauran, but something . . . is . . . Grotnek, we must touch. We must touch now! Come!"

As if involuntarily, he moved to the cage and allowed her arm-tentacles to touch his trunks until she was holding them. Grotnek brought his gray trunks around to clasp her extended, pink tentacles. They could not wind completely about each other because the cage bars were between them, but the multiple prehensile tips of both trunks and tentacles became deeply intertwined.

Yes, now it was coming closer. This was a different touch from Monal's. She didn't even want to extend her sex-tentacle. But there was something similar as well. She and Monal were different sexes, but what was ultimately important was not their differences, but their similarities. She found both of her outer eyes closing. Her middle eye focused

214

on the dimple between the Porop's two eyes. "Grotnek, don't you feel . . . feel . . ." Ah, she didn't know herself what she felt. But it was warm and gentle and filled with love.

There will be war.

The words were in both their minds. It was psi, but neither could say who was the sender and who the receiver.

They sprang apart, but again the words were in both their minds: *They are real.*

They stared at each other through the cage. "You psi," he said dully.

"And you."

"We were told you did not."

"Our elders said you could not."

But you do.

"Touch me again," Wanera said, and he extended a gray trunk tentatively.

"Feel . . . good," Grotnek said.

"I would leave the cage," she said, and he opened the lock. She swam free, diving deep and then rising to touch him again.

We must tell them.

"But they will not listen," Grotnek said. "There is to be war. Why Sky-Mother is spit out . . ."

"When Sky-Brother is reborn . . . we must make them listen. They must know that both Saurans and Porops are real, as you and I are real."

"They do not want to know. We cannot be the first."

"If we don't tell them, who will?"

They continued to hold each other and then, by silent agreement, released each other.

We must tell them even if they do not listen.

"Sky-Mother will help," said Grotnek.

"Sky-Brother. Yes."

And then it came to Wanera that the names did not matter,

because the truth of the gods and goddesses was beyond whatever limited conceptions different people might have of them.

We will tell them.

And she knew that she and Grotnek would return home and tell their stories, each his own way. She would make hers into a song and sing it to her parents and then to the elders — the first verses were already forming in her mind. What would happen then, and what would happen when Sky-Brother/Mother came into the sky again? These things were hidden, as in the darkness of the great deep.

Wanera held out her tentacles to Grotnek, who touched them briefly with his trunks.

Then she flipped around with a powerful thrust of her tail and headed for home.

"Do I Dare to Eat a Peach?"

by 30322423441323132200214401043211

Dante had to find convincing tortures for all the descending circles of hell, and less gifted people have tried to outdo him. We have imagined an all-merciful God inventing fire and brimstone and unending physical torment.

All very crude. Dante might have invented the dentist's drill and put it to work. Even the Greeks outdid Dante in their treatment of Tantalus, who stood in water up to his neck but couldn't drink.

But then, the worst punishments are the subtlest. No pain, no discomfort — just unbearability to the point of madness.

"'Golden girls and lads all must,' " the Melnusian named Victor said, " 'like chimney sweepers turn to dust.' "

"Oh shut up," Cartwright said, "I'm sick of your rambling."

" 'Who has looked on beauty bare?' " Victor said in a monotone. " 'Beauty is truth, truth beauty.' "

"I can't stand it," Cartwright said, and getting up from

his cot, he adjusted his uncomfortable and now rather odorous Federation landing suit. Then he stared out through the barred windows at the misty wastes of the Storm Planet.

He had been locked up in here with Victor for twelve days — make it thirteen (he checked the scratchings on the far wall), and had long since abandoned any hope of communication: Victor's entire dialogue consisted of literary quotations. The Keepers, whoever they were — they appeared to be creatures consisting of pulses and flickers of light and had made no attempt themselves to communicate — had thus set up all the necessary circumstances for a self-defense homicide. Which, Cartwright supposed, might even be the idea. Except that he knew of no way to murder Victor definitively, and besides, then he would be without company of any kind.

" 'We are alone,' " Victor said with a ripe ponderousness, " 'on a vast and darkling plain, where ignorant armies clash by night.' "

"Shut *up*," Cartwright said a little desperately. In the first three days it had been Shakespeare; then Edgar Allen Poe for one day, including sixteen complete repetitions of "The Raven"; then, backtracking, one day each of Rabelais, Chaucer, Milton, Keats, Byron, Thackeray, and Austen; then George Bernard Shaw, with particular reference to the Don's conversations in hell, for two days; and now, for another two days, a mélange of them all. Cartwright had no idea where — or why — Victor had picked up his vast and excruciatingly dull repertoire of literary quotations from Earth, nor did he particularly care. And Victor wasn't talking. Just quoting. Over and over and over . . .

" 'O! that this too too sullied flesh would melt,' " Victor said, " 'thaw and resolve itself into a dew.' "

"Listen," Cartwright said, turning from the window. "We've got to figure a way out of here. *I've* got to figure a way out of here. You're driving me crazy, you know that, don't you?"

218

" 'I am too much in the sun,' " said Victor.

"I mean it," Cartwright said. "I don't know why I'm here, I don't know why you're here. All I know is you're draining my sanity with your goddamned jabbering!"

Victor seemed to shrug — a difficult gesture for a gelatinous purplish blob five feet in circumference — and said, " 'The spirit killeth but the letter giveth life.' "

Cartwright felt his palms begin to itch. In spite of himself he had an overwhelming urge to walk over to Victor and strangle him. But that was ridiculous. Not only might it be what the Keepers wanted, not only would he then be without company, it was a physically impossible act. How would you go about strangling a gelatinous purplish blob five feet in circumference?

He sighed, turned back to the window, made an effort to block out Victor's droning voice, and pondered his fate for the fourteenth time. Once every day, he tried to recapitulate what had happened to him, if only as a means of hanging on to the tenuous thread of his sanity.

Fourteen days ago, Cartwright had landed on the Storm Planet to do an advance charting probe for the Federation. This world was the farthest away of those in the Beta System, known to be uninhabited (except for a few Melnusian miners looking for a certain mineral considered precious on their home world), thought to be too swampy and methane-poisoned for colonization, ignored by previous Federation surveyors; but with habitable planets at a premium in this sector, the time had come to make a Probe I instrument sweep. So Cartwright had landed and was out of his ship, down in a mist-shrouded gully applying a prismatic scan, when something struck him unconscious without pain or apparent bodily damage. When he had awakened he was in this cell with Victor. Unharmed.

Except, that was, for Victor and his quotations.

He was baffled as to why he had been caged this way. So

was Victor, evidently. The Melnusian was one of the handful of frontier miners, which fact Cartwright had deduced from the traditional Melnusian miner's suit of a grayish shimmery material. A nametag on the suit spelled out the alien's native name, the closest English equivalent of which was Victor — or so Cartwright had decided, his command of Melnusian being a bit rusty from disuse.

According to a second set of scratchings on the wall, Victor had been captured and incarcerated twenty-six days ago. "I thought of taking 'arms against a sea of troubles,'" he had said in his early Shakespearean period, "but 'our revels are now ended.'" He had also managed to convey, through a series of other quotes, his delight that an Earthman and a Melnusian should come together this way, on a planet approximately three hundred light years from their respective solar systems. It was, he pointed out declamatorily, one of those things of which dreams were made on, their little lives being rounded by a sleep.

That was when Cartwright had first thought of murdering him.

There was a flickering of light in the corridor beyond the cell door. "It must be feeding time," Cartwright said, because the only times the Keepers came around (if you could call flickers of light "coming around") were to bring food — a sort of gruel that tasted like rice for Cartwright, different types of Melnusian greenstuffs for Victor.

"'Never,'" Victor said. His purplish eyes glinted. "'Never, never, never, never.'"

The light pulsed into the cell, cast around for several seconds, and then withdrew. In its place were two silvery bowls, one filled with the gruel and the other with a steamy substance of a rather putrid olive-green color.

"Come back here," Cartwright shouted at the retreating light. He was losing his composure and did not care anymore that such conduct was considered a punitive offense, even under stress conditions, by the Federation. "I want to talk to you, whoever the hell you are. I want to know just what I've done to deserve this kind of treatment. I want to know when you're going to let me out of here."

The light did not come back.

Victor was busily siphoning up the putrid olive-green substance with a long and rather disgusting-looking appendage that may or may not have been a tongue. " 'Never,' " he said in positive tones, between slurps. " 'Never, never —' "

Cartwright felt even more murderous than before. He took a step toward Victor. He extended both arms, hands curled toward each other, forming the shape of a noose. Victor looked up at him and seemed to realize that he was about to be attacked; a sound that might have been a sigh came from deep inside him.

" 'No, no, no, no,' " Victor said, " 'no, no, no, no.' "

"Huh?" Cartwright said.

The bars of the cell appeared to shudder and then to melt in a glittering light not unlike that of the Keepers themselves. Then the bars were gone, the cell was gone, and Cartwright found himself staring in disbelief at flattish, empty swampland decorated with garlands of mist.

"Huh?" he said again, stupidly.

" 'I will do such things,' " Victor said. " 'I know not what they are, but they shall be the terror of the earth.' "

"What the hell is going on?"

Victor was still holding, with one of his appendages, the bowl of Melnusian greenstuffs; the disgusting tonguelike appendage slurped up some more of it with a smacking sound. " 'Do I dare to eat a peach?' " he asked.

Cartwright began to walk through the mist, looking this way and that without seeing any familiar landmarks. Confusion had hold of him now, but at the bottom of it he understood that he had to find his ship, get inside his ship, seal up his ship against Victor and the sound of Victor's voice. Only then could he make preparations to escape this miserable planet.

There was only one problem: He had no idea where his ship was.

"Where's my ship?" he said to Victor. "Did the Keepers do something to my ship?"

" 'Count the clock that tells the time,' " Victor said.

"Okay, then," Cartwright said, "where's *your* ship? Do you have any idea?"

" 'We are such stuff,' " Victor said, " 'as dreams are made on, and our little life is rounded with a sleep.' "

Cartwright willed his ears shut, without much success, and kept on walking methodically across the shrouded terrain. Victor, no longer interested, it would seem, in Melnusian greenstuffs, followed him in a merry roll that brought him sometimes alongside, sometimes a few feet ahead. Federation surveyors don't think, Cartwright mumbled to himself, they don't quote, they like peace and quiet, they like to be alone. Quiet and alone —

Alone.

Alone?

" 'Because I could not stop for Death,' " Victor said, " 'he kindly stopped for me.' "

Things were happening inside Cartwright's mind; belated connections were being made, theories were being worked out. At length he said, "I asked you where *your* ship was."

Victor seemed to shrug again. " 'The Carriage held but just Ourselves,' " he pointed out, " 'and Immortality.' "

Cartwright fixed him with a baleful eye. "Meaning you don't have a ship anymore. Meaning you've been stranded on this planet, lost, for months. Maybe even years."

The Melnusian's purplish skin seemed to pale somewhat; his eyes gazed off sadly into the distance.

"There aren't any Keepers," Cartwright said. "No Keepers on this uninhabited planet; no race of beings, no prison, no cell. Just you." His hands began to tremble with rage. *"You did it,"* he said. "You knocked me out and locked me up for thirteen days in an imaginary cell. Melnusians have telekinetic and hallucinatory powers; I should have remembered that days ago. That's how you managed it. That's how you kept me captive and both of us fed."

" 'After a hundred years, *nobody* knows the place,' " Victor said, " 'agony that enacted there, motionless as peace.' "

"Does that mean what I think it does?" Cartwright said. "The one thing you craved more than anything then was companionship? Someone to *talk* to?"

Victor seemed to make another sighing sound. " 'To make a prairie it takes a clover and one bee,' " he said, " 'one clover, and a bee, and revery. The revery alone will do if bees are few.' "

"Revery," Cartwright amended, "but a captive audience for your bloody quotations would be better. "But where did you pick up so *much* of our poetry and prose?"

" 'To every thing there is a season,' " Victor said, " 'and a time to every purpose under the heaven.' "

"All right," Cartwright said, "so you don't want to tell me now. It doesn't matter. Hobby, maybe: Do Melnusians have hobbies? Never mind. Could be an Earth ship crashed here at one time. Could be anything —" A thought struck him and he broke off. "Time to murder," he said cunningly.

" 'Let us sit upon the ground,' " Victor said, abruptly abandoning Emily Dickinson and the Bible once more, " 'and tell sad stories of the death of kings.' "

Cartwright made a noise and put his hands on the gelatinous body. But as soon as he did, little surges of energy flowed through the grayish material of Victor's suit and rippled into him. He let go of the Melnusian in a hurry and sat on the damp ground, not of his own volition.

223

Some Melnusian miner's suits were outfitted with a strong electrical charge, as a defense mechanism against enemies; that was something else he should have remembered.

" 'Tomorrow, and tomorrow, and tomorrow,' " Victor said, not without compassion, " 'creeps in this petty pace from day to day, to the last syllable of recorded time.' "

Cartwright sat up, took a deep breath of oxygen from his life-pac, and said to himself, "I've got to get away from him; if I can't kill him I've at least got to have a little peace and quiet. But how am I going to find my ship? I could wander around for days, weeks, lost in these swamps . . ."

Victor said something in a bawdy, Rabelaisian French.

"How long before help comes?" Cartwright asked himself. "The Federation will send out a search party — but how long before they find me?"

" 'Unto two thousand and three hundred evenings and mornings; then shall the sanctuary be victorious.' " Victor winked at him. "Book of Daniel," he said. "Chapter eight, verse fourteen."

"Two thousand and three hundred evenings and mornings," Cartwright said numbly.

" 'With thee conversing, I forget all time,' " Victor said. " 'All seasons and their change; all please alike.' Milton. *Paradise Lost.*"

Cartwright peered out across the foggy wasteland.

" 'I can't stand to think about him waiting and knowing he's going to get it,' " Victor said. " 'It's too damned awful.' Hemingway. 'The Killers.' "

Cartwright put his head in his hands and began to weep.

... Old ... As a Garment

by 4113321113231312042303043233242423

Shakespeare's *Richard II* begins with Richard's evocative "Old John of Gaunt, time-honour'd Lancaster" and out on stage totters John of Gaunt, who is pictured throughout the early scenes of the play as the very embodiment of old age.

Do you know how old John of Gaunt was when he died? Fifty-nine! But then that was old to Elizabethans. Shakespeare himself only made it to fifty-two!

Nowadays, though, the fifties are far from old age. And why not? Think of the advantages we have piled up in this century — knowledge of nutrition; vitamins, hormones, antibiotics, surgery with anesthesia, sophisticated diagnostic and therapeutic aids. It is not just that we live longer, but we are effectively younger and more vigorous at every step.

Yet it doesn't change the dream we all share —

The night was crisp and cold — much more so than last year at this time. I hugged myself in my wraps and tilted my head far back to look up at the stars as I waited for

225

Dan'l to toil his way up the two shallow steps to the front door of the Sashay Dance Hall. Way out here there were no city lights to hide the millionteen, skrillionteen stars webbing the whole cold, midnight-blue sky with their burning brilliance.

I drew a quivering breath of pure delight. Such beauty made you feel like running a-tiptoe —. Yes, I thought, The spirit can run like anything, but the flesh —! But tonight was delight, nevertheless. Tonight of the Dance! We were here, Dan'l and I. Still together. I hugged myself again, like a child, almost expecting the crisping of a taffeta sash, as yet not wrinkled down to a string across my skinny middle. And the lovely swish-bump of long, dangling curls against my shoulders — the product of a restless night of sleeping on lumpy, stocking-wrapped hanks of hair. The anticipation — the newness. Yes! In spite of all the other times — the newness!

Then Dan'l was there, his breath laboring in his chest, his hand closing almost painfully on my arm.

"Let's get in there, Becka," he gasped. "We made it again!" And I felt the heavy down tug on my arm as he started toward the door.

Then we were through the door that closed carefully, quickly behind us, and were caught up in the happy warmth of the cloakroom. I fumbled my coat buttons, my eyes trying to take in everyone at once. Thera — John — Chewey in his wheelchair, looking, as always, as if he'd just sneaked it away from some old guy to see how fast it'd go — and Dorrie, Mildred, and Van. I turned my back to the crowd to hang up my coat and Dan'l's.

"There's Chuck," said Dan'l, "but I don't see Stacy —"

"Oh," I said, my heart catching. "I wonder —"

"Hi, Chuck!" Dan'l called. "Where's Stacy?"

Chuck's unhappy old face sagged into unhappier lines.

"She — she felt old tonight. But she insisted that I come anyway." He looked around, his eyes not really seeing anything. "I don't know —"

"I'm so sorry," I said. "Maybe next time —"

He looked at me reproachfully. "You *know* —" he said.

"I know," I admitted. "Oh, Chuck!"

He spread his hands and turned away, his fingers fumbling at the back of his neck as he went.

The laughter and sudden, quick-running steps in the hall, beyond breaking through the enchanting, evocative sound of instruments tuning up, only emphasized the desolate slump of Chuck's shoulders.

I've never tired of watching the miracle of the cloakroom — the tousled emerging of laughter and delight — the prancing away of young, vigorous feet. And afterward, the silent, limp grayness hanging from each hook in the room.

"Wake up, Becka!" Dan'l was groping to lift his hands to the back of his neck. "You've got time enough for daydreaming all the rest of the year — but not tonight! Not here!"

"True," I said, "Time aplenty any other night. Here, let me." The outer door slammed open and shut with a bang that shook the whole building.

"Sorry, folks." It was Ditmar and his two sisters. "The wind's coming up. Grabbed the gawdang door right outa my hand." He tugged at his leather jacket buttons. "You know, this place is getting pretty rickety. S'pose we ought to think of rebuilding?"

"It's not all that old," said Van.

"Older'n you," said Ditmar. "And we've given it some pretty hard usage. We ought to be thinking about the kids coming up."

"Sure, sure," said Dan'l impatiently. "But tonight's the Dance. Can't we save all this 'til later? Becka, help me get out of this blasted —"

227

There was a flurry of activity, and I had just snapped the Old at Dan'l's nape when the door opened again, cautiously, and a face peered in.

Good Heavens! A *young,* puzzled face! I drifted quickly over between us all and the door. The sight of John, half out, would have been a traumatic shock to any stranger!

"Could I help you?" I asked, knowing what the youngster was seeing. A closely crowded room of ancient men and women who had been milling about and were now frozen like a stopped film, and — and —

The young eyes winced away from the room and came back to my face.

"We saw the dance sign out front and heard the music —"

"Oh," I said. "It's our Old Folks Reunion. You're perfectly welcome to stay, if you like, even if you don't look very eligible —"

There were two faces peering now, but the first one smiled uncertainly and said, "I guess it is a little out of our class. It was just the lights — and — and it sounded like a good time. Have fun." And they were gone. The sound of their feet was audible on the old wooden porch. And, just before I closed the door, we all heard — ". . . poor old things!"

When they were safely gone, laughter filled the room and activity began again. "Yeah, poor old us!" cried Van. "Let's get with it, guys! Time's awasting!"

Dan'l, as usual, was deep in an argument, half in and half out of his Olds, and, as usual, I was lingering. It was rather as if I were out in a storm, soaked to the skin, hungry and cold, yet still pausing a bit in all the discomfort just to glory in the knowledge that all I had to do was open the door and step into warmth, dryness, and sustenance and all good things.

"— tried a regional approach way back before the First

World War. No go. This is the only place." Ditmar paused. "Trying to have the Dance there was like trying to have a private one at home. Won't work. Just won't work."

"Shame," said Dan'l. "Osgood's ninety-seven now, and those young doctors of his won't let him make the trip all the way from the coast. Picked a sure way of killing him. Wonder what they're saving him for? Bet he doesn't last out the year. After all, having a few hours free of —"

The door swung open again, and we all looked to see. I gasped and blinked, not daring to believe. Surely not! But it was! It was!

"Artemiza!" I cried, and launched myself across the room to grab the plumply rounded shoulders of my long-time friend — my best friend since the seventh grade — my —

"Oh, Miza! You're one? You're one? And we never even suspected! I've missed you so! Why didn't you write?" I hugged her breathless and pushed her back to look at her.

"Becka." She was uneasy, her hand brushing back her heavy gray-streaked hair. "Is it true? Can we really —"

"We can, really," I said, pulling her to the center of the room. "Folks, this is Miza — Artemiza Coronado Hildalgo, my friend since time began, seems like. Who brought you?" I craned my neck to look past her. The bunch looked and smiled greetings and went back to their own absorbing activities.

"Nobody," she said uneasily, her hands pinching along her small leather bag. *"Tía Berta,* my Aunt Bertha, she died last winter." Her anxious childhood was back to steal her English. "She tole me. She come once, but it scare her. She tole me, I'm the only one she knows in the family can come. So I'm tired of hurting and being slow, and lonely. Tavio's gone. All the kids marry, so I come." Her anxious eyes dropped to her bag. *"Tía Berta* tole me you here. If you here —"

"Oh Miza! I can't get over it! Come on!" I drew her over

to the door that went into the dance hall, helping her off with her coat as we went.

"Move back all of you — or get gone into the hall. This is Miza's first time." I looked down at her. "Would you like it cold turkey, or to see someone go first?"

"Someone go first," she whispered shyly, dropping her coat and bag on a chair. "I don' even know —"

"I'll go —" Chewey Escobaido wheeled his chair in a swift circle, dangerous to any number of elderly shins. "I'll go first for Artemiza."

There was general laughter and someone called out, "Chewey's always willing to oblige a lady!"

Chewey shrugged his wide shoulders and grimaced. "So I like the ladies? Why not? Something better is around?"

"It's like this," he said to Miza, bending his head forward. "Right back here —" He groped and grasped. "If you can't reach it" — he peered under his lifted elbow — "then someone who loves you, and belongs with us, does it for you." We all watched as if we hadn't seen it happen countless times before.

That place, right where the spine goes into the skull — the brief manipulations — the sigh of relieved pressure — the brisk movement of his fingers. And he grabbed the bottom of his scalp and pulled his Old up over his head and down from his face, his vigorous black hair springing up before his face cleared. Then he peeled the limp garment from his shoulders and down over both arms. Dorrie and I, since we were handy and could bend a little easier than some, dropped down to ease the Old down from his withered legs. A couple of men lifted him up enough to let the Old go by. Then his own young, vigorous arms stripped his feet clear, and he was out of his chair in one lithe, wonderful movement, standing, shaking his Old down smoothly like a — a footed sleeper for a child — remember the Dr. Dentons? He hung it across his chair to slump limply like the others. Then he turned to

230

the narrow strip of mirror next to the door and smoothed back both sides of his hair with flat palms.

Miza had grabbed me early on and nearly followed me to the floor as I knelt. Miza stood now, eyes wide and half terrified, looking at the magnificent fellow that was Chewey in all his glory, dressed in what could almost be called his *traje de luz*. He has become much more imaginative in his old age!

"Oh Becka!" she gasped. "Oh, Becka! Would God like it?"

"God taught us how, *Tontita!*" I said, hugging her. "How else would we ever have found out?" Laughter broke the silence and people began to shed their own Olds, anxious to join the laughter and music in the other room.

"I'll wait for you," said Chewey, his feet already tapping.

"No, no thanks," said Miza. "I — I —" Her bashfulness was clutching her as it used to do in school.

"You know, the first time can be shy-making," I said. "You go on and get warmed up for *Chapanecas* — or is that the one you outgrew in kindergarten? Dan'l —" But he had wiggled out by himself. His Old was hanging neatly on the coat hook by Chewey's chair, and he was gone. Probably the first thing he'd done when he got through the door was to run and slide the full length of the hall as he usually did, just to feel the lovely, unhampered motion in his body again.

"Now, Miza —" I guided her fingers to the back of her neck and moved them through the sequence. I felt her wince as the last movement loosened her Old. "And now, you do the rest," I said. "Up and over like pulling off a cap —"

Up and over indeed! The blue-black flood of her hair spilled out across her shoulders and down — oh lovely! — as it had back when we attended school together. Even then, long before it was fashionable, she had worn her hair swinging free, almost to her waist. Then her face emerged — just like — *just like!*

Now she could feel the release and freedom and needed

no urging to free her shoulders and arms and, in one glorious movement, strip her hips and legs free.

"Oh Becka! Oh, Becka!" She lifted her arms and whirled, barely touching the floor in her excitement. Then she folded her arms quickly across her chest and huddled protectively, her eyes wide at me. "Have I got anything on?" she whispered. "I feel naked!"

"Of course you do," I said. "Laying all those years aside. And of course you have something on — anything you want — any dress —"

"My — my graduation dress!" she said, with hardly a pause. And, straightening, she grabbed the sides of the long, full skirt and whirled, her eyes seeking the mirror.

"Wup, wup!" I said. "Watch out for your poor crumpled Old. You have to put it back on, you know. Don't wrinkle it any more than it is! Hang it over there by Dan'l's. There's room for both of us."

She lifted her Old and flipped it competently as if it were a towel, and turned to hang it up neatly. She looked back at me. "Why did it be my graduation dress?"

"It can be whatever you want," I said. "I've found that mine is nearly always the dress associated with whatever memory is strongest in my thinking the week before the Dance. Your *tía* told you enough that you were thinking of youth and happiness and excitement and dancing, so you'd just about have to think of graduation and your first long dress."

"My first —" She was like a flame in the room. Her dress was red with multiple ruffles around the bottom. What a scandal it had been at our high school graduation! We had all worn long dresses — formals, we called them — but they were supposed to be pastel colored. To this day there are those who remember with resentment how Miza "spoiled" our graduation promenade. Truth to tell, she almost didn't get to graduate with us because of it.

"What do we do — in there?" she asked.

"Dance," I said. "Move. Any way you like. Maybe tonight you'd rather just dance by yourself. Sort of celebrate being free. You know, the 'holiday for the body.' Or square dance or — or —" I stopped, caught by a thought. "You know, we've never belly danced yet! You don't —" I grinned at her.

"I don't!" she agreed. "You come too." Her smooth young hand reached for mine.

"I'll come too," I said. "Won't take me half a second." My hands reached toward the back of my neck.

Miza whirled back. "What if I don't put that — that Old back on?" she asked. "What if —?"

"You have to," I said, sobering. "You couldn't leave here if you didn't."

"And if I stay —" her eyes flashed.

"We aren't sure," I said. "Maybe like being flayed alive when the time was gone. Time's different at the Dance. There's so much more of it. And when the time comes, we obey." I twisted my hands together, reverting to my Miza days. "We've never tried staying. We — we give our thanks to God for our holiday and take back our Olds without rebellion." I crinkled my eyes at her. "Want to make history? *You* try not taking up your Old again —"

"Not me!" She smiled back. *"Ni modo!* How long — I mean how many times —"

"Until you feel old. Stacy felt old tonight." I sobered again. "When you feel old, the release spot is gone. We don't know which comes first, the going or the feeling —

"But you're wasting time. Scoot!"

She was a scarlet flash through the door.

My hands reached — the door swung open and Dan'l and Chuck came back through. I could believe almost that time had really turned back and we all had all of life before us. Dan'l young, vigorous — Chuck —

"Chuck —" Something caught me. "What's wrong?"

He looked at me, his smooth young face drawn and unhappy.

"I can't," he said. "I just can't." He turned and sorted through the swinging Olds, looking for his own. "I can't let Stacy stay at home, being old while I — I — It just wouldn't be —"

He turned, his limp Old clutched in his two hands. "If you love, you just can't."

"True," I said, my eyes blurring a little. "You can't."

We helped him back into his Old. Just before he flipped his face out of sight, he paused and said, "Have a good evening."

He left, slowly and heavily, feeling, I knew, the same feeling we all do after the Dance is over, as though we had just climbed out of a swimming pool. But his furrowed face was smoothed of worry and indecision. Dan'l and I clutched hands and watched him go. Then Dan'l squeezed my old bones together with his strong young hand.

"Come on, Gramma!" he said. "You should have seen Chewey when Miza swished by! But at the rate she was going, he'll never catch her tonight!"

"Isn't it wonderful that she came," I said. "Just think —"

"Come on!" Dan'l tugged.

"Okay, okay!" I said. "I'm practically there!"

I flipped my Old up over my head and down, feeling my hair spilling bright and free. Already my soul was on tiptoe inside me, waiting for that magical moment when I would emerge like a butterfly. I paused, bent over the young foaming of my skirts.

"Dan'l," I said. "If it feels so wonderful to peel our Olds off, imagine! — just imagine how marvelous it will feel when the hand of God peels our bodies off our spirits! Just imagine!"

"I have," said Dan'l, smiling, with a glance toward his own limp, gnarled Old. "Believe me, I have.

"And for a person who rejoices to be free of her Old, you're taking an awfully long time!" Quickly kneeling, Dan'l stripped my feet free, shook out my Old, threw it more or less accurately at the last free hook, and, grabbing my hand, yanked me to the door.

"My hair," I protested. "And I don't even know what dress I have on tonight!"

"You're decent," he said. And, as I stumbled through the door, laughing, I was snatched into his strong, loving arms, and we whirled away to the music.

Flatsquid Thrills

by 00403334132324212304430100200432

"Neither do men put new wine into old bottles" says the Gospel of St. Matthew.

I presume that, by analogy, we can say that one can't take people who are fixed and accustomed to a way of life and expect them to adjust to a radically different way of life. Youngsters, however, who know no other way of life, are the new bottles into which new wine can be put.

And that may be the whole point of death — to clear away the old bottles and provide new ones for the wine.

When Robert awakens everything outside the dome is red: During the night a triple conjunction of the nearer moons has pulled the sea from its shallow basin to cover the colony. Robert knows that the flatsquids will have followed the tide in onto the mainland and will even now be preparing to lay their eggs under the flat rocks near his dome or, their eggs laid, be undergoing the sex-change that egg-laying triggers in their kind, from reclusive herbivorous females to venomous carnivorous males. He has no males in his aquarium, only a number of young females he has captured on previous expeditions beneath the scarlet sea; the triple conjunction of the nearer moons that calls the flatsquids to shore to lay their eggs occurs only once every seven years, and Robert is only twelve years old.

His parents are still asleep, out cold after another night of getting drunk on the local liquor — called "Patagonian absinthe" for some unknown reason — with their usual drinking companions. They are both snoring. Plucked from middle management positions of great security but with very limited hopes of career advancement in the Terran Postal Multinational by the Outworld Conscription Lottery, they have been members of the colony here on Mabuse IV for thirteen years and will not have the right to petition for reassignment back to Terra for another twelve years. Like most of the colony's other civil service draftees, they spend as much of their time as possible trying to forget where they are while doing what they can to get back at the government that has exiled them here by performing their duties in as slipshod and inefficient a fashion as they can get away with. The colony's Political Officer, himself a draftee, is of course aware of this, making it a virtual certainty that Robert's parents' eventual request for reassignment will be denied. The closest thing to an escape from the reality of their situation that the colony offers them is Patagonian absinthe.

Robert is different: Born on Mabuse IV, he has of course been receiving attitudinal and career imprints all his life, with the result that he is destined to become one of the colony's exo-zoologists when his training has been completed. He looks forward to his career; he feels a deep abiding love for this planet and its life-forms, and he is fascinated by the creatures he will be studying more seriously when he is a little older. Even now his room is filled with aquariums, sealed and unsealed, in which his female flatsquids and the other sea creatures he has collected on his trips beneath the sea live. Though he is less interested in the plants and animals on the shore near the colony and inland, he has a number of rubbercrawlers and a mated pair of cactus mice in cages next to his aquariums.

He checks the sleep-printing console beside the bed before getting up; all the lights are green, a signal that he's free to go and that all the information with which he's been programmed during the night will surface gradually over the course of the day. He reaches out and flicks the console off, then gets up and puts on his clothes and hiking boots, slips his filterface over his head, and puts his collecting equipment in his shouldersack. He leaves the dome by the airlock without awakening his parents and heads away from the other domes, toward the meadows where he hopes to find his flatsquid.

The redness through which he moves limits his vision to a dozen or so meters but hinders his movements little more than a thick Terran fog would have done; the scarlet sea is not an actual liquid at all but rather a dense, very heavy organic gas, a sort of free-floating viral colony feeding off the planet's geothermal energies. Information from the previous night's imprinting has already begun to surface, and he is pleased to find that the lesson concerned the ways in which the various lifeforms inhabiting the sea make use of their living environment for their own ends.

The meadows where he has been told the flatsquids come to breed are a little less than two kilometers from the colony, far from all human construction and activity. The ground is rocky, covered with masses of heaped and scattered flakeshale that have limited and stunted the growth of the fatgrass and thistleskull; the hoop trees are few and some hundreds of meters from each other.

He turns the light in his filterface's forehead region to

maximum intensity and takes his flipstick and collecting
bucket from his shouldersack. The flipstick is his own invention. He picks a small rock to begin with, one that he can
flip without too much effort and that is unlikely to harbor
too big a flatsquid, and, putting the collecting bucket down
next to it, unwinds the cord to the trigger-bulb controlling
its shutter top, then carefully poses his right foot over the
switch, ready to tromp down on it as soon as he has the
flatsquid in the bucket. Taking the flipstick in both hands
he quickly inserts the proper end under the rock and flips
the rock back and away with a motion he has long been
practicing for this day, but there is nothing under the rock.

He repeats the procedure with three other flat rocks of
approximately the same size without finding anything,
though the shriveled body of a small cactus mouse under
the second rock suggests that a male flatsquid — or at least
some animal that feeds on creatures the size of cactus mice —
has been there recently.

Under the fourth rock he discovers a tiny female, not more
than twice the size of his hand even with all seven of her
tentacles spread wide. His imprinted information tells him
that she is not yet old enough to reproduce, that the triple
conjunction has stimulated her need to spawn and brought
her here to the shore before she is old enough. Furtive and
shy, she has begun retreating from him even before he has
completed his assessment of her, and by the time he turns
away she has slipped out of sight under another piece of
flakeshale.

He finds nothing under the fifth and sixth rocks. Under
the seventh rock he finds a female about to spawn. He carefully lowers the rock over her again, hoping the disturbance
he has caused her will do her no real harm.

But under the next rock he finds his male, its seven basic
tentacles wrapped tightly around its eggs, the two acid-green

tentacles that have sprouted from its yellow-pink body during spawning raised in warning. Each tentacle ends in a sort of horny hook or claw. When used together the claws serve to help pry apart the shells of the bivalves that form the main part of the predatory male flatsquid's diet, but it is their defensive function that concerns Robert at the moment: The claws are not only hooked and very sharp but contain channels leading to the fat poison glands buried in the flesh just behind the claws, glands whose growth has been stimulated by the same hormonal explosion that produced the defensive tentacles in a few hours' time, and the poison they produce is even more deadly to humans than it is to the native life-forms.

He twists the flipstick around and slips the broad hooked-shoehorn end under the flatsquid, trying to flip it up into the bucket. It resists him, clinging to its eggs and to the rocks; he is distressed to see that one of the eggs has broken under the pressure of the creature's grip. But he tries again, yanking harder, and succeeds in flipping the flatsquid up into the air toward the bucket, though not yet into it. Another try and it's draped over the edge, half in and half out, then a final nudge and the thing's body is inside. A few quick but gentle raps on the tentacles with which it's still gripping the bucket's edge and it pulls all but the two defensive tentacles in close to its body. He takes the small rubber ball he's brought for this purpose out of his pocket and tosses it gently into the bucket. When the flatsquid strikes at it with both tentacles, Robert presses his foot down on the trigger-bulb, closing down the shuttered top of the collecting bucket.

He carefully detaches the flatsquid's cylindrical eggs from the rock to which they're cemented, then puts them into one of his smaller collecting jars. Only the egg that had been crushed the first time he tried to flip the flatsquid away from them seems to have been damaged.

Flatsquid Thrills

When he arrives back at home the dome is empty; his parents have gone to the shipping office, where they both work. A note on the kitchen table —the same note that was there the day before only with yesterday's date crossed out and today's date written in below it — tells him that his parents are going to be having a few friends over for drinks and a party after work and to please set his sleep-printer to put him to sleep at seven-thirty and keep him asleep until eight the next morning. There is nothing unusual or unexpected about the note, and as soon as he's installed the flatsquid in its sealed aquarium he makes the necessary adjustments to the console.

His parents have forbidden him to keep male flatsquids or any of the planet's other venomous life forms, but by now they've become so accustomed to the presence of the female flatsquids in his tanks that he doubts they'll ever notice his new acquisition. Nonetheless, he's taken care to install the new pet in the aquarium where he'd kept his biggest female flatsquid, and now he removes that female and releases it outside the dome, to find its own way back down to the seabed where it normally lives.

He eats dinner alone and plugs himself into the entertainment channel for a while, but as usual the diversions offered have been programmed for people like his parents, who hate the planet that is the only thing he really loves and who want only to wallow in the illusion of a momentary return to the world they've left behind them; so he switches off and goes back to check his animals once again before he goes to bed.

One of the rubbercrawlers is acting strangely, stretching itself long and then contracting tight again without going anywhere. Robert doesn't know enough about rubbercrawlers to know if this means that the animal is sick. He considers feeding it to the male flatsquid but decides against doing so

241

for a number of reasons: If the rubbercrawler is sick whatever it has might infect the flatsquid, and the flatsquid will probably need more time to adjust to its new home before it will consent to take nourishment from him. Besides, he'd rather feed it in the morning, so that if it doesn't eat the rubbercrawler he can remove the smaller animal before his parents have a chance to come home and see it in the flatsquid's tank. If they saw it there they might get curious enough about what it was doing in with the flatsquid to take a closer look at the flatsquid itself and notice its two extra tentacles.

It is a little before seven. He lies down and picks up a book, something about life back on Terra, which doesn't interest him at all but which the Political Officer requires everyone his age to read; he reads until the alarm system built into the console chimes, telling him that it's time to put his book aside and arrange himself in a comfortable sleeping position. When the sleep-printer puts him out it's as if he's finally been given a chance to exhale after having to hold his breath too long, and his exhalation just goes on and on, getting smoother and smoother and softer and softer until he just floats completely away from himself on it and Robert isn't there anymore.

He jerks awake to the sound of his father's swearing. Something is very wrong. The room is still dark but the lights on the console are flashing an angry red. Somebody is laughing in the next room — a woman's voice. An instant later the room lights go on. His father is standing by the light switch, over on the other side of the console.

"Father? Are you all right?" His father's face is red, mottled, bestial. Caked with dried and drying sweat. Robert can smell him, smell the Patagonian absinthe in and on him. Like some sort of sick dying animal.

"Sorry. Stumbled against your console, didn't mean to wake you up like that." Something about what he's just said strikes

242

him as hysterically funny and he starts to laugh, red-faced, half doubled over until he begins to choke and straightens up again. "I just want to borrow one of your squids for a few minutes. Scare everybody a bit, give them a bit of a thrill for a change."

Robert can't seem to wake up, separate what's happening to him from the data he was being printed with. "But if they're in our kind of air for more than a few minutes it kills them."

"I know. Like fish." Robert is just beginning to remember the new flatsquid, the male with its deadly defensive tentacles, when his father says, "Don't worry about it, Bobby," and flicks the sleep-printer back on.

When Robert awakens the next morning the male flatsquid's tank is empty. He finds the flatsquid dead in the living room, back in a corner under a table where it must have crawled to try to hide. There's no sign that it's hurt anybody or even that anyone's noticed it's a male. He can hear his father and maybe his mother snoring in the bedroom.

The door to their bedroom is ajar. He peeks in, sees his mother and father asleep on top of the unmade bed.

He hesitates a moment, then goes back out to the living room, crawls under the table, and retrieves the dead flatsquid. Its colors have begun to fade. He squeezes the tips of the two defensive tentacles one at a time and very, very gently; the dead flatsquid's flesh is rubbery, loose, like some sort of spongy bladder full of liquid. A tiny drop of clear greenish fluid appears at the tip of each claw.

The flatsquid's poison sacks are still full; it must have been too frightened or too startled to try to defend itself before the air in the dome killed it. Perhaps it had been male too short a time to have made all the necessary adjustments in its behavior.

Robert picks up the flatsquid, holding its body cradled in

his arms and one clawed defensive tentacle in each of his hands. He walks silently to his parents' room, pushes the door the rest of the way open, and enters.

They are lying there side by side on the bed, naked, ugly, stinking of Patagonian absinthe.

He goes to the foot of the bed, where he can get at both of them at the same time, jabs them simultaneously in the heavy muscles of their calves with the sharp claws, squeezes the tips of the tentacles as hard as he can, keeps on squeezing until long after the poison sacks are empty and his mother and father are very, very dead.

The Mystery of the Young Gentleman

by 14002204330021210423140032403333

In real life, we encounter bits of dramas here and there, and no one is kind enough to fill us in on the missing parts. We hear fragments of conversation, catch isolated actions, or even watch things going on for quite a time without being able to work out the inward spring that is the driving force behind it all.

When we read a story, however, the author is usually kind enough to play God and tell us everything. Perhaps that is why a story is so much more satisfying than life — and so much less than life. Why should a story not be told as life is told, with the reader expected to fill in the chinks for himself on the basis of his experience with life — and with science fiction?

No sooner had Eliza entered her Dungeon than the first thought which occurred to her, was how to get out of it again.

She went to the Door; but it was locked. She looked at the Window; but it was barred with iron; disap-

pointed in both her expectations, she despaired of
effecting her Escape, when she fortunately perceived
in the Corner of her Cell, a small saw and a ladder
of ropes . . .

Henry and Eliza,
Jane Austen

June 6, 1885 — embarking on the S.S. *President Hayes,* London to New York. I have been reading Charcot and chuckling — the things these people manage to invent when they try to explain one another! But I know you will want all the physical science and economic theory you can get and so have sent ahead the proceedings of the Royal Society, the *Astronomical Journal,* recent issues of *The Lancet,* etc., and a very interesting new volume called *Capital,* which I think you will find useful. María-Dolores has submitted with decent civility to the necessity of skirts, petticoats, and boots, and luckily for me has discovered in herself a positive liking for bonnets; otherwise only her incapacity for proper English prevents her from the worst excesses of which she's capable. Having a fifteen-year-old from the slums of Barcelona registered as one's daughter is a tricky way to make the passage, especially since I also have my living to earn, as usual. I will continue to write to you in my spare time during the crossing; if this is mailed in New York, it will reach Denver before us. In any event the scribbling can do no harm — I will keep the stuff locked up and can use the practice in this odd skill, though it is no substitute for the real thing, as you and I (in my misery!) both know. It helps keep one's mind off the ship: One huge din only beginning to become separated from the infinitely more vast roar of London itself, which has got almost beyond bearing the last few weeks. I have bought a great many dime novels on which María-Dolores can practice her English; if these fail, I will concentrate on her manners, which are abominable. (The last few weeks have been given over entirely to lessons in Eating: Not Reaching, Not Using One's Fingers, Not Swearing, and so on.) Clatter clatter bang-bang! (María-Dolores coming down the companionway. Next will be Walking.)

"Mamacita!" (Loudly present in her cabin, which adjoins mine.)

I correct her automatically. *"Papá."*

She turns red. *"Papá."* Then, in Spanish, coming in to where I am sitting, writing: "I hate these shoes. I cannot remove them."

I reach into the tiny desk, withdraw the buttonhook, and show it to her, out of her reach. She says, "But they pain me, Papá." She then instructs her boots, in Spanish, to *chingar* themselves, whereupon I lock the buttonhook up again. She is a good little soul and clings to me, half erotically, pouting: "Papá, may I have dinner with you and the Captain tonight?" I slap her hand away; she is not to steal the key. I say, "You have twelve years, María-Dolores. Behave so."

"Tu madre!" says she. I am trying not to feel those wild, bare feet shut up in a London bootmaker's fantasy for little girls. I say in English, "María-Dolores, a gentleman cannot travel with a young woman of fifteen, however short and small. Nor can he eat with her until she learns how to behave. Now lie down and read your books. The feet will heal."

"Next time I will be your son," says María-Dolores, limping unnecessarily into her cabin. But I see her see *Miner Ned, Stories of the West,* and the others: There is the thrill, the rush, the heart-stopping joy. She thinks: *these* books! and throws herself down on the bed without a pain; I get up and go into where I have a view of her white-kid calves and her child's dress.

I say, "María-Dolores, I am your father and you have forgotten to thank me."

She turns around, baffled. We're alone.

I say, "If you always behave in private as you must in public, then you will never forget the proper behavior in public."

I have put some force into this, and she gets up off the bed, her feelings hurt. You understand, much of this is still mysterious to her. She curtseys, as I taught her. "*Gracias, Papá.*"

"In English, now," I say.

"Thank you, Papa, for the books. I am sure to be pleased with them."

"Good," I say. "Much better. Now read," and instantly she is worlds away, her long black hair hanging over the edge of the bed. What they would make of us at the Salpetrière! — but luckily Europe is now far enough away to be out of the range of my worry. England also. There is no extraordinary intelligence on board among the first-class passengers, although an elderly physician down the corridor has been observing the two of us from the first hour of boarding, with an "acute," thoroughly amateurish attention I find both exasperating and excruciatingly funny. I will have to keep an eye on him nonetheless; as they say in the mountains, even a goose can walk from Leadville to Kansas, given enough time. (There are some remarkable minds in steerage, but they are not preoccupied with us.) Joe Smith of Colorado then dresses for dinner: a flat-cut diamond ring, gold nuggets fastening the shirt front, a gold watch, solid gold tobacco case, the pearl-handled derringer, hair brushed back from a central parting with the mahogany-backed brushes María-Dolores took such a fancy to in the shop window in the rue de Rivoli two weeks ago. Coming out into the corridor I have the very great pleasure of meeting the doctor's displeasure, so I stop, causing him to stop, roll my own, and light up. Instantly the dubious Italian with the little mistress becomes a young Western gentleman: well-off, tall, lean, still deeply sunburned. One must be careful, speaking; it's too easy to answer questions that haven't been asked. I say only, "Good evening, Doctor."

"How —"

I smile. "I overheard you speaking to another passenger. Not voluntary on my part, I assure you. And if I may take the liberty of answering the inevitable question, the accent is what you fellows call mid-Atlantic. I was educated at ———."

His university, his college. We talk about that. He's looking for flaws but of course finds none. He bumbles a bit (rather obviously) about "the young lady," but when I swear and say she's an awful nuisance, makes me feel desperately awkward, needs a woman's care, unexpected wardship, aunt in Denver, second cousin fiancée, so on, it's all right. There is, in all this, a strong pull toward me, and I wonder for a moment if there's going to be real trouble, but it's only the usual confusion and mess. We are chatting. I think I have located the poker game. The doctor asks me to dine with him, and I assent — would look odd not to. He takes a deep breath and pushes out his chest, saying authoritatively, "It will be a mild crossing." This is to impress me. At table are two married women, temporarily husbandless, whom I try to stay away from, an old man absorbed in his debts and the ruin of his business, and a mother-daughter pair of that helpless-hopeless kind in which enforced misery breeds enforced hatred, all made by the locking together, the real need of one for the other. There is an enormous amount of plumes, flounces, pillowings, corsets, tight boots. (María-Dolores, stealing rabbits, was luckier.) There are cut flowers at the center of the table (the first night), too much food, heavy monogrammed glasses, heavy monogrammed cutlery and china, and a vague, generalized appreciation of all this that is not pleasure but a kind of abstract sense of gratification. (Look up *wealth*.) Everything coarsened and simplified for reasons of commerciality and the possibility of rough weather. No one notices the waiter (who is a union organizer). I make my escape after dinner but only to an interlude with the younger of the married women. We are all charming: you, I, María-Dolores; we have to be, we can't turn it off; and in this situation and class there are approaches to which a gentleman must give in, despite the rules. ("What a beautiful night, Mr. Smith. Do you like stars?") She can't go anywhere in the evening without a companion. So we walk doggedly round and round the deck, Mrs.——— making most of the conversation: "So you own a silver mine in Leadville, Mr. Smith?" "My father does, ma'am" — until that topic gives out. María-Dolores is a bad excuse for leaving, as Mrs.——— will "take an interest" in and want to "form" her. That dull, perpetual, coerced lack she has been taught to call "love," which a gentleman's arm, a gentleman's face, a gentleman's conversation, so wonderfully soothes. It's a deadly business. I get away, finally, to the poker game in the gentlemen's lounge — that is, one of the gentlemen's lounges — where the problem is not to win but to keep from winning too much. I always lose, as a matter of rule, on the first night.

"A new man! What's your name?"

"Joseph Smith, Colorado."

Unoriginal jokes about Mormons, lots of nervous laughter, bragging, forceful shaking of hands. They talk about women. No one over thirty but one older professional I'm going to have to watch out for. I allow a bit of Leadville into my speech, what they expect: Not playing with you folks, of course, just thought I'd watch.

The serious game. The fear of death, of failure. Risking

fate, surviving it. One leaves, secretly in tears, saying casually, "I'm cleaned out." I balance what I see, what I "should" see, what they think I see. It's a hot little room. I lose a little, win a little more, then lose again, then drop pretty catastrophically, more than three hundred pounds.

"You'll want to get that back," says the professional, who's clever enough to know I'm no novice. He's also been marking the deck, which makes things easier. I lose again — some — and he lets me win back about a third. Winks: "Quit while you're ahead." I go on and lose again. Which is time to leave, mentioning the rich dad and his moral objections.

"I thought you fellows were born with a deck of cards in your hands!"

A promise — (embarrassed).

"What's wrong with a bit of fun?" (pretending to be aggrieved).

He says, confident, "See you tomorrow night."

So that's done. María-Dolores is asleep. Old Dr. Bumble passes me in the hall, beams and bows, delighted, unaware that his young friend is going to the dogs. I unlock the door to my stateroom, waking María-Dolores, who calls, "Come talk to me." This means exactly what it says: I'm lonely, I'm curious, I like you, I want a little chat. She is, like most of us at that age, surprisingly transparent.

She says, honestly, "Papá, what makes the ship go?"

"Engines," I say. "Great big ones. Down there." (Pointing to the floor.) "They burn coal."

"At night too?" Amusing to see her trying to imagine this phenomenon; she knows only a coal stove.

"Men shovel coal into them," I say. "All night long."

She wakes up. *"Now?"*

"Yes, right now."

A vivid picture in her mind of a vast cave with doors about it and flame within. "It must be exciting."

"Not to them," I say.

She is surprised.

"Because," I say, to answer her, "it's very hot. And very, very hard. And they want badly to sleep."

She tries to think why they do it and then solves the puzzle: "If they make the ship go, they decide where it goes."

"No," I say. "Someone else. Not the captain, the Board of Directors — no, not wood. Men."

She thinks sleepily, embroidering the furnace room (which I can see, hear, smell, touch from a dozen vantages) into Aladdin's cave, "They are paid *very* well. They are making their fortunes."

"Later," I say. She can join the argument about how much to help the others after we get home. The answer is in the books she has been reading, but books don't count; they aren't real. Only Barcelona has poor people. And even Barcelona has been kind to orphaned María-Dolores. Not like scowling, skinny María-Elena, who worked sixteen hours a day making matches and lost the feeling in her hands, or pretty, frightened María-Teresa, sold and pregnant at thirteen, or ugly, hungry, limping María-Mercedes, with the sores on her face, whose mamá beat her. Half the little girls in the Spanish slums are named after the Virgin; their twinkling, bare legs run like mice in María-Dolores's dreams. Asleep now. Something has always protected this mouse, warned her, led her, warmed her. Something has kept her safe and happy, even at fifteen.

Like you. Like me.

◊　◊　◊

June 7 — An arch note from Mrs.——, so I become ill, stay in the cabin in my dressing gown all day, and drill María-Dolores in manners. She gets madder and madder and toward evening begins to pester me:

252

"Next time I travel as your son!"

Once we get into the mountains, I tell her, she can travel as anything she likes. Even a hoppy toad.

"I want *that*"— picture in a book of a young lady in full sail. Can she dress like that when we get home? Part of this is merely for nuisance sake, but she is really fed up with being a twelve-year-old. I say yes, we'll send to Denver for it.

"Well, can I dress like a man?"

"Like this?" (pointing to myself). "Of course."

She says, being a real pest, "I bet there are no women in the mountains."

"That's right," I tell her. (She's also in real confusion.)

"But *me!*" she says.

"When you get there, there will still be no women."

"But you — is it all *men?*"

"There are no men. María-Dolores, we've been over and over this."

She gives up, exasperated. Her head, like all the others, is full of *los hombres y las mujeres,* as if it were a fact of nature: ladies with behinds inflated as if by bicycle pumps, gentlemen with handlebar mustachios who kiss the ladies' hands. If I say *"las hombres y los mujeres,"* as I once did, and am tempted to do again, she will kick me.

"I'm bored!" She wanders to the porthole, looks out, reflecting that there's nothing interesting out there, and a whole world of people on the ship, but I am keeping her away from them.

There's something more. I have, I think, been lying to myself, as is so easy out here; she's too old; we have been together too long. I have been as cold to her as I dared, fearing this. I turn my back, put on my dinner jacket, tie my tie; she raises her eyes. An electric shock, an unbearable temptation. As when things rush together in a new form in someone's mind. Oh, my dear, what will I do? What will I say? This is a real human being; this is one of ours.

She says, "You know everything. So why even ask? I've done it before. With girls too; girls do it with girls and boys with boys; everybody knows that."

She gets out softly, after a moment's struggle, "I like you."

I say, without expression, "Close the outer door." When she has: "Sit down. No, no, on the other side of the room." Then:

"You are thinking how nice it would be, aren't you? You are thinking of it right now."

The resulting wave almost knocks me over. I continue as if it had not happened: "No. It would not be nice at all.

"Look, María-Dolores, we have talked about this before, about the difference and how, when you are a baby, you shut it off. Well, it isn't something you can choose to turn on or off, as you shut or open your eyes. One loses one's sense of oneself at first; it is like being hammered to death. With so much clamor all around you, either you will shut again so fast that nothing will ever get you open or you will go crazy, like a mouse shut up in clockwork, and I must get doctors to put you to sleep with morphia for weeks to come — and this is bad for your health and very expensive and worst of all it will bring a great deal of suspicion down on me, which neither of us can afford. Do you want them to take you away from me and shut you up somewhere forever?" (Or all the other things!)

Well, she has been following this, but she has also been taking considerable pleasure in watching my lips move; I have to hold on rather hard to the writing desk. She says, "But why — " and then stops, understanding finally that I know. "Because," I say, "this is how it happens when one is young," and knowing so much more than she, sit down, knees giving way, with my face in my hands. The two mirrors so placed that they reflect each other to infinity, as you see in a barbershop, each knowing what the other feels. That remembered fusion which opens everything, even minds. So lost that I literally do not know she has crossed the little cabin until I hear her breathing. I smelled her hair and body before I saw her. She says, "Can we do it later?" and I nod. Somewhere in Kansas, miles from anyone! She says, very moved, "Oh, give me one kiss to show you don't hate me!" and I manage to say, "I don't hate you, María-Dolores, leave me alone, please," but cannot any longer trust myself with the act of speaking. She's planning to kiss me, little liar, and after that it will be really impossible, a wonderful impossible whirling descent from which I really cannot move. But manage to get up somehow and out into the corridor without touching her — fatal! — and the door shut and locked, which helps, as you would expect, not at all. So I did deliberately what I last did involuntarily fifteen years ago, confronted with my first town (three hundred souls) and no matter that old Bumble is ambling around the bend of the corridor: First things first.

Shut it all out.

◊   ◊   ◊

The smell of orange blossoms, which becomes pungent and choking: *sal ammoniac.* Bumble withdraws, turning his back on me. I'm lying on something, not in my own cabin, and for a blurred moment can't see anything of him but his broad back. As helpless as any of them. He says, "I thought it best not to alarm the young lady."

I find myself coughing uncontrollably, sitting up on the edge of his berth, bed, what-do-you-call-it. I'm awake. He really is extraordinarily stupid. He says, "You seem to have cracked a rib." Having had, you understand, perhaps ninety seconds to get his first really good look at me, he has put

two and two together and got five: *Uranian. Invert. Onanist.*
(These are words they make up; you will find them in medical
texts.) It may surprise you that this kind of thing does not
happen often, but the division is so strong, so elaborate, so
absolute, so much trained into them as habit, that within
reasonable limits they see, generally, more or less what they
expect to see, especially if one wears the mask of the proper
behavior. His mistake has been made before, but those who
make it usually do not speak out, either from the concern
of fellowship or simply lack of interest. This one is that fatal
combination: kindness and curiosity. For under the surface
indignation he is pitying and embarrassed and would really
like to say: Look here, dear fellow, let's forget all this, pretend
it never happened, eh? And we'll both be so much happier.
But he is fascinated too. He is even, unknown to himself,
attracted. He has, you see, the genuine fixing on the female
body, but there is also its dirtiness, its repulsiveness, its pro-
found fearfulness, which as a doctor he must both acknowl-
edge and feel more strongly (and believes, because he is a
doctor, that his confusions have the status of absolute truth),
and then, worst of all, there is the terrible dullness of the
business, which comes with the half disillusionment of old
age: women, the silliness of women, the perpetual disappoint-
ments of the act (no wonder!), the uncleanliness of the whole
business, and finally the sullying and base suspicion that
it's merely "propagation," one of the nasty cheats of an impersonal and soulless Nature, unless one is fool enough to senti-
mentalize it. (He sums this up by saying from time to time,
"I'm too old for all that; let the young men make fools of
themselves!")

He harrumphs. Bumbles. Fudges. Peeks at me. Out of the
welter comes:

"You — you ought to have that rib looked at, you know."
(Thinks of himself investigating under the taping, greedy old
pussycat!)

I say, "Thank you, I have. Immobility's not the thing, I'm told."

"Accident?"

"No, fight." He thinks he knows about what. He tiptoes about me mentally with all the elaborate skill of old Rutherford B. Hayes trying to catch a squirrel, fumbling with the tools in his medical bag as if he had something else to put back there, coughing, arranging and rearranging his stethoscope — and there is such a resemblance between the two that I cannot forbear imagining the doctor caught under the corner of our front porch at home and having to be pulled out yowling, his tail lashing, his fur erect, his sense of autonomy irretrievably shattered, and pieces of dust and cobweb stuck on his elderly ginger whiskers (which they both have). He says:

"You ought to . . . lead a more active life. Open-air exercise, you know. Build yourself up."

I say, "I live on a ranch, doctor."

He bursts out, "But, my dear fellow, you mustn't — it is quite obvious — you owe it to your father — and that poor child —"

I say, dryly, "She is a good deal safer with me than with you, surely." This is calculated to enrage him. I admit the logic of the matter is hard to follow, but at its base you will find a remarkable confusion of ideas: heredity, biological causation, illness, choice, moral contamination, and some five or six other notions that have not quite got settled. There is also the back-handed compliment to the virility of a man of sixty. Why does old Rutherford B. Hayes, an hour after his ignominious handling by one of us, dimly convince himself that he has been rescued by an adorer and leap to one's bosom in gratitude, demanding liver? The cases are not unalike. Bumble is not only stupid, as I have said, but his stupidity is actually the principal cause of his kindliness. I don't mean this as cruelly as it sounds; let's say only that he has

257

a genuine innocence, something fresh that his "ideas" don't affect, still less his "decency," which is (as is usual with them) the worst thing about him. My remark takes a moment to activate the mechanism; then drawing himself up — for I ought to have the "decency" to be disgusted at myself, that's the worst of it — he levels the most damning accusation he can, poor old soul: "Damn it, sir, you know what you are!"

Let him stew a bit. I re-stud my shirt, slowly, and fasten the cuffs, feel for my tie. Adjust the artfully tailored dinner jacket. I have come out without the derringer, or Bumble would remember it and he doesn't. What would he have made of it? He is beginning to be ashamed of himself, so now is the time to speak. I say, steadily:

"Doctor, I am what my nature has made me. It was not my choice, and I deserve neither blame nor credit in the business. I have done nothing in the whole of my life of which I need be ashamed, and I hope you will pardon me if I observe that, in my case, that has been of necessity a much lonelier and more bitter business than it has in yours." Here I take from his bedside stand the elaborately gold-framed photograph of his dead wife, saying, "I assume, sir, that this lady is some near kin to you?"

He nods, already remorseful. Says, gruffly, "My wife."

I put it down. "Children?"

He nods. "Grown now, of course." Better to leave the comparison unspoken. I merely say, "You may be sure, sir, that my little Spanish cousin is as morally safe with me as if she were in church. A married sister of mine in Denver wishes to give her a home. That is where I am taking her."

Not too thick. Leave quickly. We talk a bit more, about my sister, one Mrs. Butte, and the nieces and nephews — his preconceived notions of what the family is like are a trouble to me as they're rather strong, and I have to work some not to match him too closely — and by then he is so pleased

with himself for having been so very generous and good —
and so lucky too, in comparison with you-know-who — that
he offers me a drink. I say:

"No, sir. I am no abstainer; I take wine with my dinner,
as you have seen, but otherwise I do not indulge."

He pooh-poohs.

I shake my head. "Not hard liquor, Doctor. Our frontier
offers too many bad examples. In the mining camps I have
seen so many ruined that way — good, normal young fellows
whom I envied. Those tragedies have helped to keep me
straight. What is only a temptation to you is poison to me,
sir."

He says, solicitous, "But the pain of that rib —"

I shake my head.

He's very moved.

So am I.

Then off to the poker game, with a poker face, to win back
two hundred and fifty pounds. This is how it's done: Lose
spectacularly but win little by little, and pocket some from
time to time so that you don't seem to have won too much.
This takes only a very moderate sleight of hand when others'
attention is elsewhere.

But the cardsharp knows.

◇　◇　◇

June 9 — Two days' bad weather, seasickness, almost all the
passengers down. To avoid puking my guts out because of
the bombardment of others' misery, I must mesmerize myself
more lightly than for sleep, but heavily enough to put everything into a comfortable, drunken blur. (In this condition,
the novels I have bought for María-Dolores actually make
a kind of sense.) That young lady, unaffected, eating heartily
and in an ecstasy of freedom, is running alone about the
almost unpeopled first-class deck and dining room. The list

of rules: not to speak or understand English, swear, take her boots off, show her bottom, make obscene gestures, go anywhere but first class, and so on. She laughed, hearing it. Someone's saying authoritatively — somewhere in the ship — that the weather will let up tomorrow; we are skirting the edge of something-or-other. But I did not catch most of it.

◊   ◊   ◊

June 10 — That old tomcat has been *writing up my case,* as he calls it: names, dates, details, everything that must never get into print! He even plans to bribe the steward to find out if there are women's clothes in my steamer trunk, a piece of idiocy that will land us both in an instant mess. I've explained to María-Dolores, who merely shrugged, bored to death, poor soul, and violently moody from having to restrain her feelings about me. She says, "Go tear it up."

"No," I say, "*he* must tear it up. Otherwise —" and I point significantly to the porthole.

She remarks that he is probably too fat to go through, opining that the English are all mad anyway. Her judgment of *maricóns* is that (a) they're all over the place and (b) who cares (a view to which I certainly wish the good doctor would subscribe) and (c) please, please, please, can she go outside if only for a little before she goes mad herself?

"Yes," I say, "Yes, now you must." She whoops into the other room. For I know how — now — and will tell her, although like Mrs. H. B. Carrington, whose *Mystery of the Stolen Bride* (8 vol., boards, illus.) María-Dolores is now about to fling out the porthole she has got open — I have to shout "Stop that at once!" — I won't tell you. They never do in the books; that makes the story more lifelike for them, I suppose. So you may pretend you are one of them now, and don't skip.

I'm going to brand him. So badly that he will never write a word about me — or want to think it either. I think you can guess. Not nice, but easier than drowning, and safer (in these crowds).

Now he is writing in a burst of inspiration — this very minute — that the only influence that has saved me from the "fate" of my "type" (lace stockings, female dress, self-pollution, frequenting low haunts, unnatural acts, drunkenness, a love of cosmetics, inevitable moral degeneration, eventual insanity; it goes on for pages; it is really the most dreadful stuff) *is my healthy, outdoor life in the manly climate of the American West!*

María-Dolores has just popped her head in to find out why I'm laughing so hard. Memories of the mining camps, I tell her. Bumble, you deserve it, you deserve it all.

After much thought, he proudly puts down the title: "A Hitherto Unconsidered Possibility: The Moral Invert."

◊   ◊   ◊

June 14 — First class is commodes and red plush everywhere. A new dress every day. The moral fogginess, bad enough here, takes a sharp rise two levels down — out of simple desperation — then drops to something approaching limited realism as you enter steerage. (Not that anyone really sees much more than one rung above or below them on the ladder; the rest fades into mist.) Afternoons Mrs. ———, the doctor, and I make up a party with María-Dolores as its supposed center; at dinner, María-Dolores gone, everyone eats uncontrollably (as they've been doing all day), and Mrs. ———, flushed with the day's victories, makes a very determined set at me over the wine. I dodge. Bumble, outwardly approving, nonetheless manages always to claim his young friend for the evening somehow, and then the two of us spend the next few hours in little secret orgies of sentimentality by the rail, watching the stars: "My dear fellow, a lovely woman like that!" — "But, doctor, how can I honestly — and married —" Well, he didn't mean. He didn't really. Smokes. Sighs. Points out constellations. Discusses God. His substitute for emotion (all on Mrs. ———'s account, mind you). Not that any young fellow would arouse anything but wrath by attacking Bumble on the surface, as it were. But slowly, solemnly, he asks. Solemnly, tragic and shamed, I answer. And slowly, slowly, I begin to talk *at* him, as one may say, smoke *at* him, look *at* him, from the turn of the head to the smile, to the slouch, the drawl, the hands in the pockets, until one of us would know — even stone blind — what is going on. Bumble, who is not one of us — he has not a trace of the pattern — doesn't, though it's all tailored to him. From him: suppressed memories of secondary school, memories of his wife. We have been staying up later and later, which cuts into my time at cards, so I sleep later and later but never too late for the all-important staying in shape — María-Dolores, at my ever-sleepier push-ups and workings-out: "Ugh. What *for?*"

Later: five-card draw. If you want the technical details, look about you; I've been at it too long to consider them anything but a complete bore. The company, somewhat reduced by now, is made up largely of young men, very free and easy in their manners but in fact deferring markedly to what I will call The Old Faker, the grizzled old professional with mutton-chop whiskers, the usual rank-and-hierarchy business, so it will be no hard matter to shift their allegiance if only I can get the other things to work right. Having eaten all day, they now eat more; food and drink arriving periodically, bringing nothing useful to me but a little fresh air. One's lungs are at risk.

I come in late, nod, sit down. The O.F., who has an arrangement with one of the waiters, calls for an unopened deck, which is brought in with more food, more whiskey, all in amounts I haven't the heart to describe. (There is, especially, a tray of bratwurst that is almost enough to propel one out of the room.)

T.O.F.: "Mr. Smith doesn't indulge?"

Someone makes a joke about Mrs. ——.

At this one just smiles; that's best.

Play. More play. We go on, everyone smoking ferociously. The deck is marked. The Old Faker is being careful not to win too openly, so when he decides not to take a hand, I (if at all possible) do. It's a great convenience. It also begins to look uncanny, which is good.

Nobody wants to comment, because you know what *that* means. T.O.F., understanding that I've broken his code, drops back cautiously.

I make a pile.

Then Fake, outwardly grinning, suggests that we switch our games: poker to women; the waiter can bring anything. (He does have it arranged; there are women who work this crossing, as in every other.)

I say that when I play cards, playing cards is what I do.

Now the hardest thing in the world is to wait for something that will make you look surprised. T.O.F. — he's fifty-five and all he's done for the last twenty years is eat and sit — keeps me staring at the table top an unconscionable, trying time. Then he says that of course Mr. Smith doesn't crave the new game; he has all he wants of that without paying for it.

Then he makes a joke about María-Dolores.

Well, I can't turn pale, of course, but there's a reasonable-looking way to impersonate the effect of this, done mostly with muscles and a fixed gaze, so that's what I do. I get up slowly and slowly I draw — no, not the derringer, not tonight; someone might, after all, get hold of it — but the bowie (shoulder holster), and the room goes electric.

I say slowly, *turning pale,* "Why, you goddamned skunk!"
Then the knife, extremely sharp point first, driven deep
into the polished surface of the table — see, I won't use it! —
all very stupid and out of the kind of thriller you-know-who
spends her nights reading. T.O.F., across the table from me,
seated almost against the wall, rises, expecting that I'll circle — he's worried and planning to back off, protesting he
meant no harm — but it's easy, you see, when you're aware
what the other's going to do before he does it. Even before
he knows it. The table's bolted to the floor and is pretty solid
too, so one can vault over it as over a fence, using one arm
as a lever, and skidding a bit, really, feet first into poor Fake,
that tub of lard (they all get like that at his age), staggering
the poor old thing crash! against the wall. Then a couple of
punches for show; he's had the wind knocked out of him
already.

(And that, child, is *why.* She once poked my chest and said
"But how do you breathe?" Me: "From my belly, like you.")

Breathing a little hard — no, it's *not* enough, even for one
raised at eleven thousand feet — and getting up into the marvelous scandal:

"Gentlemen, this deck is marked."

Now, that is serious. I say to one of the young 'uns: "Jones,
pick a card." And call it. And again. And again. And then
again. Several begin, aghast, "But — " with a mental sniff-
and-point at T.O.F., whom I now leave prudently on his side
of the table. (And how much will damaging the furniture
add to tonight's bill? Oh, Lord!)

I say, "Who ordered the deck?"

Turmoil. Nobody's sure. One bursts out: "But I did! I said
that Mr. ———" (follows hand over mouth and he *does* turn
pale).

Now everyone believes. Sensation. Thrill. Real horror.
These are their "standards." This is their "code." I say,

spreading out what I've won, "Gentlemen, if you remember your losses —?

"This has been no fair game," I say, "and I have no taste for further play," and go out leaving a great deal of money and a lot of conflicting feelings behind me, the latter being the direct result of the former. (Let them straighten it out.)

So now *I* am head faker. You see? And can stretch my luck a little for the next few nights. I will clear, I think, some two thousand pounds before we land, with luck.

What a species.

Still, even blind —!

◇   ◇   ◇

June 15 — This is how it happens:

A fine, balmy night, the doctor standing at the rail smoking his cigar and looking out over the sea. I'm facing him, having rolled a cigarette (no anatomical comparisons, please!): two friends under the stars. Time is pressing and the doctor very uneasy. He wants to be away from the lights, so the women who drift slowly past, in pairs or accompanied by gentlemen, are recognizable only in silhouette, the dim shape of sleeves and skirt, the massed hair and hat, the gleam of an earring. The doctor is at sea and memories are disturbing him, all the more that he's not quite sure what they are. He's also a little drunk. We've been talking ever more confidentially: his school days, his friends, then the past few days on shipboard, then his wife, their meeting, our meeting, our talks, until all have fallen together in confusion; he feels the same nostalgia for all of them. He finds this troubling. Finally I lean closer, for all must happen under water now, dream-slow, dream-fast, and I say, somehow too close although still barely half seen: hands in pockets, leaning against the rail, a low voice out of the darkness:

Bumble, your companionship and your example have meant a great deal to me these past few days.

The slight stammer excites him, the slouch, the soft, precise wording, the lifted chin. All memorable, all unidentifiable. He mutters something self-deprecatory and turns to leave, extremely uncomfortable, but I'm in his way, looking more like *it* than ever. It says:

I cannot say, doctor, how much I admire you, how much I look up to you.

He protests.

It says: *I would put this in stronger terms, but there's no need. Surely you know.*

Bumble begins to drown. I am close enough to take his arm now or he would bolt; he feels the grip and the heat through his clothes, almost as if they were gone; almost, his hand is being held. *It* says, a disembodied voice, a hard, hot touch on his arm — and this time there is warm breath on his neck —

As you told me yourself, there is an instinct in such things which can never be mistaken.

In a moment he'll go under; mermaids will tickle his ears with streams of bubbles: Who am I? Do I remind you of someone? They'll be playing with his hair, tweaking his ears. He'll be picked bones in a moment. The cylindrical people, the flounced-and-puffed people, pass by a world away.

It says in his wife's voice, with the odd, light break between the syllables, which he feels as the tip of a tongue: *Ed-ward* —?

Bumble is pulling at my arm. He's in a panic. He's about to drop his cigar and top hat and won't know it. They can't stand two kinds of knowledge that don't mix — not knowing the secret — but then he finds the way out for himself, and I wish you could see it — even Bumble! — like a switchback on a train ride: jerk! jerk! jerk! and the new track is there,

shiny and straight, as convinced as if I had said it myself.
"You're a woman!"

I do nothing. I say nothing. I don't have to, you see, I have
only to smile, all sex in my smile. He will do it all himself,
from, "My dear girl, why didn't you tell me!" to, "But you
mustn't walk alone, oh dear, no, you mustn't go alone to
your cabin!" He remembers my face on a playbill (though
the name eludes him) — must be an actress, of course, have
to be an actress; we have to learn such things for the stage,
don't we? Special dress, altered voice, dye on the skin — but
nothing injurious, he hopes, nothing that will mar, eh? Don't
want to spoil that complexion, not when one needs it for
one's work, not when one's famous for it (still searching).
And what a clever little woman, to pull it off, when otherwise
they'd be all about me, spoiling my trip with their interviews
and their publicity.

He babbles: *He* knew. Doctors *know,* you know. Little hands,
little feet, smooth face, delicate features, slender body! Quite
obvious. Quite, quite obvious. Trying to remember what he
said to the gentleman that he oughtn't to have said to the
lady — but actresses are different, don't you know — free-
thinking — though nothing indelicate — and he was only
playing along, you understand, being a little free in his language, but nothing sensible, only gabble, only a lot of nonsense —

In my cabin, not quite remembering how he got there, it
all happened so fast. Another drink. He remembers kissing
my hands in the corridor. He's in the one armless chair,
drink in hand, skittish, embarrassed, giddy with relief and
desire, all the dizzy recklessness of a man who has just made
it off a collapsing bridge — when suddenly the little actress
is straddling his knees, facing him (a position which would
strike him as queer if he were sober) but her face close enough
to kiss. Which he does.

I whisper in his ear, "Dear Edward. Dearest, dearest Edward!"

He tries greedily to get at my jacket buttons and can't; I have placed his arms outside mine, behind my back, the two boiled shirt fronts crackling like armor plate between us. He tries to get up and so I give him another kiss, a slow one with biting in it. The position bothers him but it's what I need, so I whisper "Not yet. Let me," and reaching down, undo, to his indescribable shock and utter, helpless delight, the buttons of his trousers. Actresses *are* different. I fish for and play with his pretty thing and kiss his neck and mouth and tell him about the female form divine, which he will see in just a moment: the cushioned hips and swelling bosom and buttocks, and secret, round, moist parts, all the upholstery that stiffens him and makes him push and pant. The liquor's slowing him, but it also makes things possible—I mean the doubleness of dreams: right words, wrong smells (tobacco, men's hair pomade), the armor between us, the lingering confusion about who's who, the sudden, reasonless satisfaction with a stranger who knows exactly what fondling he wants, and the magic, shameful words his wife never knew, and handles his secret self, as she never would, or put her tongue in his ear, an appalling, hideously exciting novelty. So he abandons himself to the dream, poor silky old sweet tom, which is suddenly happening much too soon—and straining me close and rigid (but my arms are in the way), he heroically tries to stop; I whisper, "Shoot me!" and he spends himself freely over my hands and my second-best pair of evening trousers. For a moment he comes back to himself to see his wife—no, the Colorado gambler—no, the actress—in one dim, ambiguous person. He dozes.

He sits, snoring, trousers open. Poor old animal. María-Dolores stirs in her next-door sleep. Then, through Bumble's dreaming ragbag of a mind, goes the overpowering glory of telling the whole story from start to finish: wonders, admirations, successes. He'll do it. He's incorrigible. And will wake up and want more — later tonight, tomorrow night, and so there's nothing else for it. I harden my heart.

He wakes. What is the dear girl doing?

I am, having washed my hands, sitting at my writing desk cleaning a Smith and Wesson forty-five, with canvas over the desk top to protect it. Also hides the bowie. The doctor says, gruffly, to an unidentifiable back, tears in his eyes: "So you fancied the old fellow, eh?"

Then, "My dear, couldn't you — that is, we're alone — something more natural?"

I say, without turning round, "It's all costume."

He chuckles. "Jewelry!" he says archly (the shirt studs, the diamond).

I say, "They're worth money. I don't collect pound notes for the sound the paper makes either."

Then I add, "Do you know, I'm quite sure that someone saw us in the corridor."

He can't remember. I say, "You were kissing my hands." He chuckles again, turning red. Hands! He says, "My dear, if you'd only turn —" So I do, and he sees what I'm doing. Very puzzling, but there is some good reason, no doubt. I say:

"Doctor, have you read Krafft-Ebing's *Psychopathia Sexualis?*"

He hasn't. He's blank.

"The German medical specialist," I say, "is less generous than you in his view of the male invert. He writes that such people have no morality; they wish only to possess the generative organ of another man by any means, fair or foul; it is their sole object; and they take delight in spreading the contagion of their moral disease, especially when they find the germs of it hidden in an apparently normal man."

No connection. Bumble is slow.

I say, "The German specialist is correct, Doctor. There is, as you yourself told me, an instinct in such matters that warns against contagion — if we desire to be warned. You, for example, did not desire to be warned . . ."

Have you ever seen a man turn really pale? The color goes like a dropped window shade; it's most impressive. But the old creature is admirable, in his way; even buttoning his pants (an act not usually considered dignified among them) he can give a good impersonation of choleric indignation: "Sir — I will — I will expose —"

I say evenly, "In that case your own behavior will hardly bear examination. Remember, we were seen."

"You lied!" he cries, desperate and sincere.

"Did I?" (and I feel for the knife, just in case Bumble decides to try some first-hand research on my person). "Why, I don't remember that. What I do remember is saying nothing at all while you made the whole story up yourself; you seemed very eager to believe it. An actress? Half a head taller than yourself? Where in Europe, on what possible stage? And this business of dye for the skin — which doesn't smell, won't wash off, and can't be detected even in the most intimate contact, not even by a medical man? Come! You lied because you wanted to. And you're lying still."

I add, more softly, "Don't make me dislike you." And then, in *its* voice, "Keep my secret and I'll keep yours, eh?"

Bumble will launch. Bumble has to be stopped by the sight of the bowie, better than the heel of my hand under his chin and so on. Then Bumble has his inspiration; I did not lie. I was telling the truth, but I am lying *now*. Reasons? None at all, but he says flatly, folding his trembling arms across his chest to indicate unshakable belief:

"You are a woman."

The stupidity. The absolute, unconquerable stupidity! Like

the best swordsman in the world beaten by a jackass. I walk round him, searching, to María-Dolores's door. Say, "Have you heard what happened at cards last night? Yes, that's me; that is how I get my living; the nonsense about Colorado helps. Well, I knocked down a man fifty pounds heavier than myself; ask about it tomorrow."

Bumble is trembling.

I turn and flip the knife point first across the cabin and into the door to the corridor — why is it that acts of manliness always involve damage to the furniture? — which is, you must understand, *something a woman cannot do*. That's faith. I repeat: what a woman cannot do.

Logic also. I say:

"If I am lying now, what is the purpose of my lie? To drive you away? The little actress would not want to drive you away, not after having gone to all the trouble of acquiring you! Why confess she's a woman unless she wanted you? And why should I lie? For fear you'll expose me? I can expose you. I could blackmail you if I wanted; we were seen, you know. To drive you away? I don't want to; I like you — although I don't fancy being attacked and having to knock you down or throttle you as I did to the other gentleman at the game last night — and why on Earth, if I wanted to drive you away, should I have taken such trouble to — well, we won't name it. But it's perfect nonsense, my dear fellow, a woman pretending to be a man who pretends he's a woman in order to pretend to be a man? Come, come, it won't work! A female invert might want to dress and live as a man, but to confess she's a woman — which would defeat her purpose — and then be intimate with you — which she would find impossibly repulsive — in order to do what, for heaven's sake? Where's the sense to it? No, there's only one possibility, and that's the truth: that I have been deceiving nobody, including you, but that you, my poor, dear fellow, have been for a very long time deceiving yourself. Why not stop, eh? Right now?"

And with a smile, I touch my fingertips to the stain beginning to dry on the front of my trousers and put the fingers in my mouth. Havoc indescribable. This is not nice, not nice at all. If only Bumble does not drop dead this minute, in which case, María-Dolores — who has just come in, in her nightgown — and I must put him through the porthole anyhow.

She sees us, imitates alarm, and darts behind the door. Her head peeps out.

Poor, gray old man whispers, "Child, has this man ever — has he ever —"

"María-Dolores," I say, "this man wants to know if I have ever kissed or touched you. Tell him the truth."

She knows, of course. She says dubiously, "You kiss me good night on the forehead."

"Have I touched you?"

She nods reluctantly, troubled. "You *push* me."

"Push?" says Bumble, grasping at straws.

"When Uncle is reading at his desk or busy," says María-Dolores, "he *push* me. On the shoulder. He say, 'Go away.' It make me sad. It's happen many time."

Bumble says, "Your uncle — is — is — is he —"

She watches unblinking, as if it were a perfectly normal occurrence for strange old men to twitch and stammer in my cabin long past midnight. I say:

"This gentleman, for reasons I shall not explain to you, wants to know something about me. He wants to know whether I am a man or a woman. Tell him."

She does incredulous surprise much better than I do. Bumble, distressingly starts to speak; I cut him short: "Not my clothes, María-Dolores, and not my behavior. He wants to know the rest of it. Do you understand me? He wants to

know what's under the clothes. Tell him you're as ignorant
as you ought to be, and you can go back to bed."
She droops, barely audible. "You'll get vexed."
I assure her that I won't.
She says quickly, ashamed and starting to cry, "I did not
know. I thought you were away so I came in. You were in
the bath they bring in. I ran right out. I will never do it
again, never!"
"Child," says Bumble, "I am sorry to — I don't wish —"
"Es muy hombre," says María-Dolores, with a sketchy gesture at her crotch, and by some miracle of acting manages
to turn bright red. She adds, looking very embarrassed, "Yes,
is a man."
"But do you know," says Bumble unexpectedly coherent,
"what a man *is,* child? Do you truly know?"
"Yes, of course," says María-Dolores in genuine surprise.
Then she looks interested. "Why? Don't you?"
Back to his cabin in a hurry to vomit into the commode,
tear up his notes and essay, and burn the pieces in the wash-
basin.
So that's done.

◊   ◊   ◊

June 16 — Somewhere north of Denver we'll camp for the
night, miles from anyone. There in the high country, under
the splendid million stars, I'll let down her black hair. María-
Dolores giggles; she's done it with girls too. "Joe Smith" of
"Colorado" slides his hands under the little girl's shirt — a
process I'm sure he could describe very well — but his face
will never be reflected in her eyes. She shivers, partly from
the cold, whispers, "I want to do things for you too." I smile
yes, remembering Joe-Bob's lion silkiness and the first surprise of your wiry hair. As I bend slowly down to the nubbi-
ness, the softness, the mossy slipperiness, the heat, that famil-

iar reflection begins back and forth between us: a sudden scatter-shot along the nerves, its focusing on the one place, the echoes in neck and palms and lips, the soles of her feet, her breasts. María-Dolores is breathless; "Don't stop!" forgetting that I know. She closes her eyes, sobs, grabs inside, clutches my head with her hand: overwhelming! And sees me, all I remember, all I feel, all I know: overwhelming! And then, out of the things I know — and can't help knowing — she sees the one thing as strange and terrible to her as the dark side of the moon: herself.

And that's done.

But not yet. I'm imagining in words, as they do out here. Odd, in a language that would fade from me in half a year if I didn't continually get it from outside. (And to you, who will know Polish and Yiddish only when I get back.) María-Dolores, innocent of either, is asleep in the next cabin, cranky at having to have so many times of the month in a month (and so irregularly too) "ridiculous even at fifteen, let alone twelve," she says to me in eloquent Spanish, in her dream. Bumble, snoring, was lively enough today to have instantly annexed Mrs. ———, not only out of self-defense but quite distinctly for revenge. I told María-Dolores and she said, "That doesn't make sense." I said when did Bumble ever make sense. So I will seal this up and mail it in a few days.

But how to end? (It's a custom here.) Why, in the style of María-Dolores's books. There are only three left, since she's taken to deliberately heaving the ones she's tired of out the porthole when I'm not around. And I really haven't the heart to quarrel with her; they *are* bad! Here's the first one, a little oddly written, *The Mystery of Nevada*, which is lying open under her bed:

Funny, them McCabes, don't look like a fambly even though there's suthin' you can't put a name to that sets 'em apart from other folks. An' they got hired hands from all over,

Chinks an' niggers (That's you, pulling the apron off me when someone comes, half speaking, half laughing, "Quick, gal!"), *even Injuns. And why they stay up in them mountains all by their lonesome, God only knows.*

The second, very florid and lurid (it's called *The Mystery of Captain Satan*), has been kicked, closed, into a corner of the room (on the floor):

O reader, how can we contemplate this disordered soul without horror? Gifted with a knowledge of self and others few mortals possess, he nevertheless ran the gamut of vice! living like a parasite, cheating at cards, refusing to aid the very race that bred him but instead inflicting elaborate mental tortures on an elderly gentleman who strongly resembled his deceased papa, and using his kind's incapability for parenthood (I told María-Dolores this; she merely shrugged, not in the least interested) *as an excuse for indulging in unnatural — and what is worse, even some natural! — lusts. What doom is stored up in heaven for these hard-hearted men and women, diabolically disguised as men and women or vice versa and therefore invisible to our eyes, speaking the language of anyone in the room, which is dreadfully confusing because you can't tell what degenerate nation (or race) they may come from, and worst of all,* PRETENDING TO BE HUMAN BEINGS? WHEN IN FACT THEY ARE??? (it goes on).

And here's the last, honorably placed on the table by her bed. It's a remarkably quiet and gentle one (all things considered) and she rather likes it. She's going to keep it. It's called *The Mystery of the Young Gentleman* (he's a not-so-young lady, we find out) and it ends accurately and simply, in a very old tradition:

They lived happily ever after.

Biographies
of the Authors

ISAAC ASIMOV was born in 1920 which, he insists, makes him thirty-one years of age right now by the New Math. He arrived in the United States from his place of birth (Petrovichi, USSR) in 1923 and has been a citizen of this country since 1928. He was educated in the public school system of New York City (Brooklyn, to be exact) and went on to Columbia University, where he got all his degrees: B.S., 1939; M.A., 1941; and Ph.D., 1948. With an appalling monotony, he majored in chemistry each time. He spent time in a chemistry lab working for the U.S. Navy during World War II and was then caught immediately after V-J Day by America's eagle-eyed draft boards who decided that, with the war over, it was safe to put him in the army. The army endured him for nine months.

In 1949, he joined the biochemistry department of Boston University School of Medicine as an instructor. By 1951, he was an assistant professor; by 1955, an associate professor. In a fit of madness, B.U.S.M. promoted him to full professor in 1979.

He began writing in 1931 and submitting to magazines

in 1938. He sold his first story on October 21, 1938; published his first book on January 19, 1950; and, to date, has published over 230 books and has something like fifteen in press, five in preparation, and even he doesn't know how many promised.

He is married to Janet Jeppson, M.D., a psychiatrist who writes science fiction as J. O. Jeppson, and has a son and daughter by his first marriage.

SCOTT BAKER is a protégé of Raylyn Moore, who was his faculty advisor when he was pursuing his M.F.A. in an extension program of Goddard College. He now resides in Paris, where he is studying for three years. The author of two science fiction novels, *Nightchild* and *Symbiote's Crown,* and a horror novel, *Dhampire,* he has now completed two volumes of his Ashlu Trilogy, *Drink the Fire from the Flames* and *Firedance.* In addition to his writing and studies, he does translations, assisted by his wife, Suzy, and is at work on an anthology of French short stories.

WILLIAM K. CARLSON had a Nebula contender in 1975 with his novella, "Sunrise West." He has since expanded the work into a novel, which was published under the same title in the spring of 1981.

He was born in Chicago and grew up in Arcadia, Nebraska. After graduation from the University of Nebraska in 1961, he went to Cornell on a Woodrow Wilson Fellowship, and earned his M.A. in creative writing in 1963. After a stint in the navy, he settled down (if such a term can be used for a man who never has the same address two years running) to full-time writing. His short stories have appeared in such publications as *Galileo, Vertex, Galaxy,* and the *Carleton Miscellany,* as well as in a number of anthologies. He is completing work on his second novel, *Elysium.*

Biographies of the Authors

ALAN DEAN FOSTER has more than twenty novels to his credit, in addition to a number of short stories, a dozen radio plays, and several TV scripts. He was born in New York in 1946 and raised in Los Angeles. He attended U.C.L.A., where he earned a bachelor's degree in political science and a Master of Fine Arts in motion pictures. He spent two years as a copywriter in a public relations firm.

His writing career began when a long letter was bought and published as a short story in August Derleth's *Arkham Collector Magazine*. Sales of short fiction to other magazines followed, and he published his first novel, *The Tar-Alym Krang*, in 1972. Other novels include *Bloodhype, Orphan Star*, and *The End of the Matter*. Among his novelizations of films are *Alien, Outland, Clash of the Titans*, and *The Thing*.

He lives in Big Bear Lake, California, with his wife (JoAnn), three cats, three dogs, 200 house plants, and assorted renegade coyotes and raccoons, but is relocating in Arizona.

PHYLLIS GOTLIEB, a lifelong resident of Toronto, Canada, earned her B.A. and M.A. at the University of Toronto, where her husband, Calvin Gotlieb, is a professor of computer science. She is the mother of three children.

She has published poetry in numerous periodicals and anthologies, as well as in three books of her own work: *Within the Zodiac; Ordinary, Moving*, and *Doctor Umlaut's Earthly Kingdom*. Her science fiction stories have appeared in *Amazing, Fantastic, If, Galaxy*, and *Fantasy and Science Fiction*. Her five novels are *Sunburst, Why Should I Have All the Grief?, O Master Caliban!, Judgment of Dragons*, and *Emperor, Swords, Pentacles*.

ZENNA HENDERSON is best known for her tales of "The People," one of which served as the basis for a recent made-for-TV movie. She has four books to her credit, as well as stories in a variety of magazines and anthologies.

She was born and raised in Arizona, and earned her B.A. and M.A. at Arizona State University. She has been a teacher all her life, serving in schools in such diverse locations as the Japanese Relocation Center in Sacaton, Arizona, an air force children's school in France, and a children's TB hospital in Connecticut. She now teaches in a country school in Arizona.

JOE L. HENSLEY is a native of Indiana, where he has served for six years as a circuit court judge. A graduate of the Indiana University Law School, he is the father of one son, also an attorney.

He divides his writing between science fiction (short stories in the main) and suspense books. His stories have appeared in a number of magazines and in such anthologies as *Dangerous Visions* and *Alchemy and Academe*. His books include *The Color of Hate, Deliver Us to Evil, Song of Corpus Juris, A Killing in Gold, Minor Murders,* and the recent *Outcasts*.

R. A. LAFFERTY is a retired electrical engineer who was born in Iowa and now lives in Tulsa, Oklahoma. He prefers to calculate his age on the Celsius or Centigrade scale and states that he was 17.78 years old on November 7, 1978 (he's sixty-four on the Fahrenheit scale, but he calls that old-fashioned).

His short stories have appeared in such divers periodicals as *The New Mexico Quarterly, Literary Review,* and *Playboy,* as well as all the science fiction magazines. His first novel, *Past Master,* was published in 1968, and since then, he has published another twelve books, including novels and short story collections. His historical novel, *Okla Hannali,* was greeted with high critical praise. His science fiction novels include *Fourth Mansions, Arrive at Easterwine,* and *Apocalypses.*

ALICE LAURANCE has been writing science fiction for more than ten years, and has had stories published in *Galaxy, Galileo, Vertex, Ellery Queen Mystery Magazine,* and several anthologies, including *Generation* and *Protostars. Speculations* is her second anthology coedited with Dr. Asimov, and she also edited a collection of original science fiction written by women, *Cassandra Rising.*

She was born in Brooklyn, New York, and was educated at the Packer Collegiate Institute and Finch College. She is employed by Princeton University in their development office. She is married and the mother of one child.

JACQUELINE LICHTENBERG is best known for her Sime series, which began with a short story sold to *If* in 1968. Novels in the series include *House of Zeor, Unto Zeor, Forever,* and *Mahogany Trinrose.* Her latest novel, *Molt Brother,* is the first in a new series.

She is married and the mother of two daughters, and says she sometimes masquerades as a "suburban housewife." She is active in Science Fiction Writers of America, serving as director of the organization's Speakers' Bureau.

ROGER ROBERT LOVIN has, at one time or another, been a truck driver, a bouncer in a bar, a singer, musician, painter, stand-up comic, seaman, and minister of the gospel. He began his writing career by publishing one of the South's first alternate newspapers, and he was a founder of the *Louisiana Poetry Quarterly.* Later, he served as an editor for a paperback house and of several humor magazines. A period of wandering resulted in his book *The Complete Motocycle Nomad.* He is the author of two novels, *Apostle* and *The Presence* (written under the name Rodgers Clemens).

BARRY MALZBERG is the author of more than seventy-five published novels, among them the John W. Campbell Memorial Award–winning *Beyond Apollo,* and some 225 short stories, articles, and essays.

Born in 1939, he is married and the father of two daughters. He lives in Teaneck, New Jersey, where, as a hobby, he plays the violin in small orchestras. In the past, he worked as a reader for a New York literary agent, a job which led to his meeting with Bill Pronzini and collaborations that include one science fiction novel, *Prose Bowl,* a score of short stories, and the editing of four anthologies.

RACHEL COSGROVE PAYES is the author of thirty-eight published novels, including a sequel to *The Wizard of Oz,* a series of teenage career-nurse romances, science fiction (written as E. L. Arch), gothics, mysteries, romantic historicals, and Regency romances. Her most recent titles include *Satan's Mistress, The Coach to Hell,* and *Love's Escapade.*

She is married to Norman Payes, a gifted amateur photographer, and is the mother of a son and a daughter, both undergraduates at the University of Bridgeport and both published writers.

BILL PRONZINI is the author of eighteen novels, including the acclaimed "Nameless Detective" series, and a recent mainstream collaborator with political columnist Jack Anderson, *The Cambodia File.*

He was born in 1943, and is married with no children. His hobbies include travel and collecting genre fiction (mysteries, science fiction, westerns, and fantasy/horror) and critical or biographical material related to them. His first professional sale was in 1966, and he's been a full-time professional writer since 1969.

His collaborations with Barry Malzberg include four suspense novels and fifteen criminous short stories.

MACK REYNOLDS is a Californian, born of '49er Gold-Rush stock. Following World War II, he rebelled against returning to a nine-to-five job and determined to become a writer. His early attempts to write mysteries were less than successful, but in 1949, he moved to Taos, New Mexico, where he became a protégé of Fredric Brown. That same year he sold twelve science fiction stories, and placed thirty-five the following year. Since then, he's written some sixty books, all but ten of them science fiction, and hundreds of short stories and articles.

In 1953, he moved abroad and began writing travel articles for such magazines as *Rogue* and *Playboy*. He visited more than seventy-five countries; his unusual journeys included crossing the Sahara by land and ascending a Borneo river into Dyak country.

Today, he lives with his wife in the art colony of San Miguel de Allende, Mexico, in a Spanish Colonial house that was built in the late sixteenth century and antedates the landing of the Pilgrims in New England.

JOANNA RUSS, one of the top ten Westinghouse Science Talent Search winners when she was in high school, went on to do her undergraduate work at Cornell University. She earned her M.F.A. at Yale Drama School and has written a number of plays, including several produced off-Broadway in the late 1960s. She has spent the last fourteen years teaching at various institutions; she is now on the faculty of the University of Washington.

In addition to some fifty short stories, about half of them

science fiction, she has written seven novels, including *Picnic on Paradise, And Chaos Died, The Female Man,* and *On Strike Against God.* She has also reviewed for *Fantasy and Science Fiction, College English, The Village Voice,* and *The Washington Post.*

ROBERT SILVERBERG was born in New York City and now lives in the hills across the bay from San Francisco. He has been a professional writer for more than twenty-five years, specializing in science fiction and science articles. Among his best-known books are *Dying Inside, Lord Valentine's Castle, The Realm of Prester John, Nightwings,* and *Downward to the Earth.*

He has been nominated for more Hugo and Nebula awards than any other writer, and has won four Nebulas and two Hugo Awards. In 1967–68, he served as president of the Science Fiction Writers of America. He collects rare books and raises exotic subtropical plants.

JACK WILLIAMSON pioneered the teaching of science fiction at the college level, and published a descriptive list of some five hundred collegiate science fiction courses, *Teaching Science Fiction.* He had begun his writing career before he entered college, and he did not earn a degree in his first brush with academia. He returned to college after his comic strip, *Beyond Mars,* expired, receiving his B.A. and M.A. from Eastern New Mexico University in 1957, and his Ph.D. from the University of Colorado; his dissertation later became the book *H. G. Wells: Critic of Progress.* He taught for seventeen years at Eastern New Mexico University.

He is married to the former Blanche Slaten Harp; they live in Portales, New Mexico. His first sale was in 1928, and he has published steadily since that time. In 1976, the Science Fiction Writers of America presented him with the Grand

Master Award "for lifetime achievement." He served as President of S.F.W.A. from 1978 to 1980. He has published more than three million words of magazine science fiction and thirty-odd books, many of which have been translated into languages ranging from Scandinavian to Japanese. His most recent novel is *The Humanoid Touch*.

GENE WOLFE is best known as a science fiction writer, though his published works include a mainstream novel, a young-adult novel, and many magazine articles. He is the author of nearly a hundred science fiction short stories and of the novel *The Fifth Head of Cerberus*. His novella, "The Death of Doctor Island," won the Nebula in 1973. He is currently at work on a tetralogy, *The Book of the New Sun;* the first book in the series is *The Shadow of the Torturer*, the second *The Claw of the Conciliator*.

He was born in New York and raised in Houston, Texas. He spent two and a half years at Texas A & M, then dropped out and was drafted. As a private in the Seventh Infantry during the Korean War, he was awarded the Combat Infantry Badge. The GI bill permitted him to attend the University of Houston after the war, where he earned a degree in mechanical engineering. He is currently a senior editor on the staff of *Plant Engineering Magazine*.

To Break the Code

The last name of each writer is given in code at the beginning of his, her, or their (there are two collaborations in the book) story. The code is numerical, with each letter of the alphabet represented by a pair of digits; the numerical assignments are derived from base five. To break the code, first write out the alphabet (omitting the letter *X*, which does not appear in any of the names) and count in base five, thusly:

A-00	N-23
B-01	O-24
C-02	P-30
D-03	Q-31
E-04	R-32
F-10	S-33
G-11	T-34
H-12	U-40
I-13	V-41
J-14	W-42
K-20	Y-43
L-21	Z-44
M-22	

To Break the Code

Begin with the last pair of numbers in the series, and work from right to left until you have spelled out the surname of one or a pair of the writers. The "extra" pairs of numerals (or letters, depending on how you look at it) are added to make all the codes work out to the same length (failing that, you would have no difficulty seeing the difference between "Russ" and "Lichtenberg"); this "padding" spells out the names of four people who have been meaningful in the work of the book: Austin Olney, our editor at Houghton Mifflin; J. O. Jeppson, in private life Mrs. Isaac Asimov; Virginia Kidd and James Allen, our agents (and it should be noted that we used their names over their protests but with gratitude).